Living the Braced Fantasy

An Erotic Orthodontic Encounter

by
Catherine Aimes

An Intraoral Press publication

Our Dr.Samantha Wrighting books:

Retainer Girl
Love and Braces
The Braced Experience

Our other Dr.Samantha Wrighting shorts:

Headgeared
Madison's Braces
Lights, Camera, Braces!

Our Erotic Orthodontic Encounter books:

Notwithstanding Braces
The Braced Tease
Bracing Times with Cecilia

ISBN: 978-1-300-49856-8

Intraoral Press
P.O.Box 286199
New York NY 10128

For additional information go to:
www.intraoralpress.com

e-mail: info@intraoralpress.com

A reminder:

Living the Braced Fantasy is a work for mature readers, involving sexual situations and stimulation.

Living the Braced Fantasy is a work of fiction and for entertainment purposes some aspects of orthodontic treatment and wear might be exaggerated and the characters' experiences should not be considered representative.

Readers should not rely on any information or descriptions in these stories. For accurate information about orthodontic treatment readers are encouraged to consult a dentist or orthodontist, or to contact a professional organization such as the American Association of Orthodontists (www.braces.org).

1.

I was stirring the last melted ice cream at the bottom of my glass, just looking around. Sitting in the shade of the large umbrella in the sidewalk café, we were both happy and full, enjoying a comfortable lull in our conversation. I had been out with Jacob often enough now that we didn't feel we had to keep each other constantly engaged and interested. We were at that stage in building our relationship where we were beginning to get comfortable with each other's silences, too. Beginning to be a real couple.

Some giggly teenage girls had sat down at a nearby table, and just as I looked at the one facing us most directly she laughed, revealing two rows of sparkling metal braces, her top and bottom jaw connected by elastics on each side that stretched as her mouth opened wide. Self-consciously she raised her hand to cover her mouth and her braces, but then she revealed them again as the waitress came to take their order.

I found it hard to take my eyes off her, and especially her braces. She was already older than most girls who have them, at least fifteen or even sixteen, even as they made her look younger. She kept closing her mouth or raising her hand to cover it, but they were having a jolly time, and she kept bursting out in laughter, revealing all her metalwork yet again. The sight stirred up all sorts of emotions and feelings in me. My breathing grew deeper and steadier, and I could even feel myself getting moist between my legs.

Braces.

All the memories that brought back. And all the desires they still aroused….

But then I shook myself, suddenly worried that surely Jacob noticed my lingering irrational fixation, and that he must be wondering why I was staring like this. I snapped my slack jaw shut and turned, ready to resume some casual conversation, like I hadn't even registered that girl's braces.

1

But when I turned, smiling, I saw that Jacob too was staring at her as if transfixed.

Could it be?

I didn't know what I had looked like just a second earlier, but I imagined I had had exactly that same dreamy look, lost in a deep, private reverie of welling urges and happy nostalgia.

Could it be? I asked myself again, completely stunned by the possibility. Could Jacob feel the same way? I knew there had to be others who felt this way, but could I actually, without even knowing it, have found someone who might understand something I had kept hidden for so long? Could it be that my boyfriend, of all people, carried in him the same deep but carefully concealed longing?

2.

Of course I had had braces when I was a kid, but even before I got them I had wanted them. My older sister, Kylie, got them when I was in third grade, and despite her not being at all enthusiastic about them, I was desperately jealous of her. Part of it was that braces were like a badge of maturity. They were something you had to be older to get, and I still had some baby teeth. One girl in my class did have a retainer by then, but with its simple wire running across her teeth that seemed to me just like a plaything. It was nowhere near as impressive as my sister's very solid set of metal bands and brackets.

Kylie wasn't excited about getting braces. She didn't really complain, since she knew they were necessary and she knew that our parents were going to make her get them, no matter what she said, but she always got grumpy when the subject came up. I couldn't understand it. Sure, they looked a bit strange but I was sure it had to be such a cool sensation to have those metal rows across one's teeth.

I wanted to be allowed to go along when they were installed, but my mother wouldn't let me. Kylie was going to have to take the whole school day off, because the procedure was supposed to take so long, and mom wasn't going to let me skip all that school just to sit at the orthodontist's office. Besides, she was sure I would be bored. They were going to sedate Kylie anyway, so even she wouldn't really experience it. I knew I wouldn't be at all bored, but there was no way I could convince mom.

Kylie was totally irritable the morning of her appointment. I was the one that was excited, but she just thought I was making fun of her. Mom made her put on one of the pull-ups I still had to wear nights for the appointment, which was like the ultimate humiliation for her. But mom reminded her, "The doctor said you should. You're going to be strapped down there half the day, so it's better to be prepared and not have to worry about that."

The fact that Kylie was somehow going to be strapped down also made it sound more mysterious and serious, like a sort of major operation. I was so incredibly disappointed that I couldn't see what was going to happen.

I rushed home after school but they weren't back by the time I got there, just the housekeeper. When mom and Kylie came back Kylie was all pale and glassy-eyed and walking with her head bowed, like she'd been through a lot.

I could barely stand it any longer, jumping up and down and begging her, "So let me see! Let me see!"

She turned to me like in slow motion and gave me a look like I was the most annoying and crazy person she had ever seen. But she slowly parted her lips and revealed her braces.

My own jaw dropped. They were beautiful, all dark, silvery metal, with thick wires running across the bands and brackets in a beautiful intricate design. I thought my sister was the luckiest person in the world.

Kylie sure thought otherwise, running up to the room we shared and slamming the door behind her. I wanted to run up after her and hear more about her braces, but mom held me back. "Give her a bit of time by herself," mom said. "She has to get used to looking like this."

I couldn't believe that Kylie wouldn't want to immediately show her braces off to the whole world, but if mom said....

I watched TV for half an hour but then I couldn't take it any longer. I snuck upstairs. If mom said anything I could say I had to get some schoolbooks.

Kylie was sulking on her bed, her eyes all red from crying. I jumped on the bed, begging to be allowed to see them again. She flashed her braced face again before shutting her mouth. "Satisfied, pest?"

"No, let me see properly!" I begged. "Tell me what it was like."

"There's nothing to tell, Sally. They gave me something so I slept through it all. I just woke up in the afternoon looking like this."

"So how do they feel?"

Kylie shrugged. "O.k., I guess. They're supposed to start hurting, but only in a couple of hours."

I knew that braces were supposed to hurt some, too, but that's not what I meant. I imagined it must be such a neat feeling to have that metal covering your teeth like that and that's what I wanted her to tell me about. I couldn't understand why Kylie wasn't more thrilled.

A couple of weeks later Mom took me along to Kylie's next appointment, since it was after school. Kylie rolled her eyes but she let me come into the examination room and watch while the orthodontist changed the wires. I was terribly disappointed that it was like a normal dentist's office and chair and that Kylie wasn't strapped down and that it all went so fast. But I was still jealous of Kylie. The way her lips were spread around the cheek retractor the orthodontist put in place when he worked on her teeth was amazing, and so was the way he tinkered with the brackets and bands as he changed the wires.

I did bare my own teeth for the orthodontist, asking for reassurance that I too would be getting braces at some point.

"Yes," he said, nodding seriously, "those look like teeth that will need to be braced eventually."

Nervously I asked how soon I could get them.

"Well, I think we'll probably want to wait until you're about Kylie's age," he said. Kylie was two and a half years older than me. That sounded way too far away.

Kylie didn't pout too much for the duration of her orthodontic treatment, but she didn't like having the braces much, and she hated that I paid so much attention to them and constantly asked her about them. She just wanted to forget she had them and wished nobody noticed – and I was constantly reminding her about them! I also went along to as many of her appointments as I could, trying to take in everything that happened in the practice and looking forward to when it would be my turn. Most of the patients in the waiting room and the examination chairs looked as sullen my sister did. I couldn't believe they didn't all realize how lucky they were.

When I was fifth grade the most glamorous girl in our class, Gabriella, got braces too. She had only moved to our school the year before, and we weren't really friends. I had always been intimidated by her because she was so beautiful and obviously cool, while I felt like such a plain girl. But after she got braces you could tell she lost her self-confidence and didn't think she deserved to be part of cool group any longer. She began to sit gloomily by herself in class, and didn't join in the games at recess, and she got all shy and mumbly when called upon in class.

After a few days I couldn't hold myself back any longer. I went up to her and told her, "I think your braces are great."

She looked at me like I was crazy, or like she thought I was making fun of her.

"Seriously, they're so cool. My sister has exactly the same kind, but she's getting hers off soon." They really did look a lot like my sister's, with the same combination and kinds of brackets and bands.

"They're awful!" Gabriella blurted out miserably.

"No they aren't," I assured her. "I mean the way those little bits of metal can pull your teeth straight. That is like beyond cool."

"I guess," she said with a shrug. "But they're still awful."

I shrugged. I knew from the way my sister was about her braces that I wouldn't really be able to convince Gabriella how lucky she was that she got to look like that. Instead I changed the subject to some monster assignment our teacher had given us and we talked about that. After that we became friends, doing more and more stuff together.

Finally, in the spring of fifth grade our dentist said I was probably ready for braces and that we should make an appointment with the orthodontist. Kylie had already gotten hers off by then and was just wearing retainers. That was fine with me. I looked forward to being the center of all braced attention in the family.

I could barely contain my excitement in the days before my appointment. When we went to the initial consultation mom reminded me to wear my pull-ups, like I did whenever I went to a medical appointment, since the nerves and butterflies of what could happen at a doctor's office always left me susceptible to accidents. This time it was the excitement. I was so happily nervous that I actually wet myself on the way there. I didn't tell mom, however. Besides, I was so focused on what was going to happen that the feeling barely bothered me.

The appointment itself was a bit anticlimactic. The orthodontist took impressions of my teeth, and X-rays and pictures, but it was all really quick and easy. I didn't get strapped down or anything, and I didn't get braces either. Just a few separators pushed between a lot of my crowded, twisted teeth. I had to wait another ten days, he told me. It sounded like an eternity.

When I finally told Gabriella I was getting braces, the day before my appointment, she said, "I'm sorry." She said it really sincerely, like she felt bad for me to have to go through this.

I tried to tell her that I was looking forward to it, but that didn't make any sense to her. She decided I was happy about it because I was going to be able to miss the entire day of school, and that it hadn't sunk in what getting braces was really going to mean. I knew different.

Getting them was sort of disappointing. The assistant led me and my mom to a room in the back which I hadn't ever been in. The examination chair there had like a harness to it, and while it looked a bit intimidating I was excited about getting strapped down too. The orthodontist explained that I was going to be strapped down because it was easier for him to work that way for the long procedure, but I didn't need any convincing. I nodded that it was ok and I got in the chair and the assistant strapped me down. It was like my old car seat with the five point harness, and I didn't mind the reassuring wide, padded strap between my legs either. It felt very safe.

Gently the orthodontist said he want to strap my wrists down to, but that was fine with me too. For a moment it felt scary, but then I relaxed, eager for the procedure to begin.

But then the orthodontist lifted a small facemask attached to a long hose to my head. "Now we're going to let you get some sleep, and when you wake up we'll be all finished."

I strained at the restraints. "No!" I shook my head. I wanted to experience the whole thing! I looked desperately at my mother. "Can't I be awake for it?"

"Oh, it takes so long," the orthodontist explained, pressing the mask over my mouth. "This is much easier for you."

I wanted to protest some more, but the mask muffled my voice and after the first two or three breaths I couldn't fight off the fatigue that overcame me. I fought it as hard as I could, desperate to be awake for this, but within a few seconds I was out cold.

When I woke up my mother and the orthodontist were standing over me, smiling. My hands were already free, but I was still strapped down. It took me a moment to realize where I was. And then I felt how different my mouth felt. The inside of my cheeks rubbed against hard uneven surfaces. I ran my tongue across the front of my teeth and felt the wonderful smooth but uneven brackets and bands and wires covering them. I sighed with relief and pleasure. I was really sorry not to have experienced getting them, but at least I had them. I wanted to yell out *Hurrah*!

"How are you feeling?" the orthodontist asked.

"Good. Ok. Great," I said. "So I got the braces?" I wanted confirmation. "Everything went ok?"

"Everything went great," he said. He picked up a mirror and handed it to me so I could see for myself.

I thought I knew what to expect, but it was still a surprise. I could recognize the familiar look and outline of my crooked teeth, but now there was this metal layer across and on top of them. Shiny stainless steel brackets and, in the back, some bands wrapped entirely around the teeth. The wires clamped inside the brackets and bands, running across the rows of teeth like two single railroad tracks. A small piece of round, straight wire jutting up and out on two of the teeth on the top, and two farther back on the bottom , with a small ball on top of each. To stretch elastics across, I realized!

I was spellbound. It was better than I could have imagined it. The reality of it was so much more vivid and clear and tangible than anything I could have imagined.

Eventually my mother and the orthodontist grew impatient with my wide-eyed fascination with my reflection in the mirror. I think my mother was worried that I was in some sort of shock. That the reality of braces had brought me crashing down to earth and that I'd be as miserable as Kylie had been about them.

"Well," she asked reluctantly, "what do you think?"

I could barely bring myself to look away from the mirror, but I beamed at them. "They're perfect!" And I really felt they were.

The orthodontist reminded me of the instructions as to how to take care of them and what I couldn't do, like eat certain foods, but I knew about all this from Kylie's time in braces. Besides, I was going to be sure to take good care of them.

The orthodontist unstrapped me and I got a small bag of accessories to help take care of the braces, as well as an instruction pamphlet reminding me of all the dos and don'ts.

I was practically floating out of the examination room, even though my first few steps were a bit unsteady, after lying for so long and having been knocked out. When we got to the waiting room I looked at the other patients, proud to be one of them now. I couldn't understand why they all looked so downbeat.

I reminded my mother that I should go to the bathroom. She took out the small paper bag which concealed a spare pull-up, and I went to get changed. When I didn't come back after five minutes mom came into the bathroom, wondering what had happened. She found me lost in happy reverie again, staring in the mirror, having completely lost track of time.

My teeth did begin to ache soon, but I thought even that was neat. It was a new kind of pain, not at all like a normal toothache. It was annoying later not to really be able to chew anything that wasn't totally soft for a few days, but it was sort of cool too.

At school I could barely suppress my newly wired grin, even though I knew that I couldn't parade my joy and pride as much as I wanted to. The other kids would think it was just too weird. It was ok to pretend braces weren't a big deal or didn't bother you that much, but being happy or proud about having them was too much. But I couldn't help flaunting them around Gabriella. I thought maybe she'd feel better about hers now that I was wired up too, but she didn't. Seeing them in my mouth was like a reminder of how she looked, and she liked that even less, I think. Unlike me.

There were some annoying things about having braces that I hadn't expected, like the way they chafed the inside of my cheeks raw. Putting wax on them helped, but I preferred the hard, smooth feel of their metal when I ran my tongue over them, so I didn't like using it. And this pain was a small price to pay for getting to have braces.

I couldn't get enough of the feel of them inside my mouth, or staring at myself in the mirror and how beautiful they looked.

Gabriella was a bit distant at first after I got them. She didn't like just the two of us hanging out at school. She had overheard someone say something about *Those braced girls ...*, and that's the last thing she wanted to be known for. But she'd come over after school sometimes. We only went to her house when my mother asked hers whether I could. Gabriella always seemed a bit less comfortable when we were at her house.

Once I was at her house, around the start of sixth grade, and she was really uncomfortable. Finally she admitted she'd been to the orthodontist a few days earlier, and she went over to her desk and got a flat, small pouch. Without looking at me she reluctantly opened it and showed me she had gotten – headgear!

My jaw dropped, and I was so envious.

Gabriella spun the facebow in her hand a few times, and then reluctantly slipped it in the tubes on her back teeth, still not daring to look up at me. Then she attached one side of the neck strap, pulled it around her neck, under her hair, and hooked it into the other end as well. It took her like ten seconds before she could lift her face and look me in the eyes, to gauge my reaction.

My reaction was of course one of wide-eyed wonder and jealousy. It was just a wire coming from between her lips, and then arched across her cheeks, but it was still beautiful. It was something I wanted!

"Well?" she asked.

"You're so lucky!" I blurted out.

She shook her head in irritation and quickly unhooked the device and pulled out the facebow. She wanted sympathy, but I was just in awe.

"How much are you supposed to wear it?" I prayed she didn't have to wear it just at night, so that I could see her with it on some more.

"As much as possible. Like I'm supposed to put it on when I get home from school, and just take it out for meals and when we go out and stuff."

"So why don't you leave it on?"

"I'm still adjusting to it. The orthodontist said I should slowly increase my weartime."

"But you can put it on now...," I said longingly, my heart pounding.

She shook her head and put it back in its protective pouch. I knew it wouldn't do any good to push her. She was so touchy about everything orthodontic. But she had headgear now, and was supposed to wear it all the time outside school, so I would get to see her with it more soon, I hoped.

Gabriella continued to be uneasy for much of the afternoon. I guess getting headgear really got to her. "I hope I get it soon, too," I told her, but that wasn't the sort of thing that made her feel any better.

"It's just so frustrating," she finally opened up, "because it's like just another braces chapter." Finally looking me in the eyes again she said, "The ortho said I wasn't even close to halfway done with my treatment. And I've already had these *a year*." She bared her teeth and revealed her beautiful silvery braces. I couldn't understand what she was complaining about.

She fell back on her bed with a sigh, close to tears, I think. There was a new boy in school that she had a crush on, and she complained how with the braces she had no chance of getting closer to him.

"I can't blame him. Or anyone," she said. "Who would even think of kissing a girl with all this metalwork in her mouth?" she asked.

I thought about boys sometimes, and I had my crushes, but I didn't ever really think about all that physical stuff. But Gabriella's rhetorical question aroused something in me, as I felt my own lips around my braces.

"If you're careful, it can't be that bad, right?" I said.

"It's not like facing a chainsaw, you think?"

I bounced down her bed next to her and shook my head.

"Do you want to try?" I suggested.

"What?"

"Kissing, silly. This way we'd both get to see what it's like."

Gabriella blushed slightly, but curiosity was getting the better of her. "Ok," she stammered, looking down at the bed shyly. Then she pulled back slightly. "But careful that we don't get them stuck together," she added.

I'd never kissed anyone in like a kiss kiss, so I wasn't too sure about what we should do either, but we cautiously brought our heads together until we just felt our lips brush against each other. I cocked my head slightly and my lips sort of naturally parted as I pressed them against hers, while my eyes sort of naturally closed. I felt the warm and slightly moist softness of her lips, and then the braces behind them.

I liked the feel of her lips, but it was coming up against the metal braces which weren't my own braces that was magical. I was drawn in to them as Gabriella seemed to begin to lose herself, her lips squishing against my mouth. I felt her arms around me, pulling me closer in, too.

10

It was an experimental kiss, but it seemed to go on for ages, both of us in a trance that excluded everything else around us except the feeling of each other's mouths and tongues and braces.

Finally, breathlessly, we moved apart, both of us flushed. Now I understood why older teens and adults were drawn to *that*. And it wasn't even so much Gabriella, but the sheer, physical sensation. Sure, I had something of a girl-crush on her, but the kiss hadn't been connected to her. It was almost disembodied, almost entirely her braces and mouth.

"I guess braces aren't a complete barrier...," I said

Gabriella sighed with some relief. "Yeah. I'm just not sure any boys can be convinced of that."

We kept looking at each other and then averting our eyes. This brief exposing intimacy had been a special moment, but it was also more than kids like us could handle. We weren't lesbians, both of us were thinking, even as we couldn't deny the power of what had passed between us. But how would this affect our relationship?

Gabriella suddenly realized what to do. "I really should wear this," she said, bounding up and getting the pouch with her headgear. She quickly put the device on, then sighed again with relief. It was the perfect solution. The chastity belt that prevented us from even considering repeating what we had just done. Suddenly, we were able to revert to our previous roles and relationships.

Her mom was pleased to see her wearing the headgear, and from then on whenever we were at each other's houses after school Gabriella would always put it on immediately. It was like a safety device that put us both at ease.

We never so much as mentioned the kiss again, even though I'm sure she thought about it just as often and intently as I did. It was years before I had my next kiss, and that and all the others were from boys and men, but few caused such a deep and lasting reaction.

At my next appointment I mustered up enough courage to ask when I was getting headgear, but my orthodontist disappointed me by telling me I didn't need it. I told him I wouldn't mind, but he said it wouldn't be of any use.

The visits to the orthodontist were a bit of a letdown generally, too. I never got to go back to that back room again, and was never strapped in place again. At least he used the cheek retractors on me, and I got to feel what that was like. I always liked lying there with my mouth firmly held so gaping wide open. And I could always hope for some new accessory to add to my braced experience, but other than stretching some elastics between my teeth he didn't do much beyond changing the archwires. Not that I could complain too much. I had a set of braces that were just what I wanted. Well, except that I wanted more. But they were still wonderful.

I plotted ways to prolong my treatment, too, but there was no real way of doing it. Except for the elastics everything about the braces took care of itself, and my teeth shifted into their proper positions regardless what I did. I tried not wearing the elastics at night, but I missed the feel of them pulling my jaw together as I lay in bed, so that was a short-lived plan. While Gabriella complained about her orthodontist always saying she still had so long to go with her treatment I prayed mine would as well.

I had braces all through sixth grade, and all through seventh as well. In the late spring when I was in seventh grade the orthodontist said he would soon be ready to take them off. I was crushed. It was too sudden. It was too soon. I racked my brain for what I could do to convince him to leave them on. The best that I could come up with was telling him at my next appointment that I was worried about making the transition to the retainers. From Kylie's experience there seemed so much to worry about, including losing them, and since it was almost summer and we were going to be travelling and away from home a lot of the time and if anything happened I couldn't get back to see him quickly....

"Wouldn't it be better to leave the braces on until fall when school starts again?" I asked. "I mean it would be great to get them off now, but if I have any problems with the retainers it would be such a nightmare...."

He was a bit surprised, but he said if I really didn't mind then, yes, maybe that would be better.

I had to grip the examination chair armrests really tight to keep from jumping up in jubilation.

It was sad to know that the braces were coming off at the end of the summer, but at least I still got to have them for a few more months. And I loved every minute of it.

Going to get them taken off I was miserable. Part of me was of course curious about what my teeth now looked like, but I knew I would miss the metal tracks on them terribly.

The procedure was a bit scary too, although it went fast and wasn't too messy. But I did feel totally naked and exposed afterwards with those incredibly white, smooth bare teeth, and I wished I could get my braces back.

A few days later I at least got my retainers. Pink upper and lower Hawleys, so at least I had the look and feel of a wire running across the front of my teeth again, and a smooth hunk of plastic supportingly behind the teeth. The feel of the plastic was cool, and I loved the lisp it gave me. They were an ok substitute for the braces.

I only had to wear them fulltime for six months, and then I only had to wear them at night, but I still put them in more often, like when I watched TV or did my homework. And Gabriella just got her braces off around that time and was now also wearing retainers, and so I'd often wear them when I did anything with her, even though she was embarrassed by that.

The retainers were at least something I could always fall back on and return to, but of course they weren't braces. I was growing up and had grown out of them, but they were something I wished I could have clung to. Or had them clinging to me.

The first boy I kissed had braces. That was why I let him kiss me. It was why I went out with him in the first place, hoping he'd want to kiss me. And even with all my high and pent-up expectations it was a good kiss. I liked the sensations of his metal-covered teeth against my lips. But of course it wasn't the same thing as when they were on *my* teeth. And when I said I wanted to put my retainers in the next time we kissed he looked at me like I was crazy and shook his head. "Gross," he said. Which was less romantic. And since there wasn't much else romantic about him either I gave up on him pretty fast.

Braces remained mostly fantasy and memory. The retainers helped. I wore them faithfully. Even religiously. And alone in bed, under the covers, the feel of the smooth plastic, and at least the wires running across my teeth offered constant stimulation. Even if they weren't quite braces.

My wisdom teeth started erupting when I was a junior in high school, and our dentist decided they had to go. I asked him how that would affect my retainers, but he said I should worry, he would just make a new set after the teeth were pulled.

I didn't like having so many teeth pulled, but I was looking forward to getting the new retainers. I wanted to convince him to make me bigger ones, since I only had to wear them at night.

It took a while for my mouth to heal sufficiently for him to take the new impressions. Showing him my old Hawley retainers I explained to him that I wanted him to make the new ones bulkier. But he had different ideas. "We'll get you those invisible Essix retainers," he said cheerily.

I explained to him that I didn't want that kind. I wanted the kinds with the wire, like I had, but he treated me like I was just being silly and refused to change his mind. He must have had some sort of deal with the lab that makes them or something.

The new retainers were even more disappointing than I had expected. They were just plastic sheaths for my teeth. Sure, you could barely see that I was wearing them when I had them on. But I only had to wear them *at night*, when I slept alone, with my mouth closed....

I really missed the feel of the old retainers.

And of course I didn't really bother wearing the new ones that much either.

By the end of high school there were not many kids with braces any more, but I still caught myself staring enviously at the junior high girls with their silvery grins. Almost whenever I saw a girl with braces a feeling of nostalgia would come over me. And if I stared and reflected, sometimes I would go all soft – except my nipples, which would go all hard. And there would be that anticipatory moistening of my pussy, and that sense of disappointment as I ran my tongue over the smooth front of my teeth at never being able to have those sensory sensations again.

At college I occasionally saw someone with braces, but few kids had them, and none of the ones I was friends with. Then junior year one of my classmates, Cecilia, suddenly showed up with an awesome set of stainless steel orthodontia. I didn't really know her well before that, but I was so curious that I had to get closer to her. She explained that she was actually thinking of becoming an orthodontist, and even though she had had braces as a kid her teeth had shifted a bit, and she wanted to get them fixed perfectly. Besides, she said, there was no better way of figuring out whether or not this was what she wanted to do with her life than immersing herself fully in the orthodontic experience, which is why she went with the whole full tin-grin look, rather than some kind of less visible sort of treatment.

14

She was pretty cool, and I liked hanging out with her. But I would have been happy to hang out with her even if she was totally obnoxious, just in order to stare at those amazing braces. Cecilia actually had a boyfriend who I guess didn't mind the way she looked with them, so she spent a lot of time in the city, too, and we never became really close friends, but I did manage to do things with her regularly. She still had the braces when she graduated, too, on her way to dental school.

When I slept with my boyfriends at college, often I would fantasize about Cecilia's braces. It wasn't anything lesbian or anything like that. I didn't want to sleep with her; I wanted to be her. Yes, my sexual fantasies weren't about my partner being someone more handsome or exciting, but about me being someone else. Or more exactly, me having braces.

It's a fantasy I continued to have. But what could I do? How could I possibly act on it?

3.

I looked at the way Jacob couldn't take his eyes off that girl's braces. I recognized the look in his eyes. I recognized that longing.

Could it really be? I asked myself.

Over the years I had tried to hint to some of my boyfriends that braces turned me on, but none ever really got it. The mention of braces usually just brought back memories of middle school, and if they recalled their own experiences it was dismissively, like having braces had been some forgettable phase they had to go through but barely even remembered. Or they'd mention the girl they had a crush on – *until she got braces*. Or: *except, she had braces*.

Yes, none of the guys I had gone out with had gotten it. But here, suddenly.... Jacob really seemed to get it.

Or was it just wishful thinking on my part? I had learnt enough from experience that if he *wasn't* into it and I said I was he'd find that really, really strange. And probably not want to continue our relationship.

But if he *was*...?

Gingerly, I tried to broach the subject in a way that wasn't too obvious. "That poor girl," I said, injecting a proper note of pity in my voice.

Jacob turned suddenly, like he'd been caught peeking, and flushed slightly. "Pardon me?" he asked all innocently, like he didn't know what I was talking about.

"That girl," I explained, tilting my head in her direction. "Having to wear braces like that at her age."

"Well...," he stuttered. "It's good she's getting it done, right?"

"God, I remember having braces...," I said, hoping to sound slightly wistful.

"How old were you?"

"Oh, younger. Around sixth, seventh grade. It actually went by too fast, I think. Maybe I could have appreciated it more if I had had them longer, or later."

Jacob perked up a bit. Was I sending the right signals?

"Honestly," I added, "I kind of miss them."

"Really?" he asked, a quiver in his voice.

"There was something...comforting about them," I said, staring at the girl's braces. Turning back to Jacob and staring him straight in the eyes I asked, "You think you would have gone out with me when I had braces?"

He laughed nervously. "Of course...."

"What about if I still had them now? If I looked like that?" I asked, tilting my head in the direction of the girl at the other table.

"Of course," Jacob spluttered. "You'd look great. Still."

I leaned forward over the table towards him, and said in a much quieter voice, "Because, you know, I kind of *wish* I did look like that. That I had that on my teeth." I looked him in the eyes. "More than kind of. I *really* wish it."

Jacob was breathing hard now. "Yeah," he said, "that would be ... cool. I would like that, too."

I leaned back in my chair and drank the last of my melted ice cream from the glass. I didn't know what else to say, or where to take it from here. Ok, it seemed like Jacob had a thing for braces, too. That was good. But now what?

4.

At home we had sex, and we both seemed preoccupied while we did it. I know I was, and I know why. And Jacob seemed to be having the same thoughts.

We had changed the subject at the café, and it had been a bit awkward for the rest of the afternoon. It felt like an elephant in the room, but we were both too scared or confused to bring it up again.

Tired and more relaxed after sex I decided I just had to find out for sure. I turned over, and leaning on one elbow asked him, "So you'd find it…sexy if I had braces?"

Jacob was still panting, and he seemed to be thinking about how honestly he wanted to answer. But he finally pulled himself together. "I would. Honestly? I'd find it *really* sexy. It would be like a dream."

I let myself fall back on my pillow, so happy to hear that. "That's how I feel," I admitted. Then, turning to him, I had to ask, "You don't think it's weird that I'm…turned on by the thought of having braces?"

"I'm turned on by the thought of you having braces," he said with a smile, and took my hand and pulled it under the sheets to his cock, which was rock hard again.

I held onto his cock and sighed. "A shared fantasy…."

"Yeah," he said. "Maybe we can do something about that." It was almost a question.

"Like what?"

"Well, do you still have your retainers? At least a set of wires running across your teeth…."

I leaned back in frustration. "No," I said, annoyed. "After I got my wisdom teeth pulled I only got those clear plastic ones, and I haven't even worn those in years…."

Jacob looked disappointed, but he kissed me, slowly. "Too bad. Even that hint of metal would be…wonderful. Well, we still can share in the fantasy," he said, as he rolled onto me again. I smiled as he guided his cock into me again, knowing we were both think about that same girl's braced smile while we were making love.

17

It was good. All this was good, but after that the fancy really seized hold of me. Braces. I *wanted* them so desperately. I knew it was silly. I had had them, and gotten that out of the way. I was an adult now. Not too many years out college, but a grown-up, with a nice, straight smile, and a nice boyfriend.

But I couldn't get braces out of my mind.

I did dig up my old, plastic retainers, but just opening the container was a disappointment. They were so small and limited, just thin layers of plastic. And they didn't really fit any longer either, when I tried them on. Not that they would have done much good anyway. These were definitely *not* my fantasy.

But the fact that they didn't fit properly any longer did give me an idea. Maybe it would be a good idea to get a new set of retainers. Real ones. Like I had had at first. Bulky pink plastic behind my teeth, and wires holding them in place. They wouldn't be braces, and it wasn't exactly my fantasy, but they would let me pretend a bit better. And Jacob would like them too.

How does one get retainers? My orthodontist had retired, and my dentist was still the same one who had gotten me these awful see-through ones. I guessed that any orthodontic practice could make them for me, so I could just look up where the nearest one was and make an appointment.... But I wanted to be sure I got what I wanted.

I decided to contact Cecilia. Her orthodontist had been in the city, and she was at dental school nearby and she might know how I could make sure to get what I needed. No one else I knew had had anything to with any orthodontist recently.

I emailed her at her alumni address, and hoped it would get to her. I was pretty vague, just saying I had an orthodontic question I thought she could help me with. She answered the next day, suggesting we meet for a drink over the weekend.

I hadn't seen her for a couple of years and so I knew she had to be long out of her braces by now too, but I was still a bit disappointed to see her plain, perfect smile when we met. Sure, she was really beautiful now, without the braces – but all that metal had been something really special too.

We took a corner booth at the local bar and caught each other up on what we had done since graduation. I wasn't surprised that Cecilia was still on course to become an orthodontist, but of course that was a long road. "But I can't imagine doing anything else," she told me, and you could see how she was completely sure of that. Unlike me, who had a decent job but no career yet, and had no idea what she wanted to do when she grew up....

"So you had an *orthodontic* question you said?" Cecilia asked.

"It's silly, but yes. And when I thought orthodontics I immediately thought of you. The orthodontist I went to when I was kid retired, and you seem right in the thick of things. Even without the braces."

"So what's the problem?"

I explained to her about the retainers, and how I didn't like the ones my dentist had prescribed, and how I thought it was a good idea to get new ones, just to make sure, but that I really wanted ones more like the ones I used to have. "They can even be bulkier," I said, "since they're only for nighttime wear."

"I'm sure my orthodontist could handle that," Cecilia said. "Whatever your specifications are. I help out in the office a couple of days a week, too, and I'd be glad to introduce you and help you set up an appointment."

"I think I'd like that."

"I do have to warn you, she's not your usual orthodontist. Well, you saw my rack, so you know that she takes her work very seriously and isn't too concerned about appearances and things like that. Not that that applies to your situation, if you're just getting retainers. But she can be a bit intense. And, for example, she only treats girls."

"Really?"

"Yes. She has enough patients, and she finds it easier dealing with just girls. And then there's also that she usually straps down her patients."

I froze. "Straps them down?"

"Yeah," Cecilia laughed. Like a harness – shoulder and lap belts. And then restraints holding the wrist to the armrest." She laughed again, seeing my expression. "But don't worry. Adult patients can opt out if they want to. And if you're just getting the impressions made and then the retainers she might not even want to bother anyway."

"No, no, that's fine," I interrupted overeagerly.

"Fine?"

I blushed, then sighed. "Actually, I think that would be ok. It would be good." And, in fact, it was like a dream fulfilled.

Too good to be true. I *wanted* to be strapped down. It would be worth going to this orthodontist just to experience that.

Cecilia looked at me carefully. "That is how a lot of the patients feel. Though most initially have reservations." She leaned forward and stared at me more closely. "Tell me, honestly. Is it really just that you are worried about your teeth shifting a little, or is there something more to this?"

I blushed a bit. "Well...."

She cocked her head. "At college most people were pretty nice about my braces, pretending they didn't matter much, even though they shook their heads in disbelief at what I looked like behind my back. But you, you seemed genuinely...*happy* about the way I looked. You'd light up when I smiled. Like you thought it was the greatest thing in the world that I had them."

I blushed some more. "I did," I said hoarsely, taking a quick sip of beer.

"Look, if there's something more you want or need, why don't you tell me or Dr.Wrighting about it. Maybe we can help."

"It's so silly."

Cecilia shrugged. "I live and breathe for orthodontics. There's nothing silly to anything about them."

I couldn't look up at her. "It's so embarrassing," I said quietly. "But, well, I kind of want to have braces again. I miss them."

Cecilia nodded seriously. I dreaded her follow-up questions. I knew couldn't bring myself to tell her that I was aroused by the thought of having them. That the night before I had masturbated while fantasizing about her and her braces.

Fortunately she didn't probe any deeper. She just said, "Well why don't you come in and talk to Dr.Wrighting about it, and maybe she can be helpful."

Cecilia told me when she would be working at this Dr.Wrighting's office, and told me to call then so we could schedule a mutually agreeable time for a consultation.

Leaning over and putting her hand on mine after we had drained our beers she said, "Dr.Wrighting really is great. And non-judgmental. Trust her, and let her know what it is you're after."

But what was I after? Recapturing a long-lost feeling, and making it all sexual? That had to sound sordid, even to an open-minded orthodontist.

5.

It wasn't easy to make that call to Cecilia, but I did. I told myself it should be easy. I could stick to the story. I needed a new set of retainers. But I had to admit to myself that I wanted more.

A few days later I went to Dr.Wrighting's office after work. She had her practice in a townhouse. Cecilia, in a white lab coat, was in reception when I got there, and she greeted me and took me to the waiting room. It was already early evening, near the end of office hours, but there were still a few patients and their mothers there. Cecilia told me it might be a quarter of an hour or so before Dr.Wrighting could see me, but at least that might help the butterflies settle in my stomach.

Some more patients were called in and others released while I waited, and after twenty minutes an attractive woman in a lab coat came out, speaking encouragingly with a girl wearing a headgear. The girl looked a bit shell-shocked, but it's hard to look normal wearing headgear, I guess. Especially when all eyes immediately turn and stare, as they did in the waiting room. A mother got up and joined the girl, and they left – the girl still wearing the headgear. Was she going to go out on the street wearing that I wondered, staring after them.

I hardly noticed that the woman in the lab coat now stood in front of me. "Sally Magny?" she asked.

I looked up, startled to hear my name, and then nodded.

"Hi, I'm Dr.Wrighting. Cecilia said you wanted to talk. Why don't you come with me?"

I followed her out of the waiting room.

Down the hall she turned to me. "Do you mind if we look in on one patient before we go to my office?"

I shook my head and followed her. We went into an examination room in which there was just a single dental chair. A girl of about fourteen lay there – strapped down, I saw, and her wrists cuffed to the ends of the armrests. Her mouth was pried wide open with a cheek retractor, revealing two rows of beautiful stainless steel braces which a dental assistant was in the process of working on. A shiver of pleasure went through my entire body as I looked, my heart pounding in my chest. I even peed a little out of excitement; thank God I was wearing a pad. At that moment I would have given anything to trade places with that girl.

21

Dr.Wrighting watched the assistant, who was apparently securing the archwires. The assistant moved away when she was done, so Dr.Wrighting could inspect her work. Dr.Wrighting quickly pulled on a pair of latex gloves and then examined the braces more closely, then nodded with satisfaction. "Looks great. I think we're all set for today."

She removed the cheek retractor and the vacuum tube hooked into the girl's mouth, and asked her whether she had any questions. When the girl didn't she pulled off her gloves and threw them away, and led me out of the room again, leaving the assistant to release the patient.

Dr.Wrighting led me to her office and I took a seat in front of her desk.

"So Cecilia says you need a new set of retainers?" she said.

I nodded and explained, but Dr.Wrighting interrupted me. "I'm sure we can do that. But Cecilia suggested that there might be more you'd like."

I blushed and shrugged. Where to begin? What to say?

Dr.Wrighting didn't press me to respond. "Lots of my patients often miss their braces when they're finished with them. Usually their retainers tide them over. But there's also a small number of patients whose longing is ... stronger. Who find themselves aroused by having braces. Cecilia suggested that you might have some feelings like that."

"Maybe?" I said uncertainly.

"My patients have all sorts of feelings about their orthodontic journeys. I don't judge. In fact, I find it interesting, and I'd like to understand a lot better. Orthodontic fetishism isn't that uncommon, but apparently far more prevalent among males. Since I only treat female patients, I'm particularly interested in cases of a woman who is sexually aroused by braces."

I was blushing deep red now, mortified. I shuddered at the word *fetishism*. Me, some sleazy fetishist?

Dr.Wrighting tried to reassure me. "It's nothing to be embarrassed by. But I would love to study it in greater depth. I get some feedback from my patients, but most of them don't seem to qualify as true fetishists. You, however, seem more ... responsive. Perhaps we could help one another out."

I didn't dare ask how.

"Is it the wearing of braces that ... stimulates you, or your partner wearing them?" she asked.

22

"Me, I guess. I miss having them. Terribly. The feel, the look."

"And your partner?"

"Well, that's the thing, he seems to like them too. On his partner. That's one of the reasons why I thought of getting retainers again. With the wire running across the teeth."

"Of course. And that's easy enough to accommodate. But ideally. If you could have things anyway you wanted…. I mean, it's fairly simple to make fake braces nowadays, brackets and wires mounted on a clear or Hawley retainer, for example."

I hadn't even thought of that. "That would be something, I guess. But I guess what I really want are *braces*. Secured and cemented to my teeth, the whole two tracks all over again. And some of the accessories, I guess. Finally see what it's like to have headgear, for example."

Dr.Wrighting nodded seriously in her chair. "Fascinating," she said. "I'd really love to study and document this. There's far too little about it in the literature. Would you be open to sharing your experience? Privately and entirely anonymously, of course."

"What do you mean?"

"I propose I give you exactly what you want. For a specific period. A year, say. And during that year you provide me detailed feedback on every aspect of the experience. Why you like or don't like certain things. What is arousing, what not. Whether you get bored or tired of it. Ideally, your partner offers feedback too, from his perspective."

"I'm not sure I understand…."

"I outfit you with real and proper braces for … yes, I think exactly a year is good. There will be a treatment plan of sorts, which includes a variety of other orthodontic appliances patients encounter and deal with. Like headgear. And you keep track of your reactions and answer all my questions. To help me learn why these appliances might have this effect, and how these feelings can best be … guided. If your partner is able to contribute as well, that would be extremely helpful. I understand part of it would be embarrassing. Letting me into your bedroom, as it were. But maybe you would get a lot out of it too."

I was numb. I could get braces? It would be wild. And wonderful. And, yes, terrifying and embarrassing. But it was also for science, right?

"I would want to publish my findings," Dr. Wrighting explained. "But you would not be recognizable as the case study."

I was too dazed by the whole idea to know how to respond. Getting braces at my age? When I didn't really need them? Just to indulge in *sex*? Ok, no one had to know that was the reason, but I would know it.

Dr. Wrighting saw that I was overwhelmed by all that she had given me to think about. "Why don't you give it a few days to sink in, and we can consider the possibilities then."

I nodded.

"But would you like me to have a look and maybe take some impressions so that if you do decide you just want the retainers we can get those to you quickly?"

I nodded again.

"I still have a few patients to see," Dr. Wrighting said. "Do you want to wait in the waiting room, or do you want me to set you up in one of the chairs."

"I'd ... that ... I'd like to see what it's like, strapped down and whatnot."

Dr. Wrighting smiled. Like she saw right through me. She led me out and handed me off to one of her assistants. "Can you get Sally comfortable in one of the examination rooms? Number four should have a free chair, right?" She paused for a second. "And why don't you put in a cheek retractor already? I may be a bit, but this way we'll at least have her all ready." She smiled at me and went off to see her other patients.

I followed the assistant, wondering whether this was for real. And what I was getting myself into.

The room she led me to had two chairs, and there was a patient in one of them and a concerned looking mother hovering by her side. "Do you know when Dr. Wrighting will be back?" the mom asked the assistant anxiously. "Morgan really wants to take this device out. It's so big!"

The assistant smiled reassuringly. "Oh, they always feel big at first. It's just a question of getting used to it. Dr. Wrighting should be in soon to check on her."

The mom did not look convinced, and I caught a sight of the girl, who was probably eleven or so, looking unhappy, her mouth held slightly open by the bulk of some device that was in it.

24

The assistant took me to the wall where there was a sort of ruler running straight up it, to a height taller than I was. It had several moving parts in a track in the wood, too, including thinner perpendicular rulers, all with thin wooden pieces the size of pencils sticking straight out. She adjusted these to get measurements between my legs and on top of my shoulders, and to measure the width of my hips. "To adjust the harness on the chair so it fits properly," she explained.

She went over to the free chair and made some adjustments, and then motioned for me to sit down. I smiled awkwardly at the other patient who was watching me, and then lay down on the reclined chair. Deftly the assistant pulled the strap between my legs and the seatbelt across my waist, buckling them securely before I even could say a word. Then she pulled the straps over my shoulders and buckled them in near my waist to. I could shift slightly back and forth, but I couldn't sit up.

"Your wrists go in here," the assistant said, taking my hand and guiding it through a loop at the end of the armrest. Quickly she tightened it so the loop of fabric closed around my wrist and then the Velcro tab secured it down on the armrest. Then the other wrist, and before I knew it I was completely secured.

It was just like it had been when I got my braces, and a warm feeling of bliss came over me. Finally, I got to relive that feeling – and now I'd be allowed to stay awake to enjoy it.

"Dr.Wrighting said I should put in the cheek retractor too...," the assistant reminded me. She pulled some latex gloves on and then got the clear cheek retractors. Obediently I opened my mouth so she could stretch my lips around the device, pulling them wide open. It had been ages since I had been in this position, and this too was a wonderful feeling.

The assistant hooked a small vacuum tube over the cheek retractor, to suck away the saliva that accumulated. "Everything ok?" she asked.

I nodded. Everything was perfect. I couldn't imagine anything better. And if Dr.Wrighting had come in at that moment and asked whether she should put a set of braces on me there and then I would have nodded enthusiastically and let her do anything to my mouth.

It didn't matter that the minutes passed and Dr.Wrighting didn't come. I savored every second, held happily in place by the straps holding me down.

The mom of the other patient paced nervously and gave imploring looks at the assistant. She stroked her daughter's forehead, and asked her how she was doing.

"Now gway," the girl said.

Not great, I guessed. But mom's attitude certainly wasn't helping.

It was at least twenty minutes before Dr.Wrighting came in. She smiled at the other patient but came over to me first. ""How are you doing? Ok?" she asked.

I nodded happily, hoping she understood.

"Is it ok if I leave you like this a while longer?" she asked. "I should take care of Morgan first," she explained.

I nodded vigorously, to make clear that she should take as much time as she liked.

Dr.Wrighting went to the other chair and all the mother's concerns suddenly flooded out, about how this appliance was much too big for Morgan and she couldn't even talk with it, and can't she take it out now.

Dr.Wrighting kept her cool and smiled and nodded, letting the mother get it all out before coolly explaining to Morgan that she realized this was a cumbersome functional appliance, but that she'd get used to it and after a while and lots of practice she would be able to talk fairly comprehensibly again. What was important was that she wore it constantly and always, except when eating or doing sports, and that she never give in to the temptation of just taking it out for a bit. Or for longer....

"But until she gets used to it...." The mother blurted out.

Dr.Wrighting gave her a sharp look, but she still controlled her anger. Smiling at Morgan she asked, "Do you think you'll be able to manage that?"

"I'm naw shoo," Morgan slurred. *I'm not sure.*

Dr.Wrighting crossed her arms and looked like she was thinking about something. You could see in Morgan's eyes how much she hoped Dr.Wrighting would come up with some alternative. Or just tell her she didn't need to wear it after all. While I just looked enviously at Morgan's mouth and the wires across her teeth and the bulky plastic filling her mouth and wished I had to wear a device like that too.

"Well, maybe for a start we should make it a bit easier for you," Dr.Wrighting said. "So you can't give in to temptations to just take it out whenever it feels a bit uncomfortable."

She went to the cupboards and pulled out some things from one of the shelves. Morgan's bug-eyed look of shock when she recognized what was coming almost made me laugh.

Dr.Wrighting sat down on the stool beside Morgan and put a facebow and the straps for a headgear on the tray hovering over her chest. "Alright, let's take this out now," she said, reaching for Morgan's mouth. The girl opened wide, and Dr.Wrighting pulled the large functional appliance free. It looked like both and upper and lower retainer molded out of one large pink piece of plastic, and with about a finger's width of space between them. It really was huge.

"We have some small tubes at the back of the appliance," Dr.Wrighting showed Morgan and her horrified mother. "We can slide the facebow in those – and then lock it in, like this," she demonstrated. There were two small clicks, and then Dr.Wrighting just held the facebow, the device dangling securely from the end.

"Let's put that back in," she said. Morgan opened her mouth less eagerly but in a flash the device was back inside. Except now the rest of the facebow hugged her cheeks. Dr.Wrighting stooped the straps of the headgear over the top and back of Morgan's head, and then hooked the ends into the two ends of the facebow.

"So we'll say that for now you should wear your appliance with this headgear from, say after dinner through the night – so it doesn't 'fall out' while you're sleeping. And then if there's any time you're having trouble wearing it during the day, like when you're watching TV or doing homework, and you're too tempted to fiddle around with it, well then you just snap the headgear on it and strap it on. And if we find at your next appointment that you've had trouble wearing the device as prescribed – like at school and so on – then we'll just weld the headgear on and have you wear it strapped in place all the time."

"To school, too?" the mother asked.

"Well, she has to wear the appliance. If she can't bring herself to wear it all the time at school on her own, or if she keeps taking it out, then we'll have to use the headgear to make sure she wears it."

Morgan looked terrified by this turn of events, but I was even more jealous of what she got to wear. I would have given anything to trade places with her.

Dr.Wrighting began unbuckling Morgan. "Why don't you go wait in the waiting room, and I'll have a brief chat with your mother, and then we'll show you how to take care of the appliance and so on."

"I ha do go aw waying dis?" Morgan asked. *I have to go out wearing this?*

"Well, of course," Dr.Wrighting said, as if it was the most natural thing in the world. She put her hand on Morgan's shoulder. "This appliance is a very, very important part of your treatment, and you're going to be wearing it for a while. You're going to have to get used to wearing it quickly. I know you can handle it."

The girl didn't look convinced, and sullenly shuffled off to the waiting room. Once she was gone Dr.Wrighting's expression changed and I could see how she was ready to explode at the mother. But she kept her cool and even smiled as she asked her to accompany her to her office. She winked at me, and I nodded. She could take as much more time as she needed.

Seeing the girl lisping in the headgear I got all moist between my legs, and with the comforting pressure of the fat padded strap pressing my legs slightly apart I couldn't help but move slightly up and down to rub against it. Closing my eyes, my hands gripping the armrest I couldn't stop myself, until I came. I couldn't stifle the sigh of pleasure that rose from my spread open mouth – and then quickly opened my eyes to check if the assistant had noticed. She had her back turned to me, but I suspected she knew....

It was another twenty minutes before Dr.Wrighting came back and finally sat down on the stool beside me. "So let's have look," she said, and turned on the overhead spotlight and shone it on my still gaping open mouth.

"You haven't been wearing any retainers for a while, I take it," she said when she was done, finally but disappointingly prying the cheek retractor loose.

I shook my head.

"There's just been some slight drift," she told me. "I would certainly recommend taking up consistent retainer-wear again."

"Yes, I figured that would be a good idea."

"But there's hardly been enough damage to warrant any form of active treatment. Although of course we would get everything perfectly lined up if you did take up my suggestion."

It still seemed such a radical idea....

Dr. Wrighting looked at me. "How would you have felt if you were in Morgan's shoes?" she asked. "That girl who was in the other chair."

"I don't think I'd want to wear that headgear out on the street…"

"Oh, no, I didn't make her do that. I just had her get a feel of what it's like in the waiting room, with people staring at her. I let her take it off afterwards. It's just a reinforcement measure. The kind of thing I think she needs at night, to keep herself from succumbing to temptation. And it's the threat that she might have to wear the headgear as well fulltime, and to school, that should be enough to scare her into wearing the appliance itself like she should."

"Well, honestly, even with the headgear…I would have floated out of here on cloud nine if you had made me wear something like that."

Dr. Wrighting laughed. "Well, why don't we hold off on taking the impressions. You decide how you want to proceed, and we'll deal with everything next time."

"You're convinced that I'll opt for the braces?"

"I recognize that gleam in your eyes. It's a once in a lifetime opportunity, right? Why not take it?"

Why not indeed?

I was disappointed when Dr. Wrighting reached over and began to release the straps, handing control back to me and allowing me to rise from the chair.

She suggested I call or email her in a few days, telling her what I wanted to do, and then depending on what I decided we could discuss the details at my next consultation. I should ask Jacob what he thought of the idea, too. And whether he'd be willing to participate – answering all of Dr. Wrighting's questions, keeping track of his reactions over the course of the whole year, and so on.

I left the office dazed but elated. I *liked* the idea and the possibility of having braces. It was like a dream from which one doesn't want to wake. And the thought that it could actually get better, that I might actually get braces…it was almost too good to be true.

6.

It was hard not telling Jacob where I had been and what I had done over dinner, but I knew it was better to bring it up when we were alone. He suggested a movie after we finished at the restaurant, but I said I wanted to go home. "We should talk," I told him.

"Talk?"

"Don't worry, I'm in a playful mood too. But we do have to talk first."

At home on the couch it was hard keeping his hands off me, and we made out for a while. I guess he was trying to soften me up, in case I was really trying to bring up something serious. Me, I was just horny, and it took all my concentration not to throw myself right on him.

"So you know how we were talking about what it would be like if I had braces?" I reminded him.

He perked up right away. "Oh, yeah. I can hardly get the picture out of my mind."

"So how high would you rate braces on your list of desirable features?"

"Honestly? You won't think is too creepy? Look, you're like perfect. These breasts...." He cupped them in his hands and planted a kiss on each. "The whole package...it's fantastic. But braces? That would be something off the charts. If you're a ten, then you with braces would be a twelve...a fifteen."

"So if tomorrow you saw a reasonably attractive woman at a bar, and she flashed a smile revealing a set of braces, and she motioned with her finger for you to come over and she whispered in your ear that she wanted you to take her home, you'd jump at the chance?"

He barely hesitated, but you could see him play it out in his mind. "I'd resist. I have a girlfriend. But honestly, if she had real braces – not those pretend clear kind, but the proper metal ones...well, I wouldn't exactly regret not acting on it, but that's something I'd remember every day for the rest of my life, and wonder, *What if?*"

"And what if I got braces?"

30

"Don't toy with me," he said. "I mean, just imagining it…my balls get sore from the thought alone. I almost wish there was some reason you had to get them again, at least for a while."

"Well, there's no real reason for me to. But there is a slight possibility…." I didn't want to get his hopes up too high, too quickly. I carefully explained that I had seen an orthodontist, and I told him about Dr.Wrighting and what she had suggested.

Jacob looked at me dumbfounded. It was all too good to be true. "You're really thinking of doing it?" he asked, and you could hear his desperation in every syllable.

I nodded.

"Even if it means having to go around with braces?'

"But that's what I want. I'd actually *love* that."

"But with work, and your friends…."

"I guess I should ask at work whether it would matter. But everyone else…I could explain it. Just something that had to be done."

"Oh…my…God," Jacob said, like he was just inches away from realizing his biggest dream, too scared to really believe it might come true. "So what do I have to do to help convince you?" he asked.

It was when he said that that I realized I had some real leverage over him, too. He seemed to want this as badly I did. I wondered what he was willing to do to see that it actually happened?

He fucked me urgently after that, unable to hold himself back. Not that I wasn't just as eager and riled up by the thought of my having braces. He pounded into me. It was wonderful, except it went much too fast. If this was sex with braces still just a fantasy, what could it be like if I actually had them, I wondered.

If I didn't call Dr.Wrighting back first thing the next morning it was because I wanted her to think that I was really thinking about it, and weighing all the pros and cons. But I couldn't hold out long, and it was only a few days before I called to say I thought I did want to go ahead with this. We set up the next appointment.

I did go to my boss and asked him whether having braces would be a problem at the workplace. I work in public relations, and even though I am still a lowly underling I do have to present my smiling face sometimes, so I was worried that he'd say it was out of the question. I didn't know what I'd do then, though the

31

thought of getting the braces was enough to make me consider quitting. I was still right at the start of my career, I told myself. I'd be able to start over somewhere else....

Fortunately it didn't come to that. He made a bit of a face and admitted that it might put a small brake on my advancement, since there might be some assignments he wouldn't want to consider me for, but that I shouldn't worry. "If it's necessary...," he said.

I nodded with a disappointed shrugged, like I hated the idea. "But the dentist says it's really important," I claimed.

He bought it, which was good, since I was going to have to use that line a lot, I realized. But why shouldn't he buy it? No sane person could imagine that I was doing this *voluntarily*. Much less that I was actually *lusting* for it.

I was practically trembling with nervous anticipation when I went to Dr.Wrighting's for the next appointment. She had said there was still a lot to discuss, so I knew I couldn't expect to really get started. Sitting in the waiting room, looking at the sulky girls with the mouths full of metal I could barely repress my thrill at possibly soon being one of them. They didn't realize how lucky they were!

An assistant led me to Dr.Wrighting's office. There was another woman there, about her age, whom Dr.Wrighting introduced as Dr.Allegretta. "She's a braces counselor," Dr.Wrighting explained, "and a trained psychologist, and she'll be co-authoring this study with me. It's something we're both interested in."

Dr.Allegretta seemed nice enough and not too intimidating, though I was a little embarrassed by all this, and the fact that yet another person knew about my secret. And Dr.Allegretta jumped right in. "So you're sexually aroused by the thought of *having* braces, right?"

I blushed deep crimson and hoarsely admitted, "Yes."

"And also by your partner having braces?"

I took a breath. "No," I admitted, "that's not so important. I mean, I like seeing them, and I guess even the feel of them in someone else's mouth. But the most important feeling is in mine. That I have them."

"Interesting. And your partner? You are in a relationship, right?" Dr.Allegretta asked.

I nodded. "Jacob...he seems turned on by the idea of *my* having them. I don't think he wants them so much himself."

"Interesting." Dr.Allegretta took two packs of paper out of a folder, each consisting of at least twenty pages stapled together. "We've come up with these questionnaires which we'd like you and him to fill out." She handed the packs to me. "Look through them. See if there are any questions you have."

They began with simple personal questions – name, sex, age, height, weight, education – and then got much more intimate. Lots of questions about *When did you first become aware of braces? When did you first find them attractive? What did you like about them? Describe the circumstance when you first found yourself aroused by them?* Then all sort of questions about my own orthodontic treatment. Then all sort so of questions about my sexual experiences. Right down to *How often do you masturbate?* and *Do you use any sort of sexual aids when masturbating?*

"Do you think you can answer all that honestly?" Dr.Allegretta said, while I was still looking through them. "We guarantee your anonymity, but we do need you to be completely honest."

Why not? I thought to myself. Sure this was embarrassing. As all hell. But if this was the price for getting to live out a fantasy…. "Sure," I said, with conviction.

"And do you think your boyfriend can, too?"

I nodded.

"Good," Dr.Allegretta said. "But what's also really important to us is to be able to chronicle your reactions to having the braces over the period we settle on." She turned to Dr.Wrighting. "We thought a year was appropriate, right?"

Dr.Wrighting nodded.

"So we'd need you to record your reactions constantly, answer our questionnaires, and so on," Dr.Allegretta said. "For the entire year. And your boyfriend too, if he lasts that long."

Dr.Wrighting interrupted. "We'd also like to experiment with different kinds of appliances, to measure the different reactions. You mentioned headgear, for example, so we'd like to have you wear that for a period. And a variety of removable or maybe not so removable other appliances to go with the basic braces. Which you would have to wear as instructed. In that sense you'd be treated like any other patient, and if you fail to wear an appliance properly, or for the required hours daily, there would be consequences. Less flexibility for you, for example, and longer hours with what might be less comfortable appliances."

"Understood," I said. "That's fine. That's great."

"I'd also like to retain some elements of surprise," Dr.Wrighting said.

"So that you can't always prepare yourself mentally for what's next," Dr.Allegretta added. "As is often the case in actual orthodontic treatment. So that we can measure those reactions, too."

I nodded. It was a bit scary, but I liked the idea of some element of surprise.

"And are you willing to carry on even if you and your partner...go separate ways?" Dr.Allegretta asked.

I didn't like thinking of that, but in the back of my head that worry had already cropped up. What if Jacob grew tired of the braces? But if he couldn't handle me with braces for a year, what kind of long term relationship could we ever have? "I guess...."

"Well, we would like you to be certain," Dr.Allegretta said. "For our purposes, of course, it would also be interesting to see the psycho-sexual impact on someone who does not have an outlet. As well as what other outlets you might eventually find – would there be other men attracted to you, for example."

"Yeah, I guess," I said, without too much conviction. I didn't want to lose Jacob, and I didn't like thinking about that.

"As far as your partner goes," Dr.Wrighting said, "remember that if this is something he is...*into*, that that gives you some power over him. Now, we don't want to suggest you take advantage of that too much..."

"And if you do, remember to let us know!" Dr.Allegretta interrupted.

"...but we do have one specific suggestion." Dr.Wrighting and Dr.Allegretta exchanged glances. "This would be interesting both for our study, and it would also give you a certain amount of...control."

I liked the sound of that, but my jaw dropped when Dr.Wrighting explained to me what she meant. I didn't think anything like that was even possible! But Dr.Wrighting even had a brochure from the doctor. And I understood how it would make the feedback they would get from us more interesting.

"Why don't you talk all this over with him," Dr.Allegretta suggested. "The questionnaires and the feedback we'd like to get from him. And as to this one particular possibility, you should decide whether it's best to make that voluntary or present it to him as an ultimatum...."

I could see what she meant....

"And I would like to have a session with him before we proceed," Dr.Allegretta added. "Just to get a baseline reading, and to see how he feels about everything."

I nodded, still a bit overwhelmed by everything they were suggesting and expecting.

"So you think you'd like to go ahead?" Dr.Wrighting asked.

I nodded. Scary though it was, especially now that it seemed more real, I really did.

"Why don't we take some X-rays and molds of your teeth, to see what we'll be working with, and I can begin to draw up a treatment plan."

"And if you could fill out the questionnaire, and have Jacob do it too, and have him get in touch with me so we can set up a session...."

I nodded and followed Dr.Wrighting out. I barely registered what was happening then, almost completely spaced out as Dr.Wrighting took the X-rays and then made the impressions of my teeth.

It was all so exciting, and so scary.

7.

Jacob knew about my appointment, and so there was no way I couldn't immediately tell him what had happened and how it had gone. I gave him one of the questionnaires, and I could see how his face got white when he saw how personal a lot of the questions were. I told him Dr.Allegretta wanted to talk to him, and that she'd be able to allay many of his concerns, about privacy and stuff like that. He nodded his head, trying to convince himself that it was worth it.

He *really* wanted me to get braces, so he was ready to put up with a lot. But I was still worried that he wouldn't put up with what Dr.Wrighting had also suggested. But the more I thought about, the more I thought it was something I liked. I wanted some control too. I wanted him to have to pay a price for the pleasure he'd be getting. And there was my history. I had had three serious boyfriends in high school and college, and each of them had cheated on me. If there was a way to prevent that, then I wanted to take it.

I introduced the subject carefully. Like me, he couldn't believe you could even do that. But I showed him the brochure and said it was fairly simple. And I also said it was something I had to insist on. If I was getting braces he would have to do this.

Before he could say yes or no to the ultimatum I told him he should think about it. And that he should talk to Dr.Allegretta first, and then decide.

I didn't want to discuss it anymore because I was so afraid he'd just say *No way!* and I knew if he did I'd give in and still get the braces, because it was an opportunity I couldn't pass up. And I knew if he saw me cave like that he'd probably cheat on me at some point too, just to get away from the braces sometime during the year, no matter how much he liked them.

Even though we both had a lot on our mind as we considered all the implications of the steps we were thinking of taking the thought of my getting braces overwhelmed them all, leaving us incredibly worked up and randy. The love-making was great once we got to it – and we got to it pretty fast. We both laughed how it was almost not necessary that I get the braces, as long as we convinced ourselves that I was getting them!

Jacob made an appointment with Dr.Allegretta right away. She made time for him very quickly, which only made him more nervous about going there. I was on pins and needles too, about what he was going to decide and whether he could really go along with everything. He had filled out the questionnaire by then, but we had both decided not to show each other our answers. Even though we were lovers, some of the things were scary personal. We were going to ask Dr.Allegretta whether we had to share all the information with each other. Both of us were fine with not being quite so completely open with each other.

He came to my apartment after his appointment, looking a bit pale and spent. But he was smiling and his head was bobbing up and down. "Yes," he said. "We can do this. I can do this. I want to do this."

"Everything?" I asked.

He looked me in the eye, realizing the price he was paying. "Keeping a diary and submitting to her questions. I can do that. Absolutely. And the rest...." He hesitated. "No. Yes, I can do that too. Absolutely."

I sank bank on the couch in ecstatic relief. We were actually going to do this. And in part on my terms. "So I guess we can plan on getting started."

"Dr.Allegretta already made the first appointment. For me. So that we can get that taken care of. And then it's your turn, with Dr.Wrighting." He showed me a notebook. "Dr.Allegretta already gave me one, to start documenting everything. She gave me one for you, too," he said, pulling another out of his bag. "Like all our feelings about starting this. And our sexual routines and practices before we really get going."

I put my arms around him. "Oh, I like the idea of some sexual practices. Now. And later. And again and again...."

I couldn't believe that this was all happening. It seemed so fast too, even though there were still several steps until I had the braces on my teeth. But not too many.

The first step was Jacob's appointment with Dr.McDarmon, which Dr.Allegretta had arranged. We both felt a bit uneasy about what was awaiting us there, and I worried that Jacob would chicken out at the last moment. Or earlier. But I was also pleased that this was even possible.

Dr.McDarmon was a gynecologist, which sort of surprised me. But this part of her practice was solely a sideline. Jacob felt distinctly uncomfortable in the waiting room, with all the women. But he probably would have felt more uncomfortable if there were one or two other men there.

An assistant called our names, and led us to an examination room. I was going to ask whether I was supposed to come along, but then decided it was assumed that I should.

The room was like your usual gynecological examination room, dominated by the intimidating examination chair with the stirrups, where you lay there with your legs spread wide apart, as exposed as you could be. I liked my gynecologist, but even I felt a bit uncomfortable when I sat like that, and when she probed me.

Dr.McDarmon came in and introduced herself. She was in her late-forties, and looked like a real no-nonsense doctor. She immediately got right to it. "So this is what we'll be doing today," she explained. "We're going to fit you with a flexible metal cage like this," she said, holding up a round piece of wire-mesh some six inches long and an inch or so in diameter and with a bulbous tip. "Fitted to your dimensions, of course," she added. "And that will attach to a metal ring that will fit around the back of your scrotum, allowing it to be locked in place. Once secured, the device won't prevent you from having an erection, but it's practically impossible for you to self-pleasure yourself, or engage in any other kind of sexual activity. Urination is not a problem, though it can be messy until you get the hang of it, and you're probably better off not using urinals. Good hygiene is obviously more time-consuming and complicated, but can be maintained even if the device isn't removed for extended periods of time. You are circumcised, right?"

Jacob nodded.

"That does make it much simpler. Now as I understand it, your partner here will be entrusted with the keys, and I assume you have reached some sort of agreement about what constitutes appropriate use. If at any time you feel the need to be released from it and your partner can't or won't that you can come to me and I will immediately unlock it. I will, however, also immediately contact your partner, and I note from experience that such breaches of protocol tend to lead to the dissolution of the partnership in question."

"And this actually works?" I couldn't help asking. A chastity belt – for a man! I had never even heard of such a thing.

"Deceptively simple, and, when properly fitted, essentially 100% effective. All the lore about female chastity belts is wildly exaggerated. For reasons of hygiene alone, it's not very satisfactory. But male chastity is easy to impose."

"And there's no...danger?" Jacob asked, understandably nervous about his testicles.

"Obviously some care must be taken. No sliding across wooden floors in the nude. And there can be some discomfort and chafing. But overall patients have little reason to complain."

"Do you...fit a lot of these?"

"Not many doctors do this, but yes, I usually have a couple of patients a week. Obviously, a lot of mothers want their sons fitted with preventative measures like this. Their daughters, too, but I can't help them there...."

"They don't refuse, kicking and screaming?" Jacob wondered.

"Oh, no, I'd never do anything like this entirely against their will. Some cooperation is required. But in contemporary culture it's possible to convince impressionable young boys that removing temptation is for their own good. In households where masturbation is treated like a terrible sin they're pretty easy to convince. We try to get to them young, before they've really figured out the habit for themselves, and can usually keep them confined until they're sixteen or so, when they either get too rebellious, or they've achieved enough self-control that the device is hardly necessary any longer.

"There are also boys who have been convinced to try to save themselves for marriage, and they welcome this as a pre-marital aid. Devout Christians are my best customers. Of course, there are also many mature adults, such as yourself. In some cases fiancées insist on it during the engagement period, or young women who have concerns about their mate's fidelity. And there are married couples who have a variety of reasons for keeping the family jewels locked up.

"Of course, if I ever could get female chastity figured out – except for the most temporary measures – then I'd really be on the right track."

"You do the... temporary measures?" I asked.

"Oh, sure. But it's little more than a novelty act. Useful in some situations, but not a long term solution."

"You're sure it won't...like cut off the blood flow, or cause permanent damage?" Jacob asked nervously.

Dr.McDarmon laughed reassuringly. "I haven't lost a penis yet," she said. "And that's why you're coming to a professional. I make sure it's just the right fit, so that it's both safe, for your sake, and secure, for hers."

Jacob looked at me like I could somehow save him from this, but this was a step I wanted us to take.

"So, shall we get started?" Dr.McDarmon asked.

Reluctantly Jacob nodded.

"Alright, why don't you take your pants and underwear off." She turned around and put some latex gloves on.

Jacob looked pretty hapless, half disrobed.

"On the chair, please," Dr.McDarmon said, and then, "Legs in the stirrups."

Jacob looked miserable with his legs up and in the stirrups.

"I'm just going to secure these," Dr.McDarmon explained, as she secured Velcro straps around Jacob's ankles, fastening them in the stirrups. "And now I'm going to spread your legs a bit farther apart," she said, and spread the stirrups apart.

Jacob's flaccid penis dangled down. It looked pretty sad.

"First we'll measure around the base," Dr.McDarmon explained, maintaining her professional demeanor. She took a white plastic loop attached to a thin rod and slipped over Jacob's penis and around his balls, and then slowly tightened it. Jacob's penis briefly perked up a bit at the touch, but then deflated again once it was inside the noose.

I could see there was a small readout on the rod that told Dr.McDarmon the circumference of the loop. "That's not too tight, is it?" she asked, wiggling the loop around a bit.

Jacob was cringing. "It feels pretty tight."

"Tight, or snug?" Dr.McDarmon asked.

"Snug, I guess," Jacob admitted.

Dr.McDarmon noted down the measurement and then widened the loop so she could slip it off again. From a set of drawers she then pulled out a piece of metal. She held it up for Jacob and me to see. "So this is the base," she said. "Made of titanium, so it's very light, and appropriately contoured to minimize chafing and discomfort."

It wasn't quite round. More like a triangle, with two of the sides slightly dented in, and a flat piece jutting out from the top round side. "It goes on like this," Dr.McDarmon demonstrated, "with this side on top."

The ring could be spread slightly, so that it could be slipped around the penis and scrotum. "When the cage is attached and locked in place, the base no longer widens like this," Dr.McDarmon explained, "so it can't be removed."

She asked Jacob how it felt. He wasn't very happy, but he had to admit it sat comfortably in place. It really was vaguely contoured to his body, and with the curved edges seemed to be about as comfortable as anything could be in that area of the male body.

"Alright," Dr.McDarmon said. "Now for the next part we're going to need the penis in a...tumescent state. Is there any way we can help you achieve that? Some manual assistance?"

Jacob blushed. "I...I don't know...."

Dr.McDarmon looked at me for some help, so I moved closer to Jacob and drew one of his hands onto my breast. I ran my tongue over my teeth and reminded him, "Just think of what these are going to look like in a few days. Close your eyes and just imagine...."

That did the trick. With her expert touch Dr.McDarmon quickly measure the length, and then pulled the same loop-device around the swollen gland to get a precise measure of the width. She was just fast enough, before Jacob started to go limp again.

Dr.McDarmon went to another set of drawers and came back with a wire mesh cage shaped somewhat like a penis. Like she had shown us, just a bit smaller. The wire of the mesh left gaps more than a quarter of an inch apart, and one end had a round opening. It was also made out of titanium, and appeared to be fairly flexible, although it did not bend nearly as limply down as Jacob's penis now was.

Dr.McDarmon easily slipped the cage around his flaccid cock. At the base there was a protuberance that slid easily into the ring secured around Jacob's balls. Dr.McDarmon produced a small unusually shaped flat key and turned it in the part connecting the two titanium pieces, locking the cage in place.

It was an ingenious design. As Dr.McDarmon demonstrated by lifting the cage in all different directions, the way the two pieces were locked together made it impossible for even Jacob's shriveled penis to be pulled out of it.

"Now let's make sure that in the erect state we have the right fit, too," she said, looking at me. I went to work on Jacob again, but it was a bit harder, because he kept turning his attention from me to the metal cage his penis was now imprisoned in. But I got him around.

The cage was even more impressive now. Widening slightly towards the end, I saw that when Jacob had an erection, no part of the top half of his penis came into contact with any part of it. It was not flexible enough to be bent towards it, or squeezed around it, and there remained a gap of at least half an inch to the slightly bulbous end of the tube even when Dr.McDarmon pulled the cage as close to Jacob's body as possible. I saw what that meant. There was no way Jacob could masturbate while the device was in place. The penis, and especially the sensitive tip, was truly inaccessible!

"Perfect!" Dr.McDarmon said, after manipulating the cage in every imaginable way, to make sure that it really did fit perfectly, and functioned the way it should.

Next she showed me how to lock and unlock the device, and had me practice taking the entire thing on and off several times. I was amazed how light but solid it was. Finally Jacob was allowed to get up, with the device dangling around his cock.

He stood up gingerly, but soon saw that it didn't really get in the way of normal movement. He didn't want to admit it, but I

41

could see he was surprised that it wasn't nearly as much of an uncomfortable inconvenience as he had thought it would be.

Dr.McDarmon smiled. "My clients are usually surprised by how easy it is to get used to. Though I do warn you that urinating and proper hygiene will prove to be a bit frustrating."

Dr.McDarmon had Jacob put his underwear and pants on again. There was now a slight bulge in his crotch area, but it wasn't too noticeable.

"For the first two days, I suggest you just wear it at home. Put it on after work and wear it while sleeping. Tonight I suggest separate beds, too. No sex tonight, but then I would suggest sex every night before sleeping. Get it out of your system. And then by the weekend you should be ready for full-time wear. And whatever celibacy program you're following."

Dr.McDarmon gave me two keys, and said that if I ever needed another she would immediately provide it. "And if there are any issues whatsoever," she told Jacob, "come to me *immediately*. Any injuries, or even just bad chafing, or any other problems. That's not something you want to be playing games with."

Jacob nodded and we thanked her and left. I held Jacob's hand, and noticed he was trembling slightly. It was all quite overwhelming.

We immediately had another appointment with Dr.Allegretta and Dr.Wrighting, who tried not to sound too curious about how everything had gone. They explained that they wanted to allow for an adjustment period, until we were sure that this new device worked like it should. Then the plan was for me to get spacers in at the end of the next week, and for the braces to be installed a week later. Jacob couldn't suppress a slight moan at the sound of that, and I could see the bulge in his pants expand.

"Now because we are particularly interested in the sexual reactions to the treatment we'd like you to try to follow a certain routine," Dr.Allegretta reminded us. "In particular, we'd like you to abstain from any sexual relations for specific set periods. Starting with the lead-up to the braces getting installed, and then for the first week they're on. And then for specific times during the treatment. Do you think you can do that?"

"Sure," I said. Jacob seemed a little less certain, but it looked like his desires would be also be easier to keep in check.

Dr.Allegretta gave me a print-out of a calendar for the next two months, with large blocks in red. "This is the tentative schedule we'd like you to follow. If everything else goes according to plan. We'll have to discuss masturbation separately. I'm inclined to let you indulge in it if you want. But obviously we would want Jacob to be strictly limited in his outlets. Sex or nothing."

It was weird discussing this, but I was so happy about how everything was going that I didn't mind. Having the keys to all of Jacob's sexual activity was proving to be really empowering, and being so close to my dream of having braces again coming true I couldn't imagine anything better. Except actually having the braces. And that was going to happen so wonderfully soon!

8.

"God, am I glad I didn't try to take a piss at the office," Jacob said when he came out of the bathroom. "That is going to be a challenge."

"But otherwise?"

He looked at me. "Honestly, I don't know. It's so weird to have that dangling there. But it's surprisingly light and…not as much in the way as I figured it would be. But keeping things clean…."

"And being prevented from using it in other ways…."

Jacob nodded, looking unsure. I didn't dare ask him how much he masturbated or otherwise played around with his cock, but I assumed that not having easy access to it would quickly get annoying. But for now at least there was still some novelty value to this game.

We went out for dinner, but I didn't go home with Jacob afterwards, not wanting either of us to succumb to temptation. I promised to come by early in the morning to release him, and I called him when I got home, to see how he was doing. We were able to joke about it, so that was good.

The next morning he was pretty glad to see me. He said it had been a bit difficult to sleep, because that was a lot of metal there – and he was constantly afraid he'd catch it on something.

"Like your sheets? Your blanket?" I said incredulously.

"Hey, you don't have a cage attached to your family jewels," he reminded me.

He admitted it was weird having an erection inside the cage too.

"Did you try to see whether you could...manipulate anything?" I had to ask.

He blushed slightly but admitted he had. "There ain't no satisfaction to be found there, let me tell you."

I was pleased to hear that. But also a little scared. How long could it be kept penned in like that before he blew?

I released his penis from its prison – glad to see that I could do it easily and quickly – and Jacob took a shower. I reminded him that that night I'd make up for what we'd missed the night before. He deserved more than a reward, and I was going to make the evening special.

I met him right after work and immediately locked his cock in place again before we went out for dinner and a movie. I could see him shift uncomfortably in his seat in the dark, half aroused, half constrained. Cruelly I put my hand in his lap and grabbed the metal cage through his pants, holding on. But at the end he just wanted to get home fast because he didn't want to use a public bathroom and he really had to pee.

When we got home he briefly pleaded with me to take the cage off right away, to make it easier for him to piss, but I reminded him that he was going to have to get used to it and I was in no rush. His bladder was too close to bursting for him to argue.

I teased him some more when he joined me on the couch, and we made out, with his penis still barred from the action. Only when we moved to the bedroom did I finally relent and unlock his chastity device. I took his freshly freed cock in my mouth and only had to suck on it briefly before I could taste the salty drops of his semen leaking out. Then I pulled back and guided his cock into me, so I could get properly fucked too. Of course he was way too primed for it, exploding into me almost as soon as he'd plunged halfway into me. But I gave him a few minutes of recovery time, and fortunately he was ready, willing, and able to give it a good and more satisfying second go.

"Wash up," I told him after we had caught our breaths. "Time to lock it up for the night."

Jacob protested a bit, but he knew there was no choice in the matter. He showered quickly and then presented himself to get caged up again, which I quickly did.

"You sure you're going to be alright with me spending the night here?" I asked.

"Sure," he said. "I'm supposed to get used to this, right?"

He did toss and turn more than usual, and the feel of the solid metal when he pressed against me was odd, but we both made it through the night.

In the morning I released him again, and we repeated the routine over the next few days and nights. He barely had any chafing and no other complaints, so everything was going well. But with the weekend coming we knew there was going to be a change. Saturday morning I didn't take it off, even as we spooned in bed, and he had to wear it all day long. I let him take it off for sex and a shower in the evening, but then locked him up until the next night. And Monday he wore it to work.

Monday evening I reminded him that this was now it. One last fuck, and then abstinence was going to be imposed for almost three weeks. I had my appointment with Dr.Wrighting later in the week, and then a week after that I was due to get the braces installed. And then we still had to wait a week until we were allowed to have sex again.

Even just the mention of my appointment with Dr.Wrighting was enough to get him rock hard in his little cage. With both of us sitting naked on my bed I cradled the round wire mesh in my hands, fascinated by how inaccessible his penis was, and how effective this metal barrier was.

"Are you going to manage all that time?" I asked.

"I'm going to explode, I'm sure of it. I haven't gone anywhere near that long without sex in...years. And it'll be worse than any usual period of abstention, because I'll have the most titillating vision so close by. Separated from me just by your lips...."

I took the cage in my mouth to tease him more, feeling the heat coming off his pulsing purple member. But one more time I released him from the cage and allowed him to have his way with me.

After he showered and returned to bed I slid his cock into my mouth one more time. "A parting kiss," I reminded him, slipping his immediately hard organ into the cage and locking it in. Where it was going to remain untouched for almost three weeks.

9.

That week I watched all the braces episodes of *Family Does It* on DVD, envying Tabs and knowing that I was soon going to follow in her footsteps. I always loved that show. There aren't that many TV shows where a character has braces for a long time, and Tabitha Martin was my favorite. I couldn't believe that the actress who played her was one of Dr.Wrighting's patients. I even have her *All Braced Up and Everywhere To Go* poster that Dr.Wrighting has in her practice. Sometime I think about hanging it up on my wall, but maybe that's too weird. So I just use a picture of it as a screensaver on my computer.

Jacob watched some of the episodes with me, but he would get all restless. Like an animal in a cage, I joked. But it really was too much for him, so when he came over we tried not to focus only on what was about to happen.

We both kept our diaries for Dr.Wrighting and Dr.Allegretta, writing about all the sensations we had and what was going through our heads. At first I was embarrassed to write some of the things. *Nipples getting all hard while I watch Tabitha on Family Does It.* Or *Running tongue over my teeth, imagining not being able to feel the smooth surfaces soon. Getting all moist as I think about the metal that's going to be there. Can't keep hands off myself. Have to masturbate. Come immediately.* But after a while I didn't mind. It was for science, I told myself. But Jacob and I agreed not to read each other's writings unless one of us really wanted to share. We couldn't help but still feel a bit self-conscious about this whole experiment.

My next appointment was scheduled at a time when Jacob could come too. I wasn't getting the braces yet, but it was for the final prep work.

Because of his chastity cage there was always a slight bulge to Jacob's pants, but once he sat in the waiting room, surrounded just by girls and women, half of them wearing noticeable orthodontic devices, I could see that he was practically bursting at the seams. He tried hard not to stare, but lecherous curiosity got the best of him, and he sat there with his mouth drooping and eyes wide open, taking in this braced paradise. Even I was a bit excited in that way, too. Having Jacob there made it more exciting, too. I would have loved to take him in some back room and let him fuck me right there and then. He didn't even have to take the cage off. He could just shove it all right into me....

An assistant came and led us to an examination room, where she strapped me into the chair. I could see Jacob's eyes grow even wider. At least strapped down like this I was similarly chastised like he was, the broad padded belt that went between my legs blocking any access. Of course, unlike his cage that didn't permit any satisfaction, the soft resistance of that strap actually enhanced my own sexual feelings, and I had to resist from thrusting my pelvis back and forth to rub against it. My hands tied down as well I felt both vulnerable and protected. Blissfully happy at the journey I was about to begin.

Dr.Wrighting came in and greeted us. She explained that she had settled on a course of treatment – "Non-treatment is more like it," she added – and that she wanted to see that everything was in order for the big day.

She turned on the spotlight and shone it on my mouth, and then began inspecting my teeth. I didn't think there was anything that was wrong that could possibly stand in the way. I never had cavities, and my gums were in good shape. And Dr.Wrighting did look satisfied when she finally pulled back.

"I am going to insert some spacers to make some room for the bands that are going over some of the teeth," she told us.

I shuddered with pleasure under the straps. Bands were better than just brackets. Hugging the teeth. More metal. More secure. I was glad to hear it.

She got out the tiny colored rubber circles that she then proceeded to force between a lot of my teeth, both upper and lower.

"These will probably cause you the most discomfort of anything we do," Dr.Wrighting said. "The slight shifting they cause is like the pain patients feel when they get braces, or when they're adjusted. But since we're not putting much tension into your braces, they'll probably never hurt as much as when these take, in a few hours."

I didn't care. I didn't mind. I kind of wanted to feel that bracey ache of teeth being forced against their will into new straight positions.

I knew the spacers were going to be slightly annoying. Like bits of food stuck between my teeth that I would be tempted to pick free. But I could keep myself from doing anything like that, because I knew what the reward for leaving them untouched for the next week was going to be. My dreams and wish fulfilled.

Dr.Wrighting was done quickly, and there was no good reason to keep me strapped down. She reminded us of the upcoming schedule and what was expected from us, and then we could go.

Dr.Allegretta interviewed us each one more time too, to record our final feelings and expectations before we actually reached the stage we were so looking forward to. By now I found it fun to talk about all this. I still felt a bit self-conscious, but Dr.Allegretta made it easy for me to completely open up and reveal my wildest fantasies. I worried a bit that having braces wouldn't live up to all my expectations, but Dr.Allegretta remained a neutral counselor, neither reassuring me nor telling me I should dial back my expectations.

The waiting was *tough*. The slight aching in my teeth the spacers caused helped, a pleasant reminder of what was to come, but I knew they were nothing compared to what would be on my teeth soon. Not even like the preview to a movie. More like a black-and-white print ad compared to the 3D cinematic spectacular to come.

Jacob complained too. Unable to get any sort of sexual release, he grumbled about how tough it got. He tried *not* to think of what was coming. "Just the thought of your wired-up mouth makes me all stiff and desperate," he moaned. So of course I teased him by running by tongue over my teeth and describing what was soon going to be covering them. I know it was cruel, but it was fun too, and even if he suffered from not being able to relieve himself I knew he liked it too.

10.

And then the day came. The day when I was getting braces again. I could barely sleep the night before. My appointment was in the morning, but Dr.Wrighting said it was going to take several hours. I took a personal day from work, so I could devote the entire day to nothing else.

Jacob couldn't take the time off from work, but he spent the night with me, just as restless. Or even more so, his engorged penis locked in its cage, desperate to ram itself into me, but unable to do so.

We kissed long and hard before he went to work, one last kiss with my unfettered teeth against his, his tongue running across my teeth and deep inside my mouth, imagining all the obstructions that would be there when he next encountered it.

I finished my last meal without the braces, and brushed my teeth one last time without the braces, and then I went to Dr.Wrighting's practice.

I practically floated over, grinning ear to ear. I was elated. I signed in at the reception desk and then went to the waiting room. The other girls and their mothers stared, maybe wondering what I was so happy about. I couldn't understand why they didn't share in my overjoyed feeling of expectation. I envied those who already had devices in their mouths, and I couldn't understand why they didn't bask more fully in the incomparable delight of being braced. Didn't they understand that this was the best time of their lives?

I was nervous and jumpy, but in a good way. Like when you're anticipating something great, like being awarded first prize for something important, or being hailed as some kind of hero. Except what I was anticipating was better. I wouldn't trade it for anything in the world.

It wasn't more than a quarter of an hour, but the wait did seem endless. When my name was finally called and I got up, my legs almost buckled from the excitement of where my steps were taking me. I hurried after the assistant and savored the empty examination room, and the chair in which I was going to lie down, and where my life would be changed.

I sat down and let the assistant strap me in, appreciating the feeling of the harness that held me tightly in place. The broad padded strap between my legs was tighter than usual, but I didn't complain. I liked the pressure there, and the way it forced my legs slightly apart. When she strapped down my wrists, I told her, "Tighter." I wanted to feel the securing strap wrapped like an iron hold around my wrist.

When she was done I sighed blissfully, ready for the long journey ahead. Dr.Wrighting came in soon to say hello and see that everything was ready, but she warned me that today was going to take a while. She directed the assistant to prepare everything, and so trays of silvery bands and pieces of wire and various tools were laid out on the tray hovering over my chest and on a cabinet nearby.

49

Dr.Wrighting left for a while, while the assistant was getting all the things ready. I could feel my heart pounding against the straps across my chest.

Finally Dr.Wrighting was ready to start. She began by removing the spacers, making sure all were accounted for. There was a small sense of relief, like the pressure was suddenly missing, between my teeth after she had taken them out. Running my tongue over and around them, I could detect the thin new spaces between them.

Next came the scraping and polishing and cleaning and swabbing of my teeth. It was a bit unpleasant, but I knew it was important. I really didn't want any bacteria trapped behind the brackets and bands, rotting away my teeth while I had the braces!

Then she spread my lips far apart and secured them with the cheek retractor, leaving my mouth entirely exposed. I loved the feel of the plastic forcing my lips completely apart and making it impossible for me to close them. Now I was really at Dr.Wrighting's mercy, and now she could start actually putting the braces on.

She did hook one of those vacuum tubes on the side of the my mouth, so it would suck out the saliva. And she wadded in some pieces of cotton between my cheeks and my teeth.

Then she picked up the first metal band from the tray with a pair of pliers, holding it up for me to see. It was beautiful, a silvery metal, and with a raised part on one side where the wire would fit, as well as a thin, straight piece of silvery tubing. "That's where the headgear goes," she said, making me shudder in happy anticipation again.

She made sure the band fit over the molar before actually installing in, swabbing the tooth with something, and I guess brushing some glue on the inside of the band. She had to apply some pressure to force it over the tooth, but with the help of a hard metal tool it slid perfectly and securely into place.

Dr.Wrighting repeated the procedure, with small variations, on tooth after tooth, working her way around all my top and bottom molars and premolars first. She showed me some of the bands she was installing, some of which only had the raised groove where the archwire fit, while others also had small hooks with balls on the top or other small metal fixtures whose purpose I couldn't identify.

50

Dr.Wrighting took a break after having done a lot of my teeth, leaving me there with my mouth wide open, halfway to where I wanted to be. It was fine lying there in that open-mouthed limbo. On the one hand I was eager to be done, on the other hand I wanted this installation procedure to be drawn out forever.

Dr.Wrighting came back and continued, and I was happy that she kept holding up bands even for my front teeth. They slid over my incisors much more easily, and I liked the firm hold they had over each tooth, which I felt as Dr.Wrighting pushed up or down against the front of the band after it had been cemented in place. Only a few of the lower front teeth just got brackets, which were simply glued on to the front of the teeth.

"The banding and bracketing stage is complete," Dr.Wrighting said with a satisfied smile as she pulled off her latex gloves. "We'll give it a bit, and then I'll be back to install the archwires."

Waiting for her to come back it began to hit me what I had done. I now had a full set of braces attached to my teeth. What were people going to think? In all the excitement I hadn't even really considered how I was going to explain it to my family or friends. Not that I suddenly had any regrets, but it began to dawn on me that having braces was going to be more complicated than … just having braces.

I was practically shivering with excitement when Dr.Wrighting came back. Now I was just moments away from having my finished set of braces.

Dr.Wrighting picked up a parabola-shaped piece of wire and held it up. "We're using the widest diameter possible for the archwires," she explained. "So they'll really be noticeable. But it should also be more comfortable for you."

That sounded fine with me.

The bands and brackets Dr.Wrighting had used were self-ligating, so the wire fit in the groove on each, and then there was a piece of the band or bracket that covered it and held it in place, which locked into place. So attaching the archwires was very easy. The protuberances on the front of the bands and brackets were bigger, to accommodate all this, but I liked the finished all-metal look better than the kind of braces where the archwires were held in place by colored rubber-band ligatures.

Dr.Wrighting gave a satisfied nod when she looked at my finished set of braces. "And we are done," she announced.

I closed my eyes and tried to float in that moment, my mouth still held wide open by the cheek retractors. But this was it. I was braced.

Dr.Wrighting removed the vacuum tube, and then the cheek retractors. My slightly numb lips sank down and came up against the metal of the braces, which now replaced the formerly smooth front of my teeth. The metal was all uneven, but the surfaces were also very smooth. It felt wonderful and weird. With my tongue I could feel the flat back of the bands on many of my teeth, and then I carefully ran it cross the front. The metal on my teeth felt huge!

Dr.Wrighting still scraped and picked at my teeth, getting a few areas where small bits of cement had oozed out. She had me rinse several times.

"Can I see now?" I finally asked.

Dr.Wrighting smiled and shook her head. "No mirrors here. I let my patients get used to the feel of their new accessories first. They'll be able to stare long and hard enough at them at home."

I was a bit disappointed, but I understood what Dr.Wrighting meant. And it was sort of cool to be braced without yet knowing what the full extent of that meant.

Dr.Wrighting reminded me of some of the instructions as to how to care for the braces, like not eating certain foods or drinking coffee or sugared sodas. And she reminded me that I had taken a fairly permanent step. "We've set a one-year timetable," she reminded me, "but that also means that we won't be able to remove them any earlier. The strength and mix of adhesive I used makes it unsafe to try to remove them any earlier, so for better or worse you are literally stuck with them for the entire year."

But I knew it was for better. I knew that was just fine.

Dr.Wrighting also reminded me that I should keep a close record of my reactions and feelings, including all the intimate ones. "No kissing for the first three days at all, and Jacob stays locked out of action for the entire week. If you choose to pleasure yourself, or have him pleasure you in another way before then be sure to document everything about that."

Then I was released, another braced patient sent out to face the world again. I must have been grinning ear to ear when I walked through the waiting room. Everyone stared, surprised by someone my age with such an extensive set of braces, I guess. I

52

couldn't understand why the braced girls waiting their turn didn't smile back. I, for one, was thrilled to be part of this metal-mouthed sisterhood.

I got my appointment slip for my next appointment and then went outside, taking my first steps as a rebraced girl. Dr.Wrighting wanted me to see Dr.Allegretta immediately, so that was my first destination.

I was tempted to look at my reflection in the glass windows I kept passing, but I kept myself from doing so. I wanted my first glimpse of what I looked like to be one in front of a good mirror, where I could take the time to examine everything closely. So in the meantime I just smiled at everyone I passed on the street and looked at their reactions. My braces certainly attracted a lot of stares!

In the waiting room at Dr.Allegretta's there was a girl with headgear with her mother. Both stared at me when I came in, eyes transfixed by the silvery metal in my mouth. I gave them a friendly smile, but they both looked pretty aghast.

"Did you just get those?" the mother asked.

"My braces?" I nodded enthusiastically. "Uh-huh. Just now."

"It must be so hard, at your age."

"Are you kidding? I'm so lucky!" I leaned forward to the girl with the headgear and added, "Except I don't get to wear anything like that yet."

They must have thought I was making fun of her. Or that I was just plain crazy. They didn't ask anything else.

The girl went in ahead of me. I didn't mind waiting. I just couldn't read any of the magazines spread out there. All I could think about was my braces. And getting used to the feel of the braces against the inside of my cheeks, and exploring the front of them by running my tongue over them. They felt enormous, like everything in your mouth feels magnified hundreds of times over by your tongue.

After half an hour it was my turn.

"Congratulations," Dr.Allegretta said.

I squealed. "Thanks! I haven't even seen them yet, but they feel...perfect!"

"Well, they look very fine, too," she assured me. "Do you mind not having seen what you look like yet?"

I shook my head. "I like the sense of anticipation. And I already get to feel them. And see how others react to them!"

"How are people reacting?"

"Dazed," I giggled. "Confused. Shocked."

"You like those reactions?

I shrugged. "If people don't immediately understand how *wonderful* these are...."

"You're not worried about the reactions wearing you down? Because you know you can't remove them, right? You're stuck looking like this for the next year."

"I guess I'm a bit nervous about it, but I know the pluses totally outweigh any minuses."

Dr.Allegretta had a lot of questions from a sort of checklist she had prepared, and we went through all of those. Then she reminded me to keep recording all my sensations and thoughts and she said we were finished for today.

I took my time getting back home. I was dying to see how I looked, but I also wanted to put off that wonderful, once-in-a-lifetime moment.

When I got home I called Jacob, telling him I was all braced up – and that I hadn't looked at them yet. He wanted to hear all about them, and to have me describe what they looked like.

I put the phone on speaker and then put it down next to the large mirror that I approached close-mouthed. I put my hand in front of my mouth to describe it to him. "Even with my mouth closed, I can see the bulge behind my cheeks and lips. The two rows of braces pushing outwards."

I got right in front of the mirror, still holding my hand in front of my mouth. "Okay," I said. "I'm in position. I'll count to three and then take my hand away. One.

"Two.

"Three."

I pulled my hand away, my mouth in a huge, revealing grin. But I couldn't say anything at that first sight. Was that even me? I looked totally different. The two white rows of teeth I had had.... Now there were only two densely metal-covered rows of braces there, with just the top and bottom edges of most of the teeth visible.

I didn't just have braces, I had like *super*-braces. They were stunning. And terrifying. And awesome.

They were all that I had expected and imagined and they were so much more.

They were beautiful. A dark silvery stainless steel, with a thick, flat piece of wire running straight across the bands and brackets, each of which was like a beautifully wrought piece of jewelry. Intricate attachments on the bands and brackets and then all connected by the archwire, like an elaborate metal-superstructure.

I gasped. They were *perfect*. *Awful* and perfect. This must be the nightmare of every girl who gets sent to the orthodontist, imagining that this is what they'll be outfitted with. And also every patient's secret dream. And they were *mine*! My dream-nightmare come true!

I shrieked in pleasure and picked up the phone. "Oh my God, oh my God! They're awesome, Jacob! You're not going to believe it!" I couldn't get my eyes off my reflection in the mirror, and this silvery perfection that completely changed how I looked and who I was.

Jacob tried not to sound too disappointed that he couldn't see me right away. He begged for a photo, but I told him he'd have to wait. "You have to see them up close and personal," I told him. "To see them in all their grandeur. And we are really talking grandeur."

After he hung up, saying he'd be by as soon as possible, I must have sat there for another half an hour just staring and inspecting the braces. They were like beautiful jewelry, with their intricate design and perfectly manufactured small components, all out of hard steel. And secured immovably to my teeth. They were a part of me now. And I felt so much bigger and better and randier than before. It was like a huge chunk of me had been missing, and now everything was in place. Yes, all that metal looked *unnatural*. But the braces were like the perfect, vital extension of me. I was on top of the world.

11.

"Are you ready?" I said when Jacob came by, holding my hand in front of my mouth as I stood in front of him.

He nodded.

I lowered my hand and beamed my widest grin.

His legs almost buckled under him, and he gasped. "Oh, wow," he finally said, when he had caught his breath. He grabbed on to me and pulled me close, his eyes at my mouth level, trying to take it all in. He hugged me, and I could feel his caged cock, stiff in its prison, against me.

Letting me go again he tried to kiss me but I pulled away, reminding him of the rules.

"Just one kiss…," he begged.

I shook my head. "We stick to the schedule."

He practically swooned, and there were real tears in his eyes. "I don't know how I'll be able to take this. And another week before we can fuck?"

"That's right," I smiled, enjoying this incredible power I had over him. Men have lusted for me before, but I had never seen anyone want me this desperately. Not that I didn't want to feel him inside me, right there and now, but I knew we had to wait.

We sat down on the couch and he stared at my mouth, and then he ran his thumb across my braces, carefully and slowly. He pulled my lips back, so he could see the tubes where the headgear was going to go. "They're more perfect than anything I could have imagined," he said. Overcome with emotion and desire he buried his face in my breasts. "Oh, Sally, please…," he begged. I let him nuzzle my breast, but didn't let his lips get nearer to my mouth.

We had already decided that he wouldn't spend the first few nights with me, because it would just be too much to be so close to each other but prohibited from doing anything, but even just seeing me seemed to overwhelm him. It took him a while to gather himself, but all he could do was stare at my teeth and ask how they felt. We both just delighted in my new appearance.

He took a couple of pictures with his phone, close-ups he could look at when he wasn't with me. "The kind of pictures you'd masturbate to," I teased him. "If you could masturbate.…"

I had him take some with my phone, too, so I could admire what I looked like even when I wasn't near a mirror. God, they looked great.

We decided to go out for dinner, to force ourselves to be on better behavior in public. My teeth barely hurt. Not any more than when the spacers had been in place. But they did pose some limitations when I tried eating. Because Dr.Wrighting had used bands rather than simple brackets I could actually eat most harder foods, but biting and chewing was a different experience. Plus no red wine. No coffee.

I didn't mind the stares we got. Or that my braces got. I could see people didn't think they were as beautiful as I thought they were, but it didn't matter. They couldn't make fun of me or humiliate me. I had everything I wanted. Except Jacob's cock thrusting into me.

When he brought me home I let Jacob kiss me on the cheek, even though he tried to go for the mouth, and then I went up to my apartment alone. Just me and my braces.

I went to brush my teeth, giddily smiling and jumping in front of the mirror as I got to see my braces up close again. I could have stood staring at them all night. I was like a young girl who had just been crowned with a princess's tiara and felt on top of the world. Except that my treasure was in my mouth, where I could constantly feel it and was constantly aware of it, which was even better.

In bed, with the lights out, I was more conscious of the metal against the inside of my lips and cheeks. It felt strange. Both smooth and bumpy. And I constantly ran my tongue over all the new metalwork I had acquired.

I felt horny, too, but I didn't need that kind of immediate relief of actual sex. Just having and feeling the braces was like an endless, drawn-out session of very satisfying foreplay. No orgasm, but a deep, warm, lingering satisfied feeling.

Waking in the morning, I felt the slight tension of the braces that ran like a solid piece of reinforcement across my teeth. For a moment I felt a wave of panic, realizing the metal was really immovably part of me. For the *whole next year* I would not experience a single second without this feeling. I was well and truly and absolutely braced. There was nothing I could do without them, and no escape from them. I had to brush my teeth with them, eat with them, smile with them, even at the most awkward moments.

It was a realization that was both terrible and wonderful.

Going to work, and then at work itself I constantly was stared at. I didn't mind, mostly, but it was frustrating that the stares were inescapable. I couldn't turn them off for even a minute. Everyone saw I had braces, and everyone stared.

At work my coworkers asked about them and why I had gotten them and how long I needed them and even why I needed braces *like that*. "Don't they have those braces that you almost can't see now?" several people asked me. *Who would want those?* I wanted to tell them. *Who wouldn't want **real** braces like these?* But instead I just said, "My orthodontist said she had to use this kind." And everyone just nodded and sympathized and felt bad for me, not realizing how good they should feel for me.

I had dinner with Jacob again, who could still barely contain himself. I was still so focused on the braces themselves and the sensation of having them in my mouth that I didn't need him yet, but I felt bad for how desperate he looked, like the saddest puppy, starting at my mouth.

"At least a kiss, tonight," he begged.

"Not yet," I said. I tried not to show it, but I liked having this much power over him. I could see how girls can enjoy being a cock tease. In high school some girls had been in this position, thrusting out their big breasts, and I remembered how the boys had suffered. Now my braces had the same effect on Jacob. But I reminded him, "We're on a schedule we have to keep to."

He leaned over the table. "I don't know how much longer I can take it. I can barely think of anything else, and I'm constantly…ready for action. And come is constantly oozing out of my cock, that's how desperate I am for release. You know that when we uncage it, I mean I'm just instantly going to explode. It won't be very satisfying."

"But I assume you'll recover fast and we'll be able to try again, right? It's not just a one-shot deal, after all. Next week we'll release your inner beast, and get to play with it for like three weeks before we have to lock it up again."

"Can't we just get to it already?" he pleaded.

I tapped my braces with my fingernail – God, how I loved the feel of the metal there! – and reminded him there was nothing we could do. We had to play by the rules.

At home in bed, alone, I rubbed myself, kneading the moist, fleshy zones between my legs with my fingers and palms while I ran my tongue across my braces. This was ecstasy. Just the feel of everything, the sensations in my body, all heightened ten times by the knowledge and awareness of what I had in my mouth.

I knew I didn't look sexier or more beautiful, at least not to almost anyone else, but with my eyes closed in the darkness and just the feel of the metal harnessing my teeth I felt erotically super-charged. Maybe this wasn't any sort of ideal that the magazines and media and advertisers would have you believe, but this was the sexiest I ever felt for myself. The braces were like the perfect, final touch. Like when you're a teen and one day you stand in front of the mirror and you realize you've grown into a woman's body. Now I felt I had taken another step and moved into a different dimension, one I hadn't even been able to imagine before.

My climax, when it came, was so violent that my whole body contracted and I twisted on the bed, and I couldn't keep myself from groaning loudly. My first braced orgasm.

I fell asleep completely happy.

The third day after I got my braces Jacob and I were allowed to kiss again. He insisted on coming to my apartment as soon as he got off work. No meeting at a bar or restaurant, or somewhere in the city. He had only one thing on his mind, and he wanted to be able to concentrate entirely on that.

He got there soon after I did, out of breath from rushing as fast as he could. Standing in the doorway, a glazed look in his eyes, his tie slightly crooked, he stared expectantly. I could see the bulge in his pants, too, and knew how he felt.

He closed to door behind him and wordlessly drew me to him. I had expected him to practically try to bite my head off, but instead he pressed his lips gently against mine, slowly and carefully kissing me, and then exploring for the metal in my mouth first with his lips and then his tongue. I could feel him trembling in my arms, overwhelmed by all the sensations. And then we just lost ourselves in each other, in the passion of the kiss. It felt wonderful, and I pulled his hand down to my breasts and let him open and take off my shirt and open my bra. Only as we moved to the couch, in a further state of undress, did we realize that we could only take it so far.

"Please...," Jacob said looking down at his fully erect cock in its iron cage.

I kissed him again, pressing the metal of my braces against his lips, but shook my head. "Not yet," I reminded him. "Not yet."

There was so much emotion and anticipation built up in him that he actually sobbed. He *needed* sex, more desperately than he ever had even as a teenage boy. But he wasn't going to get it. I was going to remain strong. Of course, it was easy for me. I wanted it, but not that badly. I already had what I *really* wanted. The braces on my teeth.

That and the following nights were tough on Jacob. He looked much more haggard, and he told me he was getting much less sleep. "I feel like some girl waiting for the next *Twilight* movie to come out," he said sadly.

The night before the week of waiting was finally up we decided he should try to spend the night. We made out like we had for several days now, kissing and licking and sucking for what seemed like hours, completely lost in each other's bodies. But in bed it was different, because sex was the obvious final act, and we soon found ourselves nude, the only thing separating us from sex the cage that engirded Jacob's cock. He tugged at it in frustration, but we both knew it wasn't coming off. But we couldn't keep ourselves from going through all the motions as though it wasn't there. I spread my legs and he lay between them, his caged cock rubbing in frustration up between my engorged labial lips up to my belly.

I took the cage into my mouth too, loving the feel of the warmed metal and the musky taste of his unreachable cock within. Jacob cried in frustration and not being able to feel a thing.

He tossed and turned during the night, too, sleeping badly. He woke me up a few times, but I was in a much happier place and didn't mind. I had practically everything I wanted.

12.

I had a check-up with Dr.Wrighting exactly one week after the braces had been installed. The day of the night when Jacob and I would finally be able to consummate a braced union. The day of the night when he'd finally fuck my brains out.

It had been a while, I realized.

Strapped in the examination chair, the padded wide strap pressing between my legs, I realized it had been a *very* long time.

"So how are we doing with the braces?" Dr.Wrighting asked.

"Couldn't be better."

"Everything you hoped for?"

"And more."

Examining my mouth, Dr.Wrighting nodded. "Well, everything looks fine. The oral hygiene looks good, which is important."

I was half worried and half hoping that she would already accessorize my braces, but she didn't change anything. Instead she just asked me about how carefully I was keeping a record of everything.

I told her I was writing reams, and filling out Dr.Allegretta's daily questionnaire – a short set of ten questions rating how I felt on a scale of one to ten – every day, and that I was emailing everything to Dr.Allegretta every day.

Dr.Wrighting nodded approvingly. "And what about tonight?" she asked. "Are you ready for that?"

"I think we're both *very* ready for that."

Boy, were we ever.

Jacob and I had agreed he'd meet me at home after work and that we'd get right to it. There was no way we could put this off any longer. Then we could have dinner and regain our strength and try again....

He kissed me as soon as he was in the door, but it probably didn't even take that to have him all revved up and close to bursting. He began to tear off his clothes quickly, and mine too. There was no need or possibility of seductive foreplay. We just wanted to fuck. We stumbled to my bedroom, and by the time he we fell on the bed he was naked except for his socks, and me except for my panties.

"One moment," I said, pulling myself away from him. "I have to get the key...."

"Hurry!" he said desperately, lying on his back, his caged cock standing upright.

I had already taken the key from its hiding place and put it on my nightstand. "I hope I remember how to do this," I joked. Except that I really wasn't sure I remembered exactly.

Jacob just lay there, eyes closed. "Just get it off, get it off!"

And then with a click and turn and gentle pull I had it unlocked and open, and I squeezed his balls through it and then freed his cock for the first time in weeks. He sighed with relief as he looked down at it.

I put the cage on the nightstand and then turned my attention to his purple member, wetting my lips before slowly sliding it into my mouth. He groaned with anticipation and pleasure. Even though he kept it pretty clean it had a bit of a salty, funky taste but I loved the feel of the rod of flesh in my mouth, its throbbing veins giving it some added definition. Careful not to suck too hard on the end, lest he explode right there and then I pulled away and then straddled him, gently and very slowly guiding his cock into me.

Both it and I were so wet that it slid in easily, but I could feel even as it just moved into me how he was beginning to come. He barely thrust two or three times before I could feel his body first tense in paroxysmal seizure before going limper as he came inside of me. I rocked a few more times on top of him, to enjoy the feel of his cock inside me, before it began to deflate, then rolled off.

He was breathless and spent. "Sorry," he said apologetically, "but that's been building up for a *long* time."

I kissed him, to give him the full feel of my braces, and mumbled, "Well, I hope there's a whole lot more of that where that came from."

Just kissing him I could feel his cock get hard again, but we took our time before he entered me again. This time he teased me, kissing and fondling and licking before finally spreading my legs and getting between them and then thrusting himself in. This time we both got a lot more out of it, as he rode me long and hard before finally coming again.

We didn't really want to take a break for dinner, so we just ordered takeout. We continued to fondle and play over Chinese while watching some TV, then moved back to the bedroom for a final, glorious fuck, complete with classical music accompaniment blaring in the background.

I let Jacob remain uncaged overnight, and of course we fucked again in the morning, rocking gently, half awake, our mouths on each others'.

He got up to shower, and when he was done I was waiting for him with his chastity device.

"Come on," he protested. "Can't we leave it off for now? It's really torture wearing that."

I smiled but shook my head. "You know the rules. It's not allowed to roam free outside my presence. It goes back in the cage. But don't worry, we'll take it off again…tonight. Maybe."

"*Maybe?*"

I kissed him. "You never know," I teased. "Maybe I don't need to be…pleasured so often now, and every couple of days is enough. Or weeks."

"Sally…!" he said, really worried.

"You'll just have to wait and see," I said, not willing to give him the satisfaction of any certainty. I grabbed his cock, which immediately grew hard again. I quickly slid it into my mouth, eliciting a purr of satisfaction from him, but then I just as quickly stooped the cage over it, and locked it in place again.

"Fuck," he said.

"Maybe," I said.

I had an appointment with Dr.Allegretta that afternoon, to talk about how things were going. I was a bit embarrassed about having to talk about all this stuff which she knew we were doing, but given the pleasure we were having a bit of embarrassment was a small price to pay.

She admitted she was entering largely uncharted territory here. "Obviously, most of my patients are too young to be sexually active, and even the older teens that have had sex...well, once they're in braces of course they're no longer having sex. So at most there's a lot of talking about yearning and self-pleasuring, instead of actual experiences with a partner. Which is why this study is kind of exciting for me too."

She thanked me for all the notes I was constantly sending her. "I appreciate the way you open up. Keep it up. There really is no detail that's too small that it might not be significant."

Dr.Allegretta was getting notes and talking to Jacob too, but she didn't tell me anything about what he was telling her. I was curious, but I knew she wouldn't tell me.

"Do you worry about the novelty wearing off?" she asked me.

I hadn't really thought of that. "No. The sensation is so...incredible. I can't imagine...."

"What about for Jacob? Do you think he might get tired of them?"

"He seemed pretty into it. Completely into them."

"But a whole year of kissing a woman with braces? Of sleeping with a woman with braces?"

"I don't know. I don't think so."

"Do you think you'd manage if he did decide he had enough of them? And of you?"

"It would be disappointing...." I wondered what kind of seeds of doubt she was trying to plant in my mind. What did she know that I didn't? Had Jacob had his fun, his one wild experience, and was he now fed up with it?

"Chances are you wouldn't find anyone to replace him, at least not until the braces came off."

"It's not that long. But it would be disappointing not to have someone to share them with. I love the way Jacob feels about them. How he really enjoys them with me." I did believe that. That's why I didn't think he'd quit on me. Or on my braces. He wanted more.

13.

Can even the thing you most desire grow old? Can you get tired of it? Was it bad that I had the braces fulltime? Wouldn't it be more exciting if we only had them on special occasions? I knew there would be some variations and additions. Headgear, Dr.Wrighting had said.... That might spice things up if the braces alone became all too routine.

Running my tongue over my metal-covered teeth, I couldn't imagine it. The braces seemed as special and wonderful and different as when I first got them. Sure, I guess I'd sort of get used to the feeling of them there, but I couldn't imagine getting tired or bored of them. Or of not getting aroused by the feel or even just thought of them.

But what about Jacob? Maybe that was why Dr.Wrighting and Dr.Allegretta insisted that he be kept under lock and key, and that sex be withheld from him for an entire week every month. So that he'd have something to look forward to. Just the release, regardless of whether or not he grew tired of the braces. But after a few months would even that be enough? Wouldn't he be tempted to say it wasn't worth the trouble anymore and just get the cage removed and toss it and me and my braces aside?

I didn't want to worry about this, but I couldn't help it. Looking in the mirror, at the way I looked with the metal on my teeth, I was the happiest I could imagine. But I knew Jacob was part of that happiness, and if his lust and longing, and his willingness to satisfy me sexually wasn't part of the package that I would be half lost. I couldn't imagine finding another man who could fill his role. And even if I could still continue to take some satisfaction in the devices in my mouth, I'd be back to the times when I was a lonely teenager, masturbating alone in my bed at night.

For now, for the most part, the days and then especially the nights were incomparably wonderful. Jacob rushed over eagerly after work, and we could barely bring ourselves to go anywhere together – dinner, the movies, anything – because we wanted to focus on each other and on my braces. Whenever we were side by side we couldn't keep from kissing, Jacob eager for the feel of my braces, and me eager for my braces to be felt. And then we'd fuck, again and again, as often as we could. And I was amazed how often we could.

Yes, I was sore and exhausted by the end of the week, and so was Jacob, but just a smile that revealed the silvery glitter of my braces was enough to draw him back in, first his mouth pressed against mine, then his hands on my breasts, between my legs, then all of him between my legs, thrusting, pounding into me.

I always liked sex, but I never thought or imagined it could be this good. It was like a whole different world. I felt like I had moved from being a girl who just does cartwheels in the grass to an Olympic gymnast, flying and tumbling with perfect confidence on all the apparatuses, right up to the uneven bars.

Could this really go on?

But it did, weeks spent in an almost uninterrupted daze, where I did my work efficiently and quickly but barely knew what I was doing, always with just one other thing on my mind as I was eager for nothing else but to rush back to our braces-fiesta.

Among the small interruptions that did shatter my beautiful braced illusions and bring me back to reality were facing other people looking like I now did. At work it was somehow manageable. Embarrassing, but since we all were constantly rushing around getting things done there weren't too many occasions where anyone could really settle down and stare and try to fathom what the hell I was thinking.

Family, on the other hand, is more complicated. I hadn't told mine that I was getting braces, and then of course I put off telling them I had them. A casual mention, *Oh, by the way, Mom, I got braces*? I don't think so. But I knew that they were going to find out. I saw my parents pretty regularly, and Kylie was in the city several times a year, so I certainly wasn't going to be able to avoid them seeing what I had done for an entire year. In fact, I was surprised that it took more than a week before my secret was out.

It was Kylie that suddenly called one afternoon and said she was here for two days and when could we meet. With so little notice I was already all revved up for my nightly session with Jacob and it was hard to shift gears. I hated letting him down, and I wasn't pleased about going without our routine either, but there was no way I could put off Kylie. I had to meet her alone, too. I worried that if I brought Jacob we wouldn't be able to keep our hands off each other. If we went to dinner with Kylie, we'd probably wind up sneaking to the bathroom for a quick fuck. Several times.

So I met Kylie for dinner near where she was staying. And of course I grinned happily about seeing her as soon as I saw her and she of course stopped with a start.

"What the...?" she asked, totally astonished.

I pretended for a second I didn't even know what she meant, before answering. "Oh, that's right, I forgot to tell you about these. Can you believe it, I went to the dentist and she said I *had* to get these."

"Seriously?"

"Something about how my teeth were suddenly drifting. I haven't worn my retainers in like ages, and...well, I could even feel something as going wrong."

"But braces? Now? Again? At your age? And braces that look like *that*? I mean that's industrial level orthodontia in your mouth." She leaned closer. "Let me have a look," she said, and I opened up to show her. "Industrial level," she muttered again, shaking her head after she got a good look.

"It has something to do with how well they work and do whatever they have to do. Flimsy braces would take much longer and so on. It's no big deal."

Kylie still stared, but she didn't contradict me, trying to be sisterly supportive. "So how long are they on for?"

"Just a year. Exactly one year, and then everything should be fine, she said."

"Still...."

"I know! It's like I'm twelve again!"

"What did Mom and Dad say?"

"I kind of...forgot to mention it so far."

"Too embarrassed?"

I shrugged. "Kind of. I mean I feel like I sort of let them down. I mean, I *had* them, but because I didn't pay enough attention and didn't wear my retainers, I need them again...."

"God, I haven't worn my retainers since junior high or something."

"Well, everything seemed okay, and then it wasn't. But really, they're not that bad."

"But didn't you say you had started to get serious with someone. Jason?"

"Jacob, yeah."

"So that's over for now, right?"

"No, he's okay with it."

"You're kidding."

I smiled. If she only knew. "Yeah. I mean, it was a big change, but we've gotten pretty close, and he's very supportive."

"But I mean...the intimacy and stuff. Or is there no intimacy?"

"Kylie! We just have to be a bit more careful." I bit my lip. If she only knew!

She shuddered a bit. "You mean, you still...and actually...."

"They're just braces, Kylie."

"Not from where I'm sitting. And I mean if any guy I was dating showed up with a set of those...I mean, I wouldn't even acknowledge him, I'd just be out of there. And the idea of...experimenting with...physical stuff..." She shuddered again. "No, it would be just like middle school again."

"It's really not that bad," I told her.

"Well, you just got them, right? Maybe they haven't totally sunk in yet, for either of you. Although from the looks of them that's hard to imagine. And why isn't he with you tonight? Is he ashamed of being seen with you looking like that?"

"I wanted a sisters' night out."

"So he does go out in public with you looking like that?"

"Well, we're kind of at that stay at home stage in our relationship."

She nodded knowingly. "Oh, I understand, sure. Well, as long as he stays around for a while, I guess. Only a year, you said, right?"

I nodded.

"Though you know how orthodontists are notorious about extending the fun...."

"I'm pretty sure that I can count on my treatment being finished *exactly* on time."

"I'll keep my fingers crossed for you, sis. But then you were such a queer girl when we went through our braces periods. You didn't even seem to mind getting them and having them."

I shrugged.

67

"I just figure now, that you're grown up, you can see what disfiguring torture devices they are."

I shrugged again. "They barely hurt, and I sort of like the way they look and feel."

Kylie shook her head in disbelief. "I guess that's kind of cool and useful, if you can delude yourself so totally."

I wasn't going to argue the point. I wasn't deluding myself. Well, maybe about some things. I probably did look pretty weird with the braces. But there was no confusion about the satisfaction and pleasure I got out of them. I knew that whatever sex Kylie was getting wasn't anywhere near as hot as what I was into.

Kylie promised not to tell my parents, but of course she couldn't keep from telling them that I had something *big* to reveal to them, so I had to explain everything to them, too, when they called the next day, before they started thinking I was engaged or something meaningful like that. "It's just that I have to have braces again for a while," I told them, as casually as I could.

Yeah, that was easy. Like that was a conversation that I actually believed would be over in two minutes....

14.

It was amazing how time flew. Disappointing too. My next appointment with Dr.Wrighting was coming up, meaning I had had the braces for almost a month, meaning that one-twelfth of my wonderful adventure was already over.

Jacob and I had found ourselves in such a groove. Okay, it was a strange groove, where we spent so much of our time alone, together, intertwined, making out like horny teenagers and then having sex like wild animals. I mean, how long could *that* go on? But my braces were like a red cape that turned Jacob into a charging bull. It's like he lost all other control. It's all he could focus on and zero in on. And, boy, did he zero in. I mean, he'd ask what he could do for me too, and try to make things more exciting for me as well, but I didn't really need that. I mean, I had the braces, which I just had to run my tongue over or see in the mirror to be reminded of the feel and look of all their potency, and then I had him, ramming me to the heights of heaven every morning, noon – well, on weekends – and night.

He didn't stop complaining about his chastity cage, of course, and there were times when it got in the way, when in our desperation to couple I couldn't get it off fast enough. But I think he was probably glad to get some time off for his penis in between our bouts. I've heard men masturbate a lot even when they are in relationships, but I was sure that there was no way he would be up to it during the times he wasn't with me. So the cage was now really just an inconvenience, rather than keeping him from stuff he would otherwise be doing.

Until it wasn't again, of course. Dr. Wrighting reminded me of our appointment, and reminded me that it was time that Jacob was locked up longer. Time for another week-long period of abstinence. We both joked that we could use the sex-vacation, but we were both nervous about it too.

I was sort of nervous about the appointment too. Was Dr. Wrighting going to change or add anything? On the one hand, I was fine with things the way they were. I could go on like just this forever, I thought. But I knew she wanted to experiment some. And I kind of did too. But what if she decided it was time for the headgear? I was curious about wearing headgear, of course, but I was scared of *having* to wear it. And scared that it would get in the way with Jacob and spoil what we had now.

Sitting in the waiting room all of us patients were constantly sizing one another up. Of course I got stared at more than most. I was an adult with braces, and most of Dr. Wrighting's patients were kids. I'm sure lots of their mothers tried to make them feel better after their appointment by telling them they should realize how lucky they were that they got to wear braces now and not like that *poor woman* who was all grown up and had to go around with all that metal on her teeth they had seen in the waiting room.

I tried to figure out which of the appliances that the other patients were wearing Dr. Wrighting might have in mind for me. Some looked really uncomfortable, like the mouth-filling plastic appliances some girls wore, and through which they could barely talk. And there was always the headgear, which the girls who wore couldn't hide. Yes, I worried about getting any of these things – but the thing is, I also really *wanted* to get...all of them.

I had forgotten how good and comforting it felt to be strapped in the examination chair again, secured in place and completely at Dr. Wrighting's mercy. I felt a good sort of excited tension, like on my birthday when I was small, when I was the center of attention and had all the wrapped gifts all in front of me, and I knew they're going to be good, but I didn't yet know what I was going to find in them. Or, to mix my metaphors, Dr.Wrighting was like Santa Claus, ready to surprise me with something wonderful, but also reminding me that she had some control, and that what I got depended on whether I had been naughty or nice. And since there was a distinct naughtiness to what I had been doing with Jacob for the past few weeks, there was that old feeling of guilt about sex – especially sex that revolved around something so strange as *braces* – that left me feeling a bit like I deserved to be punished. But in a sort of good way. Like I was by being strapped down. And by getting something else orthodontic.

Dr.Wrighting made the usual small talk, and peered and poked in my mouth a bit. She put the cheek retractor in and adjusted the warm, bright spotlight she shone on and into my mouth, and peered more closely. Everything looked fine, she said, and she said she was very pleased with how everything was going. "Dr.Allegretta and I appreciate your detailed reports, too," she said. "Both you and Jacob are providing us with lots of useful data."

I blushed a bit, because I was kind of embarrassed about her reading about all our intimate details. Writing it wasn't that difficult, but when I was reminded that someone was actually reading all these very explicit confessions I got pretty self-conscious. But with my mouth pried wide-open I was glad I wasn't expected to say anything, I think Dr.Wrighting just wanted me to see that she didn't think any of those details were too embarrassing. That she could read all that stuff clinically, like the doctor she was.

"So, I think we're ready to try something else today," Dr.Wrighting said, smiling down at me.

My heart immediately pounded more strongly in my chest. Something was going to be changed or added. There was going to be...*more*? Headgear already? Or.... I didn't know what else it could be, but I relished that feeling of uncertainty, too.

Dr.Wrighting made me wait, going off to check on another patient. When she came back she had some pieces of dark silvery metal in her hand, which she put on the tray hovering over my chest.

"I thought it would be fun to try this," she said. "A lot of my patients get palatal expanders, which are these devices fixed

70

behind the back of the teeth and going up to the roof of the mouth, which are slowly screwed apart, pushing the palate apart and widening the mouth. Now in your case we don't want to expand any arch. But I am curious as to the effect and sensation of wearing a device like this, so we're going to install these in your mouth and see how you and Jacob take to them."

She held up one device, which had a small, flat metal block in the middle, about the size of a fingernail, and four curved pieces of wire coming out of it, looking like some contorted *X*. "Usually, the devices I use embed all this in acrylic, so it's like a retainer, with a cut down the middle to allow the two halves to slowly be pushed apart. But lots of orthodontists rely on ones that only have this metal skeleton, and since the retainer version would probably affect your speech too much we're going to use this. Personally, I find the full-bodied acrylic ones more effective, but since we don't need to effect anything in your mouth that's not an issue. I think they're more comfortable too, aside from the difficulties with speech they cause. You're going to find food wraps itself around these metal arms and pieces.... But I think it will serve our purposes well."

Dr.Wrighting brought the strange device to my mouth, and then I could feel here push the metal ends into what I guessed were openings on several of the bands on my teeth. I could feel the device slide reluctantly into place. When she removed her hands, I could feel just the slightest tickle at the top of my mouth where the top of the device barely brushed against my palate.

Satisfied that it was properly in place, Dr.Wrighting took a pair of pliers and crimped something on the inside of my bands. Securing the device in place, I guessed.

There was another device, too. Smaller and flatter. For my lower arch of teeth, I realized. Dr.Wrighting repeated the procedure, and in a few minutes she had that installed as well.

When Dr.Wrighting removed the cheek retractor my tongue immediately came up against the new obstructions in my mouth. The lower device was practically right behind my teeth, and suddenly my tongue couldn't push nearly as far forward. The upper device was contoured to my palate, the wires running up from the back of my braces to the flat piece of metal on top. The top device wasn't in the way the same way as the lower one, but especially then when I swallowed I could feel it's intrusive presence. They sort of reminded me of having retainers, but instead of the smooth plastic of my retainers they were like skeletons of them. So there was less bulk, but more texture to them.

"That feels weird," I told Dr.Wrighting, lisping slightly.

"Good," she said.

Good? But I guess she was right. That was what she was after here. She wasn't concerned with what would fix the teeth, like she had to be with a normal patient, but rather with how I dealt with the non-technical aspects of orthodontic treatment. The way the stuff felt in my mouth. What it was like to talk and eat and kiss and fuck and live day in and day out with these devices.

I slurped a bit. Like retainers, these made me salivate more.

"I would have preferred installing more substantial devices, but I realize we can't have you lisping like a typical retainer girl at your job. And I think these will give us a good general impression."

More substantial? Sure, I could imagine larger versions of these, but I had to say: these felt pretty substantial already. The braces were just on the front of my teeth, the back of the bands barely noticeable. But these expanders felt like the whole of the inside of my mouth was wired now. Like there was a scaffold installed there.

Running my tongue along all the different wires and bits of metal felt intriguing. Not bad at all, I thought. Except, as I tried to swallow yet again and my tongue pressed against the scaffold arched across my palate, I realized that they were secured in place much like the braces. A new permanent fixture that I would not be able to remove even for a moment of respite until, at the earliest, my next appointment. Could I handle that? I wondered, as I tried to swallow yet again.

Of course, Dr.Wrighting wasn't leaving me any choice. She told me about what I should pay attention to in taking care of them and then was ready to let me go. But was I ready to go? Suddenly I wondered whether I hadn't gotten more than I bargained for. And then I told myself I was being silly. For God's sake, I could have gotten *headgear*, right?

But even that thought didn't make me feel a whole lot better. Nor did the one that followed: one of these days I was going to be walking out of here with headgear too.

Jacob had already left several messages on my phone by the time I left Dr.Wrighting's practice, eager to hear what had happened to me. We had agreed that we were going to meet for dinner in public again. It was hands-off time again, and it would be easier for him to control himself if we were in public. Same for me. Still, he wanted to know whether anything had changed, and how much he would be missing and then looking forward to in the next days. I only texted him back, so he couldn't even hear whether my speech sounded any different, leaving him completely guessing as to whether Dr.Wrighting was making me wear anything new.

I had to time to go home beforehand. Looking in the mirror the first impression was still pretty much the same. But when I opened my mouth the bottom expander was pretty noticeable, the wire and metal mounted behind my teeth. The top, not so much. Or hardly at all. I had to tilt my head back a lot to see it.

Unlike the braces, however, this was something that I could *feel* a lot more than I could see. The braces were noticeable pretty much immediately to everyone, at least if I opened my mouth the slightest bit. These new appliances were something I was constantly and keenly aware of, but that even someone face to face with me would only get a hint of.

They were kind of irritating, I had to admit. But like some itches, they were right on that borderline between wonderful and terrible. One second I loved the feel of that metal scaffolding against my tongue, and the obstruction placed in my way. The next moment, as I slurped yet again, I wanted to yank them out. If they had removable been like retainers I'm sure I would have taken them out repeatedly.

When we made our plans Jacob and I had joked that maybe dinner wasn't a good idea, since maybe Dr.Wrighting was going to make me wear something that would make it even harder to eat than the braces already did. I laughed about it, because I didn't think I'd get a retainer or anything else that might really get in the way with eating yet. She'd save that for later in my treatment. But now, as I pressed my tongue against my palate, I realized the joke might be on me. These were definitely going to be in the way.

How do kids manage to put up with all this stuff? I wondered to myself. Of course, it was easier when you had no real choice. And I had to admit that if I had been outfitted with accessories like these when I had my braces I might have hated it half the time. But I know I would have loved the feel of them the rest of the time. Annoyance and pleasure seemed to balance themselves out. And it was nice that the pleasure I did get from these sensations, and from looking this way, was pretty intense. Too bad the annoyance was, at times, too....

I could see Jacob's eyes expand as he rushed over when he saw me, almost tripping chairs and tables. "Well?" he asked, barely able to contain himself.

I smiled, revealing the now already familiar tin grin, and I could see him almost deflate with disappointment, since he couldn't see anything new.

"She didn't do much," I said slowly and teasingly before opening my mouth to expose the lower expander. I pointed at it. "Except installing this," I said, and then leaning my head back and pointing to my palate, "and this."

Jacob immediately perked up again. "Wow! That's pretty good. And they're wired in?"

I nodded.

"How much in the way are they?"

"Pretty much. I can speak almost normally...well, not ridiculously abnormally, anyway. But my tongue constantly comes up against them."

He leaned forward, whispering, "Can I feel them?" He wanted to kiss me and stick his tongue into my mouth. And I wanted him to do it, but I knew I couldn't.

I pulled back. "You know the rules. No intimacy until they get settled in."

He sighed. Looking down I could see the bulge in his pants. I felt bad for him. It was going to be a while again before he could uncage that little beast and we could play with again.

Dinner itself was a bit of a chore. It was weird chewing food with these new obstructions in place. Especially with the metal on the roof of my mouth, which was really in the way. And yes, food found a way of getting stuck behind and around all the wires. I mean, I had gotten used to some food getting stuck in my braces, but those were usually only small, annoying bits. But the expanders left huge gaps and space for food to wedge itself in and wrap itself around. So I was constantly sucking and poking with my tongue and sticking a finger in my mouth. It can't have been very appetizing, but at least Jacob didn't look too grossed out. No, he still looked as eager and turned on as ever.

Of course we had agreed that he wouldn't be staying over that night. Since we weren't allowed to take his penis out to play with it would have been pure torture for us both. And I should try to get used to the feel of the devices by myself anyway.

Brushing my teeth now involved even more brushing in hard to reach places. But when I was finally in bed and had turned out the lights of course I could still feel all the wire and metal there. Like I could feel the braces, but even more upfront and obviously. And I was surprised that I also felt that tingling down below. I hesitated, but then I slipped my hand into my panties and began caressing my swollen, moist folds. Between that and the feeling of the scaffolding in my mouth the sensations competed with one another until I came in an orgasm that shook right through me.

Sure, I would have liked to have been able to take the expanders out after that, and be left overnight just with the braces. But it was ok. It was ok.

15.

It was a few days before I let Jacob kiss me. I got a bit more used to the expanders day by day, but like the braces themselves, their constant *thereness* was hard to ignore. I couldn't forget they were there, and every time I said anything, or ate anything the reminder was especially strong. But I liked having them to myself too, letting *my* tongue run along the wire and press against the metal. And, at night, letting *my* fingers explore my other cave of pleasure.

Maybe I just needed a bit of a respite from getting my brains humped out.

Still, when I invited Jacob in after going to a movie, and pulled him close as the door fell closed, and pressed my lips against his and then parted them to let him come up against first my braces and then plunge his tongue between my teeth to explore all the new hardware.... Feeling the fleshy softness of that hot, wet tongue and the eagerness with which it came up against the metal that I had already been allowed to enjoy for days I was again so happy to have him and to excite him and to give him such pleasure.

I still had to say no when he begged to be released from his chastity cage, but at least everything that was in my mouth was enough of a distraction, after so many days of not even having had access to that, that he was almost satisfied just kissing me passionately.

The next night his pleading was more insistent, but I wouldn't budge. "But you can spend the night," I told him. "And maybe you can show me how much you can do with that tongue of yours," I suggested, hoping he would get the hint.

He looked sort of sad with that metal cage wrapped around his bulging cock as we cavorted in bed, but I told him in no uncertain terms that it wasn't coming off, no matter what. We made do without the use of that particular appendage, handy though it otherwise is. The one advantage of not relying on it was that Jacob lasted much, much longer, as he attempted all sorts of oral satisfaction in a prolonged session of what was foreplay without a payoff for him, but entirely satisfying – several times – for me.

I had to give him a few cunnilingus pointers, but I have to say his tongue-thrusting really hit the spot once he got the hang and taste of it. And lying there while he went at it, while I could feel the braces and the expanders in my mouth, was even better than my solo efforts.

Now he was the one counting down the days until we could finally have real sex again. I looked forward that too, but had to admit that I was enjoying the in-between period too Especially since Jacob really seemed to be working a lot harder when he couldn't get the instant gratification. Which I found *really* gratifying. Repeatedly.

The braces had been a huge draw for him, but like for me the metal jumble of the expanders was something to really explore, so his tongue kept finding its way deep into my mouth, nestling and writhing there. Our kisses now weren't just of the surface passionate sort, satisfied simply with the feel of the braces themselves. Now my entire oral cavity wasn't just a place to peek into, but rather was a main objective. His tongue was more like when I took his cock into my mouth, an organ meant to settle in those depths and almost become part of them.

Yes, we both liked the expanders very much.

I felt weirdly self-conscious about the expanders. Obviously I felt somewhat self-conscious about the braces, especially whenever I flashed them at someone who hadn't seen me with them before. People *always* reacted to them, even if they pretended not to. But the expanders were so internal. I mean, you could see the lower one when I spoke, but the upper one, so dominant inside my mouth, was pretty much invisible to everyone, unless I threw my head back and laughed with my mouth wide open, which I never did. But I was totally conscious of it, and every word I said had my tongue come against it and worry about lisping it, or making some other *thlip*. And I was more likely to add a bit of spray to my words, which I really wanted to avoid. So I always had them in the back of my mind whenever I opened my mouth to say anything, and I tried to weigh and pronounce my words as carefully as possible.

Eating was an issue too. Food *always* got wrapped around them, or wedged behind them. So I had to keep myself from poking my finger around my mouth or trying to release the food with my tongue, neither of which looked very appealing to anyone I was with. Between worrying what was visibly stuck in my braces, and more annoyingly but at least invisibly stuck behind them eating was always something to worry about. But at least there was no question about my oral hygiene habits. I didn't just brush my teeth countless times a day, I really scrubbed them, especially after every meal. So I wasn't too worried about getting cavities or anything like that.

When Jacob's week of enforced abstinence was up we were able to return to our oversexed schedule. The first time we did it again was of course disappointing. After a week without release he was so primed he barely managed to slip between my legs before he came. But I was expecting that by now. And after that things were better again.

I was a bit worried that once he was able to get off effortlessly he wouldn't pay as much attention to all my needs as he had while he was still locked up and limited in his potential. But all the hardware in my mouth continued to be a big draw, and he definitely did not neglect that. In fact, it was pretty much a perfect balance.

I wondered whether we would be able to keep this incredible pace up for the entire year. I mean, we did it so often that I was getting sore and bruised down there. But the one week break every month was probably just enough to keep us from doing too much damage and breaking down. I would have preferred a different schedule. Like two days off a week. Not the weekend, because we had more time to indulge in our pleasures over the weekend, but some other two days. But Dr.Wrighting and Dr.Allegretta were not going to go for that.

I really didn't have much right or reason to complain. I was having the best sex of my life, under the best circumstance of my life. Sure, the braces got in the way professionally and personally sometimes. But as far as my intimate life went – and my intimate life dominated everything else – everything was perfect. I really do not think I could have been happier.

And even as things were going so well there was always that slight fear and trepidation and excitement about what was going to happen next. But as long as Jacob was part of it I was ready for anything, I told myself. And a bit of uncertainty just made everything more interesting.

16.

Naturally my anxiousness and excitement about what Dr.Wrighting had planned next intensified as the date of my next appointment approached. We lived a lot in each moment and day, but then suddenly another four weeks were behind us. Jacob abruptly found his daily periods of freedom from his cage lost, and I got to visit Dr.Wrighting.

I was looking forward to getting the expanders removed. I did like the feel of them, but most of the discomfort they caused, from making me spit and getting in the way of swallowing to food getting stuck in them, didn't get any better with time. It had been interesting having them, but I was ready to have them taken out.

Of course I couldn't be sure that whatever Dr.Wrighting had in mind for me next wouldn't be even worse.

What I wound up realizing was that it didn't matter what your age or circumstances were: you never knew what your orthodontist was going to do.

Strapped in, lying happily on the examination chair, I offered my wide-open mouth to Dr.Wrighting's inspection, ready for anything. Well, almost anything.

"So how are you finding the expanders?" Dr.Wrighting asked.

I sent her notes every week about all the things that were going on with me and the braces, so she knew how I felt about them anyway, but I guess she wanted the latest status.

"They've been pretty cool to have," I said. "But, yeah, I'm ready for them to go."

"Really? Well, we should be done with them…eventually."

"You're not taking them out now?" I asked, a bit surprised and shocked.

"No. I'd like to leave them in a while longer."

"Oh," I said, finding it hard to hide my disappointment. I mean, it wasn't the end of the world or anything, but it wasn't what I had expected, either.

"But we will be making a small change," Dr.Wrighting added.

"Oh?"

She smiled at me, letting me try to guess what she could have in mind.

It turned out just to be elastics. Small rubber rings. She stretched one from my top row of teeth to the bottom on the left side, and then the same on the right. There were small hooks on some of my brackets, so I knew which teeth she was stretching them across.

Elastics seemed pretty boring. They weren't even very tight. When I opened my mouth wide I could feel some resistance, but nowhere near the strong force I remembered from when I had had elastic when I was a girl. But since Dr.Wrighting didn't want to really move my teeth I knew she couldn't use too much force. That's how she explained it to me then too.

That was it, too. Instructions to wear them all the time, and continue reporting back to her, and another appointment in a month's time.

So was this what was going to happen for the next months? Was Dr.Wrighting going to just be layering on devices? After all, there was room to add the headgear on top of all of these, for example. But there were also still a lot of months left….

O.k., I was a bit disappointed at first. But even just walking out I realized that there was a new sensation there in my mouth. Just these two strange…threads or links between my upper and lower jaw. Allowing me to open and close my mouth pretty much as usual, but still exerting some control and pull.

O.k., I smiled, these did feel pretty good.

At home I realized that they made a different difference, too. Looking in the mirror I saw how they accentuated my braces. I mean, they were just two pale rubber bands stretched jaw to jaw, but now there was that link whenever I opened my mouth, and everything in there now screamed a little louder at anyone who looked at my mouth: *hey, I have braces.* I didn't think just these elastics could make such a difference, but they did.

I called Jacob to tell him what Dr.Wrighting had and hadn't done. He was less disappointed than I was about the expanders staying in place. "I like them in there," he said dreamily. "I like the feel of them." He worried a bit about the elastics. "So is your jaw going to like snap shut from the force," he asked, "so if I have like my tongue or...other appendage in there..."

"Yes, *snap!*" I giggled, teasing him. I liked it that he didn't feel sure just how serious I was being. I liked that my braced mouth could seem just a bit more menacing. With all that metal it already looked menacing enough, but this added some spice to any up-close action.

The elastics did change how we made out a bit. I didn't think they'd be in the way so much, but they were. I couldn't open my mouth as wide as easily, for example. And while they weren't really barriers, and while they stretched more on the side than right in the front of my mouth, between my and Jacob's tongue we had to navigate around them constantly. It took us a few days and tries to get the hang of just kissing with them.

It was interesting seeing how people reacted, too. These two small elastics really did make my braces more real for them. It felt like even everyone at work and everyone who had seen me with the braces for two months now did a double-take when they saw this latest addition, like they were reminded again of all the hardware I was sporting. Or like I was sporting a whole lot more now.

I loved wearing the braces, but the incessant stares and the way people tried to pretend it wasn't a big deal or the way some people just couldn't hide their astonishment or shock or amusement sometimes did get to me a bit. It's hard not to feel self-conscious when you have braces. I didn't mind feeling that a bit, but sometimes it got to be a bit much, too. There were times were I was so much the odd girl out that I wished I didn't have them. But those were more than made up for by all the times when I was so happy to have them. And especially all that time and those nights with Jacob, when I couldn't imagine anything better than having them.

There was that week-long wait until we could actually have sex again, which seemed to take so much longer than a week, but once we could again the elastics continued to be a nice little enhancement. They didn't make too much of a difference, but they made my braces more *bracey*. Something like that anyway. The braces were even more blatant and obvious, and we both liked that. It gave me a sort of inner satisfaction, to know I looked even more braced, and to see how Jacob reacted to them.

And of course Jacob managed to give me a different kind of inner satisfaction, too.

17.

I was pretty sure that at my next appointment Dr.Wrighting would let me know that it was time for headgear. It made sense. She was adding one thing after another, and there wasn't too much room for anything else. Braces, expanders, elastics. Headgear seemed the obvious next step.

Jacob and I talked about it a lot. I wanted headgear, but I was also a little afraid of it, and how it might get in the way of kissing and anything that involved my mouth. Jacob promised he'd be more careful, but I could see he was also thinking about the possible consequences. Certainly we couldn't be as wild in our lovemaking as we usually were, right?

Strapped in the examination chair I tried to prepare myself mentally for the headgear. I *was* excited about it. I told myself I should just enjoy getting it and the new feeling of having it and worry about the sex angle later.

The first thing that Dr.Wrighting did was remove the elastics, and then she peered around in my mouth. Then came the cheek retractors, and then when she came at me with a pair of long nose pliers I realized she was removing the expanders. And I had resigned myself to them staying in! I didn't even think she might take them out at this appointment. But, in surprisingly few yanks and tugs and twists, she pulled both free.

Well, that was o.k. with me too. But what now?

She left the cheek retractor in place and got a small tray with very small metal pieces in the different hollows on it. They were like brackets, except smaller and thinner. One by one I could feel Dr.Wrighting attach them to my braces, around where the elastics were hooked on. There were two each on the top and bottom row of braces. I had no idea what they could be for.

When Dr.Wrighting removed the cheek retractor I immediately felt the new additions. They jutted out from my braces and rubbed against the inside of my cheeks. Or dug into them, with pretty sharp edges. I immediately told Dr.Wrighting, but she just smiled and said, "Good."

That couldn't be right, could it? A few minutes with these rubbing against the inside of my cheeks and they'd rub them all raw.

But Dr.Wrighting wasn't finished yet. She brought out the material she used to make impressions, and took impressions of both my top and bottom teeth! Which was more complicated since I had the braces, and the goop solidified around them, so the impressions were much harder to take out when they had set.

"So those metal bits are irritating, right?" she said when she was done.

I nodded. They really were. They actually *hurt*.

"Well, it's going to be a bit before we can finish everything up and have it so they don't dig in there, so we'll just prop your mouth open again, all right? That way they won't chafe the inside of your mouth."

I agreed, and let her spread my lips around the cheek retractor again. I didn't really mind having that in place, and it was definitely more comfortable than those barbed pieces she had attached.

Obviously she was going to prepare something else for me, using the impressions. Some kind of cover that went over them? Or maybe they were supposed to help hold the headgear in place? But then she wouldn't need the impressions, would she?

"Do you mind if I bring a couple of patients in to gawk at you?" Dr.Wrighting asked. "To set an example, for example?"

I was a bit embarrassed by the idea of others staring at me, trussed up like this, mouth exposed, but I sort of liked the idea of showing off my braces like this. The one place where it wasn't that weird to have a mouthful of metal – an orthodontist's office. I nodded and made an agreeing sound.

"Good, thanks," Dr.Wrighting said. "And you are going to have to be patient," she added. "It is going to be a bit before we're ready to finish. And maybe the visitors will help keep you entertained."

I didn't mind at all if it took a while. I even sort of liked the opportunity to relax here. Sure, it wasn't exactly relaxing to have my lips spread all apart by this device, but even that was sort of comfortable and comforting, my lips resting in the smooth plastic groove of the cheek retractor. And being securely tied down in place certainly felt good. I was fine with it if she wanted to keep me this way all afternoon.

It was probably a quarter of an hour before she came back with a girl who looked thirteen or fourteen. Her eyes were a bit red, and her teeth clenched.

"I know the retainers take some getting used to," Dr.Wrighting said, but wearing them is *essential*. Let me introduce you to Sally here, who first finished up with her braces when she was about your age. She did wear her retainers like she was supposed to – at first. But then, when she only had to wear them at night she began to forget or not bother. End result? Well, Sally is all grown up, but we had to install these."

The sight of my gaping mouth and what was on my teeth made a big impression. The girl gasped, and I could see the wires of her retainers.

"It's only for a year, but can you imagine having to wear braces for a year when you're grown-up?" I could tell that Dr.Wrighting was having trouble keeping a straight face. She was enjoying this.

"And see," Dr.Wrighting said, moving closer, "now that she's grown up the teeth aren't as pliant anymore, so we couldn't just put on the kind of braces you had, we had to use these."

My set of bands were certainly more impressive than the usual set of braces. And I knew that laid bare as they were by the cheek retractor they looked even more metallic and intimidating.

"So this image might be something you want to keep in mind whenever you are tempted to remove those annoying retainers," Dr.Wrighting said. She leaned closer to the girl's ear and half whispered, "And you know that once I take those off her, she's still going to need a set of retainers just like yours as well...."

The shocked girl shuffled out with Dr.Wrighting, who turned back and winked at me, pleased with her performance. And if I contributed to getting a girl to wear her retainers like she was supposed to then I had done a good deed, too, I told myself.

It was another quarter of an hour before Dr.Wrighting brought in the next visitors, an older teenage girl with her mother. "I know it can seem challenging, facing the last years of high school and then possibly even starting college in braces, but it's really never too late. A good number of my patients are older. Sally here is in her twenties. Out in the working world and everything, and fully braced."

The girl cautiously came closer. I tried to smile, but of course couldn't, so I just looked at her so she could take in what I had in my mouth."

"Would I get braces like that?" she asked, clearly intimidated.

Dr.Wrighting smiled. "Sally is a special case. In many cases we can use brackets instead of bands, at least on some of the teeth. Those aren't quite as massive. But we'd have to decide what's best for your particular bite." Turning to the mother she added, "But function is definitely more important than aesthetics as far as what kind of devices we would use. And patients usually make their peace with whatever they have to wear. Sally was probably a bit overwhelmed when she was first fitted with these, but now she doesn't mind them at all, right?" she said, turning to me.

I gave my most approving grunt, trying to say, *Not at all*, but unable to pronounce the words with my lips stretched open like this.

"And the strapping down...?" the mother wondered.

"It's easier on the patients, and it makes working on them easier as well," Dr.Wrighting said. "Some are uncomfortable with the idea at first, but then after they try it out they see that it really is better that way. Even the adult patients. Right, Sally?"

I nodded vigorously.

Dr.Wrighting put her hand on my arm. "And that's even though we've made Sally here wait quite a while today," she smiled. "But it's probably easier for her this way than if she could fidget around."

I nodded some more, while both mother and daughter looked at me. They couldn't quite get the look of shock and horror off their faces.

When Dr.Wrighting came back the next time she was alone. "Thank you for letting me show you off," she said. "And I hope you don't mind the little white lies. I think explaining why you really have braces would have been...counterproductive.

Whereas this was very productive. I'm pretty sure I could convince Robyn to wear her retainers fulltime forever now if I wanted too, so that she can avoid this fate."

Sitting down beside she put two pieces of pink plastic on the tray hovering above me. Retainers. Not exactly normal retainers. They didn't have the wire in the front for example. And I was relieved to see they weren't *too* enormous.

"That's right," Dr.Wrighting said. "Retainers."

She picked one up and snapped it into place. "That's what these small metal bits I wired in earlier are for. They anchor the retainers in place." She snapped the other one on.

"Any pain?" she asked.

I shook my head. I felt some of the plastic in my mouth, but it fit like it was molded on.

Dr.Wrighting removed the cheek retractor. My lips had been stretched open for so long that it took a moment for them to close properly. I felt a bit more of a metallic bulge on the side of my braces, but at least now the little metal pieces she had attached earlier didn't stick out any more. The retainers snapped onto them in a way that pressed them flush against my teeth. The plastic part of the retainers was like a thick piece of plastic covering the back of my teeth. The top retainer didn't cover very much of my palate, but it did circle back pretty far in my mouth along my teeth. Gingerly biting down the retainers took up space in my mouth but otherwise sat securely like they were part of it.

"So how do those feel?" Dr.Wrighting asked.

"Ok," I said. "Smooth. And they fit right in." I had a little trouble speaking, the plastic getting in the way of my tongue.

"Well, since we couldn't have them affect your speech too much we had to make them pretty small, but I think they'll get the job done. They're for 24/7 wear, only to be removed after meals and so on, to brush your teeth and clean them. You *can* take them out if you really have to, for some professional event for example. But if you do those annoying metal bits are going to spring out and be a constant reminder that you should be wearing them…."

The metal bits were a strong incentive not to take the retainers out. Of course that was the idea. That was their purpose.

Running my tongue across the obstructing plastic I thought, *This isn't too bad.* The smooth plastic certainly felt less like a foreign object than the expanders had. But the realization that they were always going to be there, 24/7 also made them suddenly feel larger.

"Even when I eat?" I asked, suddenly realizing the full implications of 24/7.

"Absolutely," Dr.Wrighting said cheerfully.

Well, food wouldn't get wrapped around them like it did in the expanders, but I knew they would make biting and chewing more difficult.

Dr.Wrighting uncuffed my hands so that I could practice taking the retainers out and putting them back in. The bits of metal she had attached earlier were like an added lock to hold them in place. They weren't really locked fast, but it took a surprising amount of pressure to release the retainers. And once they were out I could feel those metal bits spring out and dig into the flesh of my cheeks again. Yes, I would definitely want to keep those retainers in at all times, to avoid that pain.

I quickly got the hang of how to take them out and put them back. Once I had Dr.Wrighting stretched two elastics back in place – I got to continue wearing these too – and then unbuckled me. I was done for the day.

I ran my tongue across the smooth retainers. They were a new challenge. A new set of sensations. I did like the feel of them there. But I worried about their bulkiness. Even though they were fairly small. But they still seemed to take up so much space. Feeling anything with my tongue magnified the size of it, of course, but even so.

Cecilia was manning the reception desk when I was leaving, and I got my slip for my next appointment from her, grinning sheepishly.

"So Dr.Wrighting decided a full set of braces are necessary?" she asked.

I blushed. I wasn't sure how much she knew. "It's just for like a year...."

Amazingly, Cecilia looked completely non-judgmental. I don't think anyone had looked at me like that since I had gotten my braces. Everyone though it was strange or funny – or hot – that I had them. But Cecilia seemed to think it was completely natural.

"You wear them well," she said encouragingly. "I guess if anyone has to get stuck with braces again at our age you can handle them as well as anyone."

"Yeah," I said, a bit more confident again. "It's a bit strange. I wake up some mornings thinking I have to rush and pack my lunchbox so that I'm in time for sixth-grade homeroom again, before I remember that it's the adult me wearing them. But they're ok."

"Another orthodontist probably would have worked with…less noticeable metalwork," Cecilia observed.

I shook my head. "Maybe, but you were right. About Dr.Wrighting. That helps a lot. That she's the one handling my case. I feel totally safe in her hands."

"She knows what she's doing, that's for sure. But she can be demanding."

"That I can handle, I think. Though I guess I am a bit nervous. I have the little tubes for the headgear on my molars, so I guess I have that in store for me too…," I admitted.

Cecilia's appraising look was still entirely neutral.

"She knows what's best, and what's needed. And she can usually convince her patients of it too."

"Well, I've pretty much decided just to put herself in my hands, come what may. It's scary, but it's ok."

Cecilia smiled. She seemed genuinely pleased that I was handling this so well.

A mother came in with her daughter, and they came up to the desk to sign in. "I'll probably see you at one of your next appointments," Cecilia said as I turned to leave and she turned her attention to them.

"I hope so," I said. And I genuinely meant it. Cecilia probably didn't understand what I was really going through, but it was still nice to deal with someone who just accepted you for who you were, even when you were as wired up as I was.

I called Jacob as soon as I was outside.

"What took you so long?" he asked. He'd been waiting. I had forgotten that the appointment had taken much longer than expected.

"Dr.Wrighting took her time," I told him. "So guess what I got."

I don't know if he had been expecting headgear as much as I had, but that was his first cautious guess.

"I thought that's what it would be," I said, "but no. Not this time."

"So...?"

"Guess," I said. "Gue*th!*" I hinted. But he said he didn't know, and so I told him I'd surprise him when we met in the evening.

18.

The retainers were a pleasant surprise. Though not as deeply hidden in my mouth as the palate-reaching top expander had been they were still something Jacob liked to explore. Their smooth surfaces pleased both of us – except when I was eating, when their presence was a bit more annoying. I could still bite properly, or almost, anyway, because the surfaces weren't totally flush with my teeth, leaving the sharp edges of my incisors and so on free to bite. But there was all this additional chewing surface now.... It was strange. And eating without them wasn't really an option: those metal spikes that poked out when the retainers weren't in place really hurt, and when I chewed they just rubbed even more fiercely into my cheeks.

The retainers encroached on my tongue, but not too much. But the unforgiving smooth surface was always there. When I woke. When I spoke. When I did anything. They affected my speech just in the slightest way. You could tell there was *something* in my mouth, but the slurring and lisping wasn't enough to be really pronounced. When I talked, people who knew me would look at me like there was something slightly off, without being able to put their finger quite on what it was. And of course I didn't go around announcing that I had retainers sitting in my mouth, too.

The flat, smooth surfaces made a nice contrast with the harder, uneven metal surfaces of the braces themselves, and the sharp, thin line drawn by the elastics. I was very happy with the combination I had in my mouth. I liked living this way. And when Jacob was allowed to roam free again and could poke and thrust into all my openings we enjoyed ourselves very much.

We argued about whether this was the *ideal* setup. The elastics, for example, were sometimes really in the way, like a wire stretched between my jaws. Or Jacob moaned that he wished my retainers were bigger. That the whole inside of my mouth was a plasticized cavern. But it was hard to really complain. All of this was *awesome*, and did feel wonderful. And it wasn't just with Jacob that I enjoyed it. Just carrying it around in my mouth brought a smile to my face. I loved the feel of the braces and the retainer, and of them being welded and wedded to my teeth. Part of me. Like some good luck charm and a security blanket all wrapped up in one. Sometimes I wondered how I was going to be able to live without them again....

This setup was great. Braces, elastics, retainers. I wouldn't have minded if Dr.Wrighting didn't change anything else for the remaining months. But part of me also remained constantly excited about what might come next....

The weeks flew by. I didn't think we could have so much constant sex. Our desire was undiminished. The sight of the braces was enough to set Jacob off, and me...I was always primed and ready to go. And so we just fucked and fucked and fucked. Like the happiest rabbits.

When the date of my next appointment came closer I began to feel that queasy vertigo that reminded me of anticipating childhood visits to the doctor or dentist. What now? What next? The fear of the unknown. But it wasn't really fear. It was a sort of anxious excitement. Because I wanted Dr.Wrighting to lead me on, even further down this braced course, to places I hadn't ever experienced or imagined. So far everything had exceeded my expectations.... The only thing I worried about was that I had already reached such orgasmic and sensual peaks that there was nothing left higher. That I could only be disappointed.

Strapped back in the examination chair I immediately relaxed completely. Here was my ultimate happy place. Sure, sex with Jacob, and lying in his arms was wonderful. But being strapped down here, immobilized and awaiting my fate, was my nirvana.

Dr.Wrighting removed the elastics and retainers and examined everything closely, looking satisfied. Would I be getting those things back, I wondered, looking at the pink retainers lying on the tray in front of me. Or was this experiment and episode over?

I was relieved when Dr.Wrighting snapped the retainers back into place. They were still mine! Still part of me! But from the way she looked at me I could tell she wasn't finished yet. And when she went to the cabinets in the back of the room and opened some drawers my heart pounded more strongly against the straps across my chest, hoping and fearing about what she was getting.

I recognized it in her hand when she turned back. Elation and terror flooded through me. It was the facebow for a headgear.

I was getting headgear.

What I had dreamed of as a girl was finally going to happen to me. I was going to have to wear headgear.

So far everything that Dr.Wrighting had done to me had been familiar. My braces were different from the ones I had had when I was kid, but fundamentally they were the same. I had had elastics, too. And while I had had another kind of retainers they weren't something so completely different. But headgear – headgear was an entirely new experience. A leap into the unknown, promising entirely new sensations.

Dr.Wrighting put down the facebow and stretched my lips across the cheek retractor. I melted with pleasure and anticipation, mouth wide open to receive my new appliance.

"Yes," Dr.Wrighting said smiling at me, "it's headgear time. But since we can't put any real tension in the appliance I've tried a little adjustment, so that the facebow still can't be dislodged easily."

As she picked up the facebow I could see that near the ends of the wire of the inner facebow there was like a tiny ball, maybe welded on, with only a fraction of an inch of wire on the other side. The balls were just slightly larger than the diameter of the wire itself, making for little more than a small bulge there. Maybe a quarter or half an inch farther along the wire there was a quick bend up and down. I assumed this was to prevent the facebow from sliding farther through the tube that would hold it in place than it should.

Dr.Wrighting brought the facebow to my mouth and I could feel her press one end into the tube attached to the side of the band wrapped around one of my molars. She had to force it through the tube, until there was a slight pop and I guessed she had pushed the ball all the way through. Then she pushed the other side through. She looked almost surprised that it worked the way she had planned. Examining how the facebow sat above my braces – I didn't think it was touching them, since I would have felt that – all the way to the front of my mouth, she looked satisfied. She tugged and pushed at it from where the inner bow met the outer bow. Satisfied that it sat firmly, she then tugged to remove it, and then to put it back in again. It sure felt like it would be hard to accidentally dislodge.

"This seems to work just fine," she said. She put the facebow on the tray again and then removed the cheek retractor. She put in my elastics, and then she picked up the facebow and inserted it again. Now I could feel the wire from the inner facebow bulging slightly above my braces. And then my lips closed around the stub of metal connecting the inner and outer facebows, which felt odd but not unpleasant.

I guess I was a bit surprised that something as major as headgear seemed to make so little difference in my mouth. Except for that bit between my lips – and that was odd! – it wasn't much more than a different sort of wire across my braces.

Dr.Wrighting got up and got a neckstrap from her cabinets. The center part was wide and padded, and then there were these white, plastic strips one each side, with evenly-spaced holes in them.

Dr.Wrighting had me raise my head so she could put it behind my neck, and then she hooked the ends of the facebow into the plastic strips. She tried different settings, and when she was satisfied she pulled the neckstrap away and snipped off the plastic ends. "The setting is the last hole on each side, she told me," as she reattached it.

"So, how does it feel?" Dr.Wrighting asked, leaning back.

There was little pressure or pull. Just the feel of the neckstrap around my neck, and then the metal bit between my lips, which my mouth constantly was closing around. I nodded. "Fine. Good."

Dr.Wrighting began to undo my restraints. "Alright then, why don't you go have a seat in the waiting room, and see if it really sits nicely, and then we'll show you how to take it on and off and all that."

I froze for a moment. I was fine showing off my braces, and I was fine with the thought of dealing with stuff like this headgear here in the examination room with just Dr.Wrighting and an assistant watching, or in the privacy of my apartment, with Jacob or alone. But headgear was a lot more than braces. Certainly a lot more visible. And to show myself in public with it? Even if it was just an orthodontist's waiting room, where one out of every four or five patients I saw there wore one....

Of course all the patients sporting headgear in the waiting room were always girls. Almost all of them ten or twelve or so. Only once or twice had I seen a girl who looked like she was a teenager wearing some kind of headgear. Even though having braces as an adult was unusual, it wasn't that unusual. I didn't mind people seeing me with them. I kind of liked it. Being able to surprise them when I opened my mouth. But the headgear was something I couldn't hide. *Everyone* would immediately see it. I couldn't show it on my terms.

Walking out there with headgear was liking walking out there naked. Completely exposing myself. But I could see Dr.Wrighting wouldn't take any excuses or allow me to just wait here. Meekly I went out, and immediately felt all the stares.

I was sometimes self-conscious about the braces. Of course I was. At fancy receptions, for example, where everyone was wearing tuxedos and fine evening gowns and there I was, a giggly girl with my mouthful of metal. But I had never felt as self-conscious about them as I did now about wearing the headgear.

The fact that there was another girl in the waiting room who had it almost made me feel worse. She was ten or so, and it seemed so appropriate on her, and so inappropriate on me. There was also the fact that I didn't even know what I looked like with it yet, since Dr.Wrighting hadn't let me look in a mirror. So I just had to sit there, and notice everyone else there staring or trying not to stare or constantly glancing over at me. Some of the mothers gave me a sympathetic smile, and I tried not to look too discouraging because I didn't want to be a bad role model for the younger kids, but it was hard.

It didn't help that Dr.Wrighting made me sit out there for over half an hour, meaning that patients were constantly coming and going, and new people got to see me and react to what I was wearing. Yay!

What was weird was that even as I felt so uncomfortable about being on display with this thing on, I really liked the way the headgear actually felt, in my mouth and on my head. There was something comforting about how it was secured to my head, the neckpad gently pushing against the back of my neck. I could run my fingers along the outer facebow, which curved around the front of my face but didn't touch the skin anywhere, unless I pushed it down into my cheeks. And my lips kept closing around that small metal bit where the inner and outer facebows met, and I really liked the feel of that there. It was halfway between something to suck on and a kiss. If I had been by myself, I would have been really happy with it.

92

Finally Dr.Wrighting called me back in. As soon as I walked back to where the examination rooms were I felt unburdened. Somehow it felt *ok* or even normal to be wearing the headgear back here, even though patients could see me with it as I passed by. Dr.Wrighting led me to another examination room, and then to a corner of it where, hidden behind a wall, there was a mirror! So there was one in the office after all!

Of course there had to be, because for some of the appliances she needed to show patients how to insert them and take them out safely.

I marveled at my headgear. It was just a simple wire, stretched across my mouth and cheeks, the neckstrap disappearing under my hair. But it was also so much. And on my own face, it was more than I had been able to imagine. Not something I wanted to be seen in public wearing, but in private....Yes, I liked the idea of having and getting to wear this.

I could have stared much longer, lost in happy thoughts, but Dr.Wrighting wanted me to learn how to take it off and put it on myself. Unhooking the neckstrap was easy, though the plastic was hooked on fairly securely. At first I was scared to tug as hard as Dr.Wrighting wanted me to to get the facebow out, but she said that as long as I held it in a specific way it was ok. With a small pop and jerk the ends of the facebow came out of the tubes, and then it was easy to remove. It took me a few tries putting it in until I mastered that. It really did require some real force, but once I knew how much to apply and where it was easy to do.

Still wearing it, I followed Dr.Wrighting to her office. She gave me all the instructions written down, too. "Now as to weartime...," she said.

Weartime! That's right. She was going to prescribe a set number of hours a day. Or maybe just night?

"Quite a few of my patients wear the headgear more or less fulltime," she said with a smile. "But unfortunately we can't do that with you...."

She sounded disappointed, and the way she looked at me, it was like she was asking, *Or can we?* But no way could I show up to work with this on.

"I understand that your work situation means you can't wear it as much as if you were a school-age patient. I'm even willing to accommodate you so far as to say that you don't have to wear it in public, which is something I never promise my other patients. In fact, I usually try to break down their resistance to wearing it in public as quickly as possible, since that allows us to proceed much more quickly and effectively. But I do expect consistent and dedicated weartime, and if you fail to achieve that I will...raise the stakes." Dr.Wrighting smiled. "There's no such thing as deciding you only want to wear it a certain number of hours a day, or not at all some nights. If you fall short of your prescribed weartime, I will no longer be as accommodating."

She sounded very serious, which was starting to make me nervous. I sucked on the bit of metal between my lips. So what was that amount of weartime she was prescribing? More than just at night, from the sound of it....

"So what I expect – no, what I insist on is that you wear it twelve hours daily, and fourteen hours a day on weekends and holidays."

I breathed a sigh of relief. Twelve hours was half the day, but that still left a lot of time.... Or did it?

"Some days, if you go out at night, you might not be able to get in the twelve hours, and you can make them up another day, or on the weekend. But by the end of each week you have to have worn it for eighty-eight hours."

She gave me a chart where I could keep track of the hours.

"Thanks to the wonders of microtechnology, your device is wired in such a way that I can get an exact reading of your weartime," Dr.Wrighting explained. She typed something into her computer and then pressed enter and turned the monitor so I could see it. My name was printed on top, and there was a graph filling the screen, and you could see a straight line that was interrupted by a series of spikes near the beginning and near the end. It represented my weartime, the spikes marking when I had been practicing taking it out, and earlier when Dr.Wrighting had been fitting me with it in the first place. "So there's no way to lie or cheat, and no getting away with not wearing it as you should."

I was properly intimidated. The little girls she fitted with headgear must have been totally terrified. Especially since their sentences were often longer than mine.

"I can do this," I said, as much to convince myself as to reassure her.

"I know you can," Dr.Wrighting said. "I just want you to be sure and know that you don't have any choice, either."

Like with the braces, and with the retainers. Everything except the elastics was more or less out of my control.

"One more thing," Dr.Wrighting said. "I always insist my patients wear their devices home, too. In your case I'm willing to let you take it off once you get outside, but I would appreciate it if you could wear it to the exit, and not let any of the patients see you take it off outside. To preserve the illusion."

I nodded.

"And if you could put it on before getting here at your next appointment. All my patients have to wear their appliances in the waiting room, and I'd rather you didn't just put it on there. It sets a very bad example."

"Sure," I said. I wanted to please. To be a good girl.

It was all a bit much to take in, and I couldn't quite do the numbers in my head as I walked out into the waiting room again. There I was immediately hit by the self-consciousness again, and I thought I could hear the gasps and rustles as I went toward the reception desk still wearing the headgear. They couldn't believe I was going to go out on the street like this.

I collected my appointment slip for the next time. It was for a week from now, and I asked the receptionist if that was right. She smiled. "With a new appliance like headgear, Dr.Wrighting wants to make sure you're settling in well."

I nodded and went to the door, taking a quick breath before opening it. No one else was coming out, so I didn't have to worry about anyone behind me, but I had to make sure no new patient was just coming to the office before I whipped off the headgear. So I had to look up and down the sidewalk for any girls being led by an adult, while trying to avoid having any regular adults see me. Fortunately it isn't a busy street, but my heart still pounded as I looked to make sure no patients of Dr.Wrighting were on their way.

Whipping off the headgear also was wishful thinking. The neckstrap was easy enough to undo, with only a bit of fumbling, without looking in a mirror, but the facebow really was stuck pretty well, and for a moment I felt the sort of panic where you think you'll never get it out. It was only a few moments before I did manage to get it out, but my heart was pounding violently. I stuck the facebow and neckstrap in the pouch I had gotten from Dr.Wrighting and quickly fled the scene. I couldn't imagine what it was like for girls who just got their headgear and who walked home accompanied by their mothers, not allowed to take the new device off. But maybe Dr.Wrighting was right that in those cases it was best just to break them as soon as possible, and get them used to being seen like that.

I waited until I got home to call Jacob. I didn't want to be overheard in public talking about having gotten headgear. I picked up the phone when I got home, but then I realized that I really should put on the headgear right away. I had been trying to work out the math and it was clear that I now pretty much always had to put it on right away when I got home. And keep it on.

Sleeping only got me in eight hours of weartime on a good night. Which left four more. There wasn't any available in the morning, between showering and breakfast. Which left four hours from the time I got home to the time I went to bed. Interrupt that for dinner, and time really got tight. Damn, I realized. This was not going to be child's play.

19.

"I got it," I told Jacob.

"What?"

"It. The ultimate orthodontic accessory. The fashion statement. The bridle and the bit."

"No...."

"Yes. Yes, indeed. I got headgeared."

"That's...fantastic. Congratulations. It is fantastic, isn't it?"

"It is. And I mean it really is. I can't get over it. I'm staring at myself in the mirror, and it really is fantastic."

"I can't wait...."

"See you soon. And you get to see it soon."

"As soon as I can."

I could hear how excited Jacob was. I was glad about that. That he was looking forward to this too. But I was a bit worried, too. This bridle and bit was more in the way than the braces or the retainers. This could actually interfere with some things. I was already worried about what it would be like sleeping with it on, but there was also the matter of things like kissing. And more intense physical activity. I mean obviously I could wear it while having sex. Plain sex. But it kind of limited what I could do, didn't it? I couldn't just shove my face anywhere any longer, could I? But I also *had* to wear it during sex, didn't I? Our sex playing usually went on for a while, and I needed to get in the hours of weartime wherever I could.

We were going to have to experiment. Carefully. But for once I was glad Jacob was locked up and that we wouldn't be able to do very much for the first week. It would give me time to learn just how much in the way this thing was and how to live with it strapped on.

I don't know if Jacob was out of breath from rushing home, or from the excitement, but he stood there staring and panting at me as soon as he got in the door.

"Wow," he said.

"You like?"

"I do like. So much. Wow."

He approached me slowly, and then bent forward slowly, and then kissed me slowly, trying to work how to deal with the metal bit and bar. I know we weren't supposed to but I couldn't resist and I was curious. And besides, we couldn't *really* kiss with this thing between us, could we?

We managed to connect our lips, but the metal was also right there in the middle of it all. Which made it more exciting, even though it limited how much we could do.

"Oh, my God," Jacob said, his voice breaking. "Sally, you've got to unlock this stupid cock age," he said desperately. "You've got to let me out. You've got to let me in. You've got to let us fuck," he said, his voice cracking even more.

For a moment, in that moment, I wanted nothing more, too, and I almost gave in. But I knew I couldn't. I could feel the hard bulge of his pants against me, and I wanted that inside me so badly, but I knew I had to stay strong. "We can't," I said.

He pressed and squeezed my breast, nearly completely out of control. "Sally, I can't…I can't take it. We *have* to fuck. Now. Here. Look at you. You're perfect. You're everything. You have headgear!"

It was like he was delirious, completely overcome by desire.

I pushed him away gently, but his glazed eyes stared at me uncomprehendingly. "Sally…."

"It's only a few days," I reminded him. I didn't dare say a week.

He seemed close to tears, like he had been completely broken. "Sally…," he said hoarsely.

He buried his head in his hands, tearing his eyes away from me. Panting. Or sobbing.

"I can't do this, Sally," he said, trying not to look at me. "It's too much. I'll explode. I can't stay here. I can't look. If I do...," he glanced at me again and then looked away as quickly as he could. He got up and stumbled to the door. "I can't do this," he repeated. "I have to get out of here. If I'm with you I have to...but we can't...."

Without looking back at me he left.

I hadn't expected that. I sat there more or less dumbfounded. Only the foreign feel of the headgear again brought me back to my senses.

What now? I wondered.

What I felt: In the way it encircles you, headgear does make you an island. It's a self-sufficient ring, fencing you in and fencing the world out. If you dare go out in public with it on, or are forced to by your parents, it's like a zone that separates you from everyone else. A halo that is anything but angelic. No one can not notice it, least of all you. And if you're too chicken to go out in public wearing it, like I was, then it isolated you at home, defining you just as much.

At home you only had to expose yourself to your family and those closest to you, who had to accept you for what you were, even when you were all braced and bridled. It was funny that the one person I leaned on, Jacob, couldn't take it because it was too much of a good thing!

I felt like I was the center piece of a scale, with the whole world, laughing at me in my headgear, on one side, and Jacob, loving me in it, on the other. The scale was in balance, because Jacob was *so* happily overwhelmed by my new get-up – but the sheer weight on each side of the scale was so much that we teetered under the strain of all of it. And there I was, stuck in the middle, trying to maintain a sense of balance. And I was the one with the headgear on.

It was ok adjusting to it by myself. Maybe it was even easier and better this way, without Jacob slobbering and swooning all over me. I kept going to the mirror to see how I looked. Watching TV I'd even forget I had it on at moments, unlike the retainers or the braces themselves, which I felt more constantly. But then I'd lift a glass to my lips to try to drink and see that it wasn't quite so simple.

I took it off to make myself some food, then snapped it back on. I didn't mind wearing it, but I realized that I would be wearing it a lot. Getting in those hours was going to be…time-consuming. Obviously.

Taking off all my orthodontic regalia to brush my teeth before going to sleep, I stared at the retainers and the headgear and the little bag of elastics. This was all fun and games, but this was also serious. I didn't have a choice. I had to put them back on again, and I would again tomorrow, and the day after. I didn't mind putting them back in. I liked the feel of the retainers. I liked the novelty of the headgear. But I had lost an element of free will and personal choice. I mean, I could convince myself that this was exactly what I wanted, and I really did feel that. But there was a tiny part of me that worried about the day when I was fed up with it. The night when I just didn't want to wear that headgear. But I was still going to have to, because Dr.Wrighting insisted and even if she couldn't force me directly she still controlled so much that was in my mouth that she could bend me to her will. The braces couldn't be removed, and who knows what she'd come up with as punishment if I didn't wear what I was supposed to?

Sure, that was what I wanted. I even liked that slight sense of terror that I knew would keep me from being disobedient. But I did worry that there would come a time when it would be too much for me to take. But then, like with any teenaged braced girl, it wouldn't matter. The orthodontist decided, not us.

I was kind of annoyed that Jacob didn't at least call to apologize after he left. Or to explain. Or that he didn't call or email the next day.

And I guess I was kind of worried. I mean, the only reason I was able to really enjoy all of this to the fullest was because it was the two of us. I mean, I *liked* having the braces and everything anyway, but if it weren't for Jacob enjoying them with me I would have gotten pretty sad and lonely pretty fast. Like in crime, having a partner in passion didn't just double the fun, it exponentially increased it. All along that was my worry, of course. That he was going to abandon me. And obviously I'd never find anyone who would want to play this game with me, so I'd just have to grin and bear it to the bitter end alone. Which would still be somewhere between fine and great but wouldn't be as deliriously blissful.

O.k., I wasn't too worried. Not at this juncture. The problem this time was that he was *too* turned on, after all. He wanted this. Bad. Really, really bad. So I didn't think he could just run away from it. But what if he went to Dr.McDarmon and had the cage removed? We could still continue being together, but it went against everything Dr.Wrighting and Dr.Allegretta had planned and organized, and they would find a way to punish us for the transgression.

Don't do anything stupid, Jacob, I kept telling myself. By late in the afternoon, when I still hadn't heard from him, I had to call. He still sounded shaken up and desperate. I liked that.

"I can't see you like that, Sally," he said. Whispering over the phone he added, "I can't get the image of my head, and it's been killing me all day and night, Sally. I took the longest, coldest shower I ever have last night. I stood there until I was shivering under the water and *blue*, and I still had a steel ramrod erection and I was still as turned on as I've ever been."

We agreed to meet for dinner, when I didn't have to wear the headgear, but Jacob insisted that he wouldn't even walk me home because he couldn't bear the thought of what awaited me in there and what he couldn't yet enjoy to the fullest. "You don't know how hard it is," he said, his voice still quivering.

I had to say I liked that. To hear that desperation and lust. Even if it wasn't quite *me* that was causing it – it was the bridle and bit and the braces, better than any push-up bra or sexy lingerie, that was really driving him over the edge – I was still part of that equation. To wield that kind of sexual power, regardless of the accessories required, was a really good feeling.

I tried not to tease him about it over dinner, but you could see his eyes trained on my braces, imagining the facebow there as well. It was hard to have a conversation because he was so preoccupied. He looked like he was falling apart. Could he really last an entire week?

We kissed passionately outside the restaurant before heading in separate directions, so full of desire but knowing that we could not act on it.

At home I brushed my teeth and then immediately put the headgear on, checking the time and marking the chart where I was keeping track of my weartime. It was hard getting enough

100

hours in, I realized. I was going to fall a bit short today, and I was going to have to make that up at some point.

It felt good to wear the headgear. I liked that additional strip pulling at the back of my neck, and the feel of the metal between my lips where the inner and outer facebows were connected. I was so lucky, I thought. And I felt bad for Jacob, sitting home alone and fantasizing about this picture, but unable even to relieve himself by masturbating. I hoped he had gone out to have a drink or a few instead. At least I didn't have to worry about him picking up anyone to get off that way. With his penis caged like it was he was mine. All mine.

In the days that followed I was still all by myself with the headgear. Jacob didn't dare come over when I wore it. And I had to wear it all the time except for work and going out to eat and things like that. Even so it was hard to get in more than ten hours on a weekday. Which meant I had to play catch up on the weekend, and saw less of Jacob then too.

I liked wearing it. I even liked *having* to wear it. But a small part of me resented not having the freedom to decide whether or not to wear it, or when. The braces were a permanent fixture, but I could sort of hide them when I went out in public. Not *everyone* would notice them, unless I opened my mouth. But the headgear was something completely different. Wearing headgear in public was like going topless in public. Way more than I dared to do. So they did constrain me in a way that was kind of frustrating. But I knew that was also part of what I liked about them. Even though they served no purpose, it felt good to be *forced* to wear them.

Even though I already had to wear it an extra two hours a day weekends – fourteen instead of just twelve – I almost caught up with the weartime then, by wearing it almost all the time. But of course I forgot to plan ahead. I should have realized that I was going to have a hard time getting in twelve hours each of the remaining days before I had to see Dr.Wrighting again, especially since there was an official function on Monday night that I had to be at. So I was going to come up a few hours short for the week. Maybe I would manage eight-five, when I was supposed to wear it for eighty-eight.

When I went to Dr.Wrighting's for my next appointment I made sure the coast was clear for half a block before walking quickly to the door. I tried to time it so that I would insert the facebow just as I reached the door, and then hook up the neckstrap right before opening the door. I had gotten pretty good at being able to put it on quickly, but I hadn't practiced doing it without looking the mirror enough, so I did stand there longer than expected fumbling with it. But fortunately no patient came out just as I was putting it on, and when I went into the office I was like every good little girl there, wearing my appliance like I should. I saw I wasn't the only one with headgear in the waiting room when I got there, but I still got more and longer stares, the grown-up with the braces and headgear still an odd sight even here.

Dr.Wrighting made me wait for a while, and after I had been strapped in and she finally came in to check on me she shook her head. "Not even eighty-three hours," she said. Her electronic monitoring system gave her an all too precise number. 82 hours and 48 minutes and 12 seconds it said on the printout that she waved ion front of me. "That's more than five percent short. That's unacceptable."

"I didn't time it right…," I tried to make excuses.

"Even my youngest patients know how to count!"

"I tried…."

"If you call this trying, then I'm very disappointed. It's all very simple, after all. All you do is strap it on, and you're done."

I felt bad and guilty. "I'll make it up."

"You will. That's an extra five hours for this week. And I'd advise you to aim higher in the coming weeks, to make sure you get that twelve hours a day average in. This isn't *entirely* fun and games, Sally, and if you fail to wear an appliance as instructed there will be consequences."

I couldn't imagine what she had in mind, but I didn't want to test her and find out. "It won't happen again."

She looked mollified. "Ok then. And how are you getting on with it otherwise."

"It's fine," I admitted. "Other than finding the time to war it, it's really ok."

"Good, because you'll be wearing it a while longer you know."

I didn't know of course. Dr.Wrighting hadn't said how long I was going to have to wear this or any of the other accessories. After a year everything was coming off – except there would be retainers after that – but until then I knew: anything goes.

Dr.Wrighting didn't do or change anything else. This was strictly a check-up, and except for the missing weartime she was satisfied and quickly let me go. Except she added, "I know you're due to let Jacob out of his...well, so that you can enjoy a night together again, but given the situation, I think it's better if you wait...let's say two more days."

My heart sank. Not so much for me, though I was looking forward to getting fucked again, and getting fucked regularly again, but for Jacob, who would be absolutely crushed. If he didn't simply explode down there.

"Do we...," I began to say, but seeing Dr.Wrighting's stern look I knew there was no questioning her decision. Two more days it was. And two more nights.

I called Jacob as soon as I got out of the office, to try to let him down easily. As I figured, he was crushed, but he knew it was hopeless to argue. After that I went home fast, to strap the headgear on again and make sure I got the twelve hours for that day in, and maybe a bit more to start making up for lost time. realized.

20.

Finally, after two more long days, it was time. Not a moment too soon.

I greeted Jacob at the door, grinning behind the headgear I sported. And hoping none of the neighbors were passing by as I opened the door. Jacob sighed with pleasure, seeing me again with the device on for the first time in a week. He carefully but passionately kissed me. It was a weird feeling, what with the wires of the facebow there between our lips, and our lips maneuvering around it. We had to be careful, because he couldn't press too hard against it, or push the facebow up or down.

Pulling me close to him I could feel the caged bulge in his pants and felt all soft in my legs, and wet between them. I wanted him so bad, and I could feel his desire pulsing through him.

Closing the door without separating my lips from his we practically danced into the room. Jacob reached up to begin to unbutton my blouse, but I raised my hand. "Dinner first," I said, smiling through all my metalwork.

"I know what I have an appetite for...," he said.

"Me too. But we'll get to it."

"But I don't want you to have to take out the headgear," he said, looking worried.

I smiled, and he melted at the sight of all my orthodontic work, the wiring and the elastics. "Trust me," I told him.

I had set the table nicely, with candles and everything. I told him to sit down and then began serving. I had made him some pork chops, just the way he loved them. O.k., lighter on the garlic than he liked, just in case, but otherwise just he loved them. He was all jumpy in his seat as I leaned over to serve him. I hadn't buttoned my blouse back up from where he had opened it, so you could just see my bra. Not that he needed anything else to get him more aroused, but it made me feel a bit sexier. I knew the headgear turned him on, but it was still hard for me to think of myself as looking at all *sexy* with it on.

On my own plate I only put mashed potatoes and vegetables. I had been practicing eating with the headgear on, to wring every last possible minute of weartime out of them. As anyone who has had headgear can tell you, it's a real trial to eat with it on. It's just that stupid bit between your lips, but surprisingly that makes a big difference. It's worse drinking from a glass or anything, because there the facebow really gets in the way. Which is why I had a straw in my glass if white wine, which at least made it possible for me to drink without slobbering all over the place. But eating was tough too.

The retainers got in the way, too. First of all, they always made it harder to swallow *anything*. But because of the space they took up I also had to open my mouth wider to chew properly. But when trying to eat with the headgear I had to try to keep my mouth closed, lips tight around the metal bit connecting the inside and outside facebows. It was not an easy balancing act. And, of course, I couldn't bite into anything because of the facebows. But I had figured out that I could sort of eat mushy stuff that I didn't really have to bite into or chew. Yoghurt. Mashed potatoes. Mushy vegetables. With the retainers it was easier to eat things off a fork than a spoon – it was sort of hard to get everything off a spoon for some reason with the retainers and everything else in my mouth – so mashed potatoes were easier than yoghurt, for example.

I'm sure I didn't look very sexy as I tried to keep the food in my mouth, but Jacob still looked totally entranced, barely looking down to quickly cut off another piece of meat and before he turned all his attention to me again.

104

We made dinner conversation, but of course all either one us was thinking was was about what was coming next. And so after the main course we decided to leave the chocolate pudding for later.

Usually I'd brush my teeth after a meal, but there was no stopping this train now and neither of us cared about anything that might be stuck in my braces, or the foody taste in each other's mouths. Jacob twirled me to the bedroom, carefully kissing me along the way, and I opened my blouse and gently pushed him down on the bed.

"Why don't you get undressed, and I'll be right back?" I told him.

I took off my blouse and undid my bra and tossed that in the hamper. Looking in the bathroom mirror I smiled at what a weird picture that was. Me with my perky breasts and hard nipples, looking pretty fit and attractive, and then that face with the headgear on. I smiled, revealing all the underlying metal of the braces too. Sure, I looked like a strange mix between tweenage girl in braces and nude model, but I was completely happy. I didn't want it any other way.

I got the key to Jacob's cage and went back to the bedroom, where he was standing naked, waiting, and eager.

I knelt down in front of him and took hold of the cage, which stood pointing out, held up by his completely erect penis. I fumbled with the key and it took me a moment before I could open it, but then I slid it off and there it was, his pulsing veined member, a drop of liquid already at its tip. Jacob sighed and then roared with relief, and pulled me up, reaching for my pants to pull them off as quick as possible.

Once I was naked he lifted me and placed me on the bed, and then lowered himself onto and into me. He tried to be careful and not go at it too hard, trembling as he tried to show some restraint, but of course it did little good. He barely pumped into me a few times before I could see he was coming. Still, it felt so good, as if a burden had been lifted off me as well. I realized how much I had missed sex.

We kissed and caressed and caroused, and I enjoyed the attention that his lips and tongue and fingers paid to my breasts and between my legs. Jacob was soon ready to give it another, longer try, and that was terrific too.

The headgear did limit what I could do, or the positions I could take. I had to be face up, and there was only so much I could do with my mouth with the facebow there. So it was Jacob who serviced me more than I did him. But he was certainly into it. I was glad, because facebow sex was obviously going to be a bit more plain vanilla otherwise.

Lying there together afterwards, Jacob still fingered my headgear lovingly. I was glad that he didn't just like it to help him get off, and then prefer it off of me as well. I was obliged to wear it, marking the hours on my timesheet, so I was glad he continued to want me to have it on, even after we had gotten the sex out of our system. Though in his case it wasn't so much out of the system, it's that his system needed to recuperate after going it so hard and so long – after not having gone at it at all for over a week.

I had gotten sort of used to sleeping with the headgear. You can't really roll your head as much when you're wearing it, and you certainly can't bury it in your pillow. The first few nights I had woken up several times by the device getting pulled or pushed or tugged when I moved around. At first it had taken me a moment or two to remember why there was something sticking *out* of my mouth and attached to the back of my neck too. But for the most part I had adjusted by now. Of course, sleeping with and next to Jacob made for a whole new learning curve, since I couldn't just snuggle up tight against him like I liked to. The headgear enforced a certain distance. It was sort of like a fence. A really simple one, but still effective.

When I woke up in the morning, Jacob was staring at me happily. "Man, do I love that headgear," he said, kissing me. I'm sure my retainer-breath was worse than his morning breath but I still liked the feel of his and my lips around the metal bit where the facebows joined, and then his filmy tongue exploring the thicker inner facebow wire, and then licking the curved surface of my retainer. Before I even knew it he was inside me again, and we were rocking gently in a slowly heightening game of mutual pleasuring. I came before he did, and I couldn't stifle my long squeal of pleasure, which just grew louder as he continued to thrust himself in and out and in and out and I came again, and again.

The braces experience was proving to be great no matter what, but I was surprised how much better it made the sex too. Maybe just because we were having so much of it, and maybe because of those enforced week long pauses in between. Or because the combination of the braces and me made Jacob so much of a more determined lover. Whatever the reason, just the act itself was beyond any of my previous wildest experiences or dreams. I didn't know it could be this good and intense and satisfying. Lying there, drained, feeling the gentle tug of my headgear, and of the elastics in my mouth, and my tongue resting between the smooth plastic plates of my retainers I was in a state of complete bliss. Nothing could be better, I thought.

We showered together, and after sucking it clean I locked Jacob's cock up again. He didn't protest too much, having gotten all out of it over the past twelve hours that he and I could and probably glad to hit the pause button until that evening. I had to put my headgear on for him briefly just before we left – "For the mental picture I want to carry with me during the day," he said – but it was just for a minute and a long kiss. I didn't mark it down on the timesheet. And then we went to work, both wondering how we were going to get anything done, sure that our minds would both be wandering right back to the same point, right back here.

Now that we could be together again we enjoyed the time. It wasn't all sex. But it was almost all headgear. After work there really wasn't time to go out and get in all the required hours, so we stayed in a lot. By the weekend Jacob was getting antsy, wanting to do *more*. He wanted to go out. And even at home he suggested we have sex *without* me wearing the headgear.

"Are you getting tired of it?" I asked, honestly worried.

"No, I love it. But it's so there, between us, when we're fucking. And we can't play around as vigorously as we can otherwise."

I wanted to keep him happy, so I timed things that we could escape for a few hours and enjoy half a night out, and I reluctantly took off the headgear for one romp in bed. Though I made sure to put it right back on when we were done. Maybe it was because his request made me worry about so many things, like that he was getting tired of these orthodontic games, even while I still had so many wired up months ahead of me, but the sex didn't feel nearly as good. Jacob was trying hard, but it didn't feel natural. It was like we were forcing ourselves to go through with it even though this wasn't really what we were in the mood for.

So then of course I started worrying about what was going to happen when I was stripped of all my orthodontic accessories and I was pretty much like every other woman out there. I mean, he had found me hot and liked fucking me before we even discovered our mutual affinity for braces and before I got them. But now that he had gotten a taste of the braced me would he ever really think the braceless me was worth paying much attention to?

Once the workweek started we got back in a better rhythm. Two nights he only came over late because he had to go out with other people for business. It was weird having to stay home like some Cinderella, obediently wearing my headgear. I have to admit I cried a bit at my plight. I would have given a lot for a day when I could go without wearing it. But I knew the numbers and the hours didn't add up.

Because of the headgear I couldn't have gone anyway, but I did ask Jacob about one of the functions he described to me. "So is this the kind of thing you'd have taken me to, if I didn't have the braces?"

He actually blushed and looked really uncomfortable. "Well...."

"Well?"

His head, bowed in shame, bobbed slightly. "But I mean you couldn't anyway, right? Because it would be such a pain to get in all the hours of the headgear time in, right? So I didn't really consider asking you."

"I could have made that work," I said. "I have to go out some nights for work, and I just catch up the time elsewhere."

"Yeah, on my watch, when we're together."

"Which you like."

"I do and..."

"But you're evading the question. Let's say I tell you I can work around the weartime. Would you have taken the braced me?"

"I...I guess...probably not."

"Are you ashamed of me?"

He looked at me like he was scared of having hurt me. A bit late for that. But he shook his head. "No, no, no. You know how much I love you. And how much I love you like *this*, with *these*," he said, running his thumb over my braces. "But it would be sort of hard to explain to everyone."

I could understand that. It didn't make me feel any better, but I could understand it. I still hadn't gotten used to the way people looked and stared and treated me, and I knew I never would. Even without the headgear, I knew I was a freak. And even though I loved my braces so much, a part of me did feel ashamed of looking the way I did.

Jacob felt bad and didn't even ask me to unlock his cage that night, realizing I wasn't in the mood and not wanting to force himself on me, or try to seduce me. He tossed and turned a bit, unable to conceal his erection, but he didn't say a word about me offering him some relief. He took his punishment like a man.

Not that it made me feel that much better.

21.

Headgear. The retainers. Elastics. And of course the immovable, massive braces themselves. It *was* a lot to deal with.

Don't get me wrong, I loved it. Most of the time. But after brushing my teeth and feeling my tongue able to move freely around my entire mouth and reach all of my palate I sometimes wished I didn't have to reinsert the retainers right away and snap the elastics into place. And there were lots of afternoons when I got home and I wished I could put off putting on the headgear just a bit longer. Or wait at least until I saw Jacob and put it on only for him. Or not have to worry about whether or not I had weartime enough to spare to be able to go out and do something. But that's not the way it worked. I knew I had to wear everything as instructed. I didn't want to find out what Dr.Wrighting might have planned if I failed or fell short.

I couldn't even imagine how it was for Dr.Wrighting's younger real patients, who weren't dealing with all this voluntarily. And who weren't just not getting laid but probably couldn't get any boy to smile at them – unless it was when the boys were trying not to laugh at them. I was wearing all this stuff for real, in a way, but it was so much more real – and so much longer for them, wasn't it?

The sex continued to be great. And so was the time with Jacob. But I had to admit as my next appointment approached that I kept my fingers crossed a bit that Dr.Wrighting might loosen up my headgear requirements, or say that I could do without it completely. No, not completely. I wanted to be able to wear it when I wanted to wear it. To put it on for Jacob to get him in the mood, and then be able to take it right off again. But not to have to wear it for any specified and significant amount of time. And not to have to sleep with it on either!

I almost forgot to put it back on when I got to Dr.Wrighting's office for my appointment, so I fumbled around with it at the door putting it on. Fortunately nobody was walking by at the time.

Cecilia was at the reception desk, and she smiled when she saw me. "So she put you in headgear, too?" she said.

I nodded sheepishly. "I kind of expected it, but...."

"Dr.Wrighting is a great believer in headgear." Cecilia leaned forward and continued in a half-whisper. "Sometimes I think she uses it even where patients could be treated without it. I think she thinks it's a good thing for her patients to experience."

"It is definitely an experience," I agreed.

"Oh, I'm sure if she's making you wear it, it's because it's necessary," she assured me. "Or helps the treatment go faster."

"It's ok," I told Cecilia. "I've always been curious about it, so now I'm learning my lesson."

Cecilia laughed. "It's no big deal. Or it shouldn't be. I've already decided to follow in Dr.Wrighting's footsteps when I have my own practice. I'm going to rely on it a lot as well."

I didn't say that I wasn't sure that this was a trend that was going to really take off.

"How many hours does she have you wearing it?" Cecilia asked in her professional voice.

"Eight-eight a week," I sighed.

Cecilia looked impressed. "That's pretty serious weartime for an older patient. But: the more the better. And like the braces, you carry it well."

"Thanks," I said.

I signed in and then went to the waiting room. Joining two other girls sitting there in headgear too, whose eyes grew all large when they saw someone my age outfitted like them. The one other girl waiting didn't have headgear. I wondered if she felt like an odd man out. Or was worried that today was clearly headgear day at Dr.Wrighting's and she was going to get it now too.

It was my turn soon, and I let myself be led to the examination room and get strapped down, hands and everything. Lying there I couldn't believe that I'd been in headgear for four weeks now!

"I'm glad to see you've been wearing it properly," Dr. Wrighting said. "Averaging almost eighty-nine hours a week. Perfect."

I took the praise silently. I didn't think saying something like, *Well, that's enough of that, then, right?* was going to help me any.

Dr. Wrighting asked the usual questions of how everything was and peering around in my mouth. It was always a bit embarrassing, because I assumed she read all the things that Jacob and I were writing, keeping track of our experiences. A lot of which was very embarrassing. At least what I wrote. And Jacob, too, if he was being honest.

Finally she unhooked the neckstrap from the headgear. But she didn't pull the facebow out. I wasn't sure how to interpret this – until she went to the cabinet and I saw what she came back with.

I should have guessed. I wasn't escaping headgear-wear anytime soon or quickly. Except now what I was getting was the real bridle to go with my bit. The combination of straps that not only went behind my neck but also across the back of my head, and over the top of my head. Brilliant.

I leaned my head forward so Dr. Wrighting could scoop the straps over and around my head, and then resignedly let her hook the facebow to them. I could feel the extra straps. It felt ok. All that more evenly divided small amount of pressure. But I could guess how it looked, too.

"Perfect," Dr. Wrighting said, smiling at me. "The same instructions as last time. Just a little more to hold everything in place."

"And I still wear the retainers and elastics too?"

"Of course," Dr. Wrighting said. Like I was asking a really ridiculous question.

So I guess I really was just getting more and more layered on every time. And there were still more than six months to go!

I didn't have to go back and wait in the waiting room this time, but I also didn't get to look in the mirror to see what the new contraption looked like. I just got to go, with my next appointment a month away.

Cecilia smiled when she saw me. "And you thought maybe she was going to tell you you were finished with the headgear today, right?"

I nodded.

111

"I think you'll find this way is sort of more comfortable. It sits really securely and everything. And you don't ever go out with it, right? So it doesn't matter what it looks like."

So I guessed it looked *really* bad, if even Cecilia was warning me about it. "Yeah, at least I've been able to manage to avoid public appearances with it on," I said. "With the earlier, sleeker version."

Cecilia smiled. "She didn't let you see what this looks like, did she?"

I shook my head. I could imagine, but I knew I couldn't really imagine. "Is it that bad?"

"I think it's really cool. But girls who are rigged up like that tend not to be as clinically neutral about their new appearances."

I shrugged. "What has to be, has to be. I'll manage."

Cecilia smiled. "Honestly, it's probably easier to wear than just the neckbrace. You'll be fine," she assured me, giving me my appointment slip for the next time.

At the door I considered for a split second just walking out and going home wearing this. I think I only even considered it because I didn't even know how bad it was. But then I realized that it had to be really bad, and that it was definitely worse than just the neckstrapped headgear had been, which I had been too scared to wear that in public. So after I slipped out of the office I quickly slipped it off. I did feel a small pang of remorse. I did wish I had the guts to wear it home. But I really, really didn't have those kind of guts.

At home I put it on straightaway. I could do it without looking in the mirror, once I figured out where all the straps went, because the plastic tabs into which the facebow hooked were just like for the neckstrap alone. I wanted the first sight I got of myself to be with me wearing it as it looked in all its glory.

Boy, was there a lot of glory. Or a lot of straps, anyway. If what I had the past month was headgear, now I had something that looked like headgear squared. And I looked pretty square too.

But I had to admit too that it was kind of nice how the straps in all directions held everything in place. It felt ok to wear this. It felt good, actually. Secure. It just looked…the way it looked. And it just looked…a lot. But I guessed Jacob would like it. And I had to admit I sort of liked it too.

"So are you still a headgear girl?" was the first thing Jacob asked when I called him.

"More than ever."

"What, you like have to wear it all day now?"

"No, Dr.Wrighting wouldn't do that. What she would do, and did do, is give me a more impressive headgear. Straps all around my head."

Jacob took that in. I could hear he sounded relieved and pleased. "Cool."

"Something like that." I wasn't sure I was willing to be quite so enthusiastic about it.

"And the same number of hours a week."

"The magic eighty-eight. Yay."

He was torn between coming to see and knowing how it would torture him not to be able to relieve the intense sexual desire that it would cause for a whole week. But of course he couldn't resist. He would come to pick me up for dinner, take a peek, and then we'd *quickly* go out, before he exploded or imploded or just fell apart.

He was thrilled when he saw me wearing it. It was nice to see that genuine pleasure. Even though I knew it was all sordidly sexual, that it was just a question of him being turned on, it still felt good. I felt lucky, knowing how all the other girls at Dr.Wrighting's who were made to wear something like that would never have anyone look at them so genuinely pleased to see it. All they could look forward to were pitying looks, or being made fun of behind their backs.

We made out for a bit – Jacob couldn't resist, and I didn't want to – but Jacob knew he had to tear himself away from this. It was going to be a tough week, no matter what. He sighed as he watched me unhook it and put it away and we went out.

"I'm so lucky," he said, staring at me. "There you are, the sexiest thing ever with that headgear on, and even after you take it off there's still all that wonderful metalwork left which I get to admire all night long." He looked sincerely happy. Just a little disappointed that he wouldn't be able to act on his admiration.

It was a holiday weekend that week, and my sister and I had both promised to visit our parents. Jacob was almost relieved that I would be far away, maybe making it just a bit easier to get through those days before we could finally have sex again. Out of sight wasn't quite enough to put me, or rather my headgear, out of mind, but the distance was the sort of barrier that was easier to rationalize and accept than when I was just a few blocks away.

I didn't mind time with the parents, but I was dreading this a bit. First of all, they hadn't seen me with the braces yet. And second of all, I had to get in all that headgear time. So I had to walk around all weekend with it on most of the time. The whole long weekend.

The braces were of course the first thing they commented on when they saw me. They were surprised at how massive they were, and why I needed them at all. I tried to smile and grin and bear all their comments, explaining that this was just the way things were. Then I gave them a good second surprise when I excused myself right after we got home to put my stuff away in my room, and when I came back down adorned with my wonderful new headgear. That really blew them away. I really had to wear that, they asked. I assured them I did.

My sister only got in much later, but I still had it on when she arrived, and it gave her a good laugh. She had seen my braces, but she couldn't believe this. "What is that orthodontist doing to you?" Kylie chuckled.

"What every orthodontist does. Fixing my teeth while making my life a continuous series of embarrassments."

"Come on, this guy is just having fun with you. He can't be serious."

"It's a she, and Dr.Wrighting is totally serious." I realized that probably didn't sound completely believable when it came from my wired-up mouth and headgeared head. "Something about the ideal use of forces and…."

"But you've got like everything in there. The elastics too. And you have that lisp – are you wearing some sort of plate too?"

I was self-conscious about the retainer lisp. I didn't think people noticed, and I hated the fact that Kylie had picked up on it.

"It's only about six more months. I guess using all this stuff is just the most efficient way of setting everything in place as quickly as possible."

"But no one gets braces like these," Kylie said. "Maybe some eleven-year-old girl, but an adult?"

"You don't know what people get. I only wear the headgear at home. No one ever sees me with it on/"

Kylie nodded. "So all the metalwork finally got to be too much for...what was his name, Jason?"

"Jacob. No, he's still in the picture. He's still supportive."

Kylie snickered. "Supportive? You have like *layers* of wires around your face. A fence on top of a barbed wire fence. The *über*-oral-chastity belt of all chastity belts. Don't tell me you...kiss and stuff with all that on."

"What we do is none of your business."

"You just chastely hold hands, while he tries not to look at you?"

"Kylie!"

"I'm sorry, you're right, it's great that you have someone who can put up with all that. It's just that I find it so hard to imagine you doing anything...."

"I think I'd rather you didn't imagine anything." Which was even truer than it sounded.

"I just remember what it was like when I had that kind of stuff. I mean, we were all just kids, but still.... And it's not enough that you just wear it when you sleep?"

"Not nearly. Twelve hours a day, and fourteen on weekends and holidays and so on."

Kylie shook her head in amazement. "I see it but can't believe it."

I was mad at her, in that way that I always got mad at her, just like about every little and big thing that we argued about when we were kids. We get along, but there's always an edge to our relationship. Always has been.

I felt embarrassed walking around the house with the headgear on, but I also liked having to wear it around someone other than Jacob. There was something exciting about being exposed like this. And I kept it on when people dropped by too. This was probably the only time they'd see me with it on, and I liked that little shock I gave them, and that slight humiliation I felt. I was too chicken to go anywhere outside with it on, but for the first time I felt really exposed with it. More people had seen me with it at Dr. Wrighting's, of course, and even though even there it was unusual and everyone stared it wasn't anything really remarkable. You knew you could expect to see patients wearing headgear in that waiting room. But here it came as a total surprise, and something very striking. And even as I felt uncomfortable about their stares and comments, I liked being in the position, the girl with the headgear.

Back in my old bed at night I masturbated happily too. There's something about that old room and familiar surroundings and the excitement of so many people seeing me looking like this and of doing something that felt forbidden but still felt so good.... Much as I liked sex with Jacob, pleasuring myself was immensely satisfying too.

Sunday morning Kylie dryly told me, "I heard you last night. Enjoying yourself, shall we say?"

I blushed beet red. I had been so focused on myself and my own pleasure that I had forgotten she was right in the next room, and that my bed squeaked and creaked, and that I didn't really manage to completely stifle those moans when I came.

"I understand," Kylie said understandingly. "You're not getting enough − or any? − from Jacob, so it's...all hands on deck, right? You do what you have to do."

I wanted to answer back, but I was so mortified that I couldn't. But not so mortified that I could keep myself from doing it again that night. I just made sure not to rock the bed nearly as much, and concentrated on not letting too many sounds escape from my mouth when I climaxed.

Back home Jacob and I still had to wait a few more days before we could take pleasure in each other again. As always, that first night back together again was wonderful. Exhausting, too. Jacob liked the more elaborate headgear even better. Not that he could really get even more excited than he already always was when he saw me in my full regalia. I liked it better too, especially when having sex. It seemed much more securely held in place with the extra straps, so I didn't worry about it as much, and I could just enjoy the feel of having it on. And the extra straps meant there was more of a feel to it, so that was great too.

Jacob couldn't stop staring, either. Now whichever way I faced him there was at least the hint of my braces, since the straps behind my head were visible even when I was turned completely away. Sometimes he said he missed just the feel of my braces, without the headgear's facebow barring the way, but he got a clear feel of them when we kissed in public, when I wasn't wearing it. And at home he seemed to enjoy pushing his lips and tongue around the facebow to get at the braces themselves. There was a lot for him to explore and enjoy, and we both got a lot out of that.

Still, I dreaded when after a few weeks of always headgeared sex he turned to me and asked, "Couldn't we have sex with you *not* wearing the headgear for once?"

Was he getting tired of it? Of me? Headgeared sex couldn't be quite as creative and contorted and physical as regular sex, but I thought we were doing pretty well. Was it not enough for him any longer?

"I need to get my weartime in," I said. "I really don't want to take it off unless I have to." That was only half a lie. I could make up the time. I just didn't want to give in too easily, and start us down a slippery slope.

He asked again a few days later, and I still said no. But that weekend I told him I was ahead of schedule with my weartime, and if he still wanted to do it without me wearing the headgear.... I wanted the suggestion to come from me, but I still didn't entirely like how he leapt at the opportunity.

I have to admit, it was good being able to move around a bit more freely and violently, and the sex was great. It felt weird putting on the headgear *afterwards*, like some post-coital cigarette. But I also knew I had to dose these treats carefully. I didn't want him to get too used to getting what he wanted when that wasn't really part of the program. Of course, maybe it wouldn't matter soon. Maybe Dr.Wrighting would change the program and move me out of headgear at my next appointment....

22.

At my next appointment I was the only one in the waiting room with the super-headgear. Or with any headgear. I wondered whether there was ever a point where you could wear that and *not* feel self-conscious. I knew Dr.Wrighting had some of her patients wear it all day, including to school. Did they just get used to everything about it after a few months? I couldn't imagine it was possible.

Once I was strapped in the examination chair, waiting for Dr.Wrighting, I thought about what I wanted to have happen. It was funny, though. I really hoped that she wasn't going to take anything away from me. Yes, the retainers were kind of a pain, but I liked the reassuring feel of that smooth plastic. And yes, the headgear was a ridiculous thing to have if you didn't need it. And the elastics were just these little irritating connecting bands between my jaws. But I liked each and every one of these things. I wanted to have to wear them longer.

"So how are we enjoying the headgear?" Dr.Wrighting asked.

"We are," I admitted. "It's weird, but we are."

"Well, that's good," Dr.Wrighting said as she unhooked it and then pulled the facebow out of my mouth. "And not even that surprising. A lot of my patients find that if they give it a chance they wind up liking their headgear much more than they expected. This kind – the combination headgear, rather than just the neckstrap kind – especially."

"Yes, this one is much better. Except I guess in public, where it is a bit more embarrassing."

"I suppose," Dr.Wrighting smiled. "I guess it still seems like so much more, doesn't it?" She sounded like she didn't understand what the problem with that was. I suspected that if she could she would have *all* her patients – and me – wear this full headgear 24/7.

Dr.Wrighting did her usual check, removing the elastics and retainers as well and then propping open my mouth with the cheek retractors so she could easily peer and poke around in my mouth. She praised my hygiene and said everything was looking good. It must be a bit weird for her, I realized: here she had a patient where she had to worry about the teeth *not* moving around, while with all her other patients the whole point of what she was doing was to move them around!

With all my accessories neatly laid out on the tray in front of me – my gleaming, spit-covered retainers, the straps and facebows of my headgear, the tiny round rubber bands – I wondered what was going to be returned to my mouth.

I tingled with anticipation but I also hoped I wouldn't find out too fast. I liked lying there with the cheek retractors holding my mouth open like this. I didn't mind at all when Dr.Wrighting got up and said she'd be back soon. She could take all the time she wanted.

She did take ten minutes at least, checking in on another patient I guess. And she didn't come back empty-handed. She had a small, clear plastic bag with her. When she opened it and put the two things she took out from it on the tray I saw they looked like retainers, except there was more acrylic in different places. They were clear, too, unlike my pink Hawley retainers.

"This is a Twin Block," Dr.Wrighting explained, holding what looked like the top one up. It didn't cover nearly as much of the palate as my Hawley did. But it wasn't flat at the bottom either. There was plastic like where my molars were. Like a continuation of my molars. Taking the other device, she showed how one fit on top of the other. Each had such blocks of plastic, one farther back than the other.

What I also couldn't help but notice was that when the two fit into each other, there was still a space between the devices. She explained how it worked, that the blocks of plastic forced the jaws of the patient into the proper positions relative to on another. "Of course, in your case, that just means a holding pattern," she added.

Dr.Wrighting pressed them into my mouth, and I felt them click into place just as my retainers always did. Dr.Wrighting asked whether they hurt anywhere, but they didn't.

Of course, when she took out the cheek retractor I understood how they worked. My teeth couldn't come together anymore, because these small blocks of plastic on both the bottom and top side held them apart. It felt weird shutting my mouth, but not being able to shut it all the way.

The blocks also fit into each other, sort of. I immediately felt that I couldn't move my jaw back and forth like I could normally, for example. Which is a *very* weird feeling. There's just this huge seeming gap between my top and bottom front teeth.

There was also suddenly more plastic bulkiness in my mouth. Not on my palate, but everywhere else. And I immediately started salivating more. And keeping my lips together and not drooling was harder, because the devices prevented me from getting my teeth together. It felt a bit frustrating.

"But I can't wear something like this to work," I exclaimed. And was about to repeat it when I realized that these also affected by speech much more than the retainers did.

Dr.Wrighting smiled. "All in good time," she said. "Did I say that's where you had to wear them?"

I was still adjusting to the feel of these things in my mouth. Swallowing was much harder than even just with retainers, because I couldn't close my mouth properly. Dr.Wrighting wiped away some of the drool running down my cheek. But the saliva kept coming.

"First of all," Dr.Wrighting said, "I'll tell you straight away that you'll only have these for the next two months. Unless of course you don't wear them as prescribed. In which case we will continue with them."

As prescribed. That was always the catch. How many hours a day?

"We are going to a whole new schedule now. At work, and for work functions or for other good excuses – and I will be asking for those excuses, so they better be good! – you can still wear the retainers. The rest of the time, it's these new Twin Blocks. As soon as you get home, you switch out the retainers for these, and it's the Twin Blocks until you head back for work. So weekends, it's all Twin Blocks, all the time."

"What about when I eat?" I asked. Obviously I couldn't eat with these in my mouth. I couldn't bite down, and I couldn't really chew, because my teeth wouldn't meet. So I had to put in my retainers to eat? I still had those strange spring clasps on my braces, so I couldn't not wear *anything*.

"What about it?" Dr.Wrighting said, much too cheerfully. "It's a bit of an adjustment, but you'll see, you can eat with them just fine."

"Really?" I said, lisping and slurring my words and spitting and completely unable to imagine wearing these all the time, and much less eating with them.

"Really. It takes a bit of practice, but they're designed for that. In a few weeks you'll have adjusted completely. Now as to the headgear...."

My mind was still on these new plastic torture devices. And I still had to wear headgear on top of it too?

"We're reducing your headgear time to more or less just at night. Eight hours on weekdays, ten hours on weekends. Sixty total. But I still want you in the headgear."

So did Jacob, I was sure. And honestly, I didn't mind that. I wouldn't have even minded a bit more. But this gave me more flexibility, so that was good.

But these Twin Blocks.... No, I didn't think they were good. I bit down hard on them, but it was like I had a pencil between my teeth. They just wouldn't come together, blocked by the plastic. It wasn't even that much. Probably only a quarter of an inch. But the gap felt huge and frustrating.

Dr.Wrighting reinserted the headgear, and hooked it back up again. She took my retainers and washed and dried them, and then came back with a retainer case, where I could store whatever I wasn't wearing at the moment, the retainers or the Twin Blocks.

She gave me a printed instruction sheet where she reminded me again of when and for how long I should be wearing each of the different appliances. "And I really mean it when I say that, except for work and work functions, you're only allowed to switch out the Twin Blocks for the retainers in the most exceptional circumstances. In fact, I strongly urge you to email or call to get permission beforehand. Or to try to get permission, and be told that you can't. You would have to sell me a good story to convince me."

Dr.Wrighting looked at me sternly. "And remember that that wonderful microchip technology allows me to monitor your weartime of each device very closely. Exactly, in fact. So there's no cheating."

She knew I always wore the retainers because it was unbearable not to have them in because of the weird metal parts that secured them, which otherwise cut into my cheeks. But she was reminding me that I couldn't pretend to be wearing the Twin Blocks, which hooked into the same mechanism, when I was actually wearing the retainers. She could tell the difference. Using her technology. I guess in the old days, before that was possible, she would have just wired everything in.

Usually I liked lying there strapped down, but with this constant drooling the urge to reach for my mouth and wipe that away – and to take out what was in my mouth was so strong that I almost wished I wasn't restrained. But I knew it was better this way, too, because once she let me go I could reach for my mouth, but I couldn't make the situation any more comfortable. Except for wiping away the drool.

But I couldn't take the Twin Blocks out. First of all, it wasn't that easy to take them out. I would have to remove the elastics first, and it was hard to do with the headgear in place too. And I knew that it was important that I kept them in as long as possible anyway. I had to get used to them. I had to. So I couldn't just be snapping them out every time they felt a bit uncomfortable. Because that would mean snapping them out every time I put them in.

Snapping the plastic pieces against each other, I didn't pay much attention walking through the waiting area, or getting my appointment slip at the reception desk. Walking absent-mindedly, concentrating on the weird feel of not being able to close my jaw, I actually walked into the street still sporting my full headgear. It was only the stare and giggle of a couple walking by that snapped me out of it and, after checking that none of Dr.Wrighting's younger patients were coming or going – since I didn't want to set a terrible example – I quickly pulled it out and off.

It's only for two months, I reminded myself. And it was good to experience something new and unexpected and different, right? It shouldn't all be predictable and familiar. It was good if it was like orthodontic treatment in childhood, where you never knew what was coming next, or how you would adapt to it, or face the world. I had had it easy as a kid, so it was sort of cool to be thrown the occasional curve now.

Though I did wonder what curve balls might still lie ahead, coming my way, with so many more months left for Dr.Wrighting to experiment. Since I was only wearing these for two months....

I called Jacob when I got home, and he immediately heard how my speech sounded slightly different. "New retainers?" he asked.

"You could say that."

"What about the headgear?"

"It's still here. Or still there. But I only have to wear it nights now, more or less."

"So what's with the new retainers?"

"Oh, you'll love these. They're called Twin Blocks and...well, you can Google them. It's kind of hard to describe. And kind of hard to deal with. And she wants me to wear them full-time, except at work, when I get to wear my regular retainers instead."

"Sounds cool."

"Oh, yeah. Definitely. Drool-worthy, let me tell you."

He came to pick me up in the evening. He wanted to check out the new devices in private first. Waiting for him, I still found it hard to get used to them. Especially not being able to close my mouth properly. I could close it so my lips were together, but it still felt strange. And when I looked in the mirror I could see that you could tell I had something in my mouth, even with my lips closed. Much more so than when I just had my retainers. And when I smiled or anything it was a strange sort of smile since I couldn't bring my teeth together, and you could sort of see the plastic obstructions between my teeth.

Frustrating!

But Jacob liked them. Exploring them with his tongue, which he could dart into my mouth through the unbridgeable gap between my teeth now. The additional smooth plastic surfaces. He liked this variation on retainers.

I was kind of scared of going out and eating in public. I had no idea how I was supposed to eat with these, but apparently kids who wore them really did manage. So I let Jacob take me out. But I did insist on a dark restaurant where we could sort of lose ourselves in a corner and no one could easily see the struggles I anticipated.

And I was not wrong.

I tried to joke about it, but it was incredibly frustrating. I hadn't been close to tears about my orthodontic work very often, but here I was. This was insane! Plastic mashing against plastic. I could barely bite, and I couldn't chew the way I was used to.

Two months of this?

Jacob kissed me eagerly and long when he said good-bye for the night, but at home I was sorely tempted to switch out the Twin Blocks for my retainers. *Just for the night...* a voice inside my head teased me. But Dr.Wrighting would know, and she would disapprove. And most of the night I was sleeping anyway. I'd hardly notice....

Yeah, right....

It was hard getting used to them. Especially just lying in the dark, with nothing else to think about or feel. I had an uneasy, restless sleep.

I took them out in the morning to brush my teeth, which came as an incredible relief. I considered putting in my retainers already after that, but Dr.Wrighting said I had to wear them as much as possible. And breakfast would be good practice eating just a bit more with them in place and trying to get used to them.

That's what I convinced myself of, and what I reminded myself of as I tearfully tried to chew on my toast.

What a relief it was then to be able to put the retainers in instead and rush off to work. How much more comfortable and insignificant these felt by comparison!

My coworkers wondered why I was so cheery all morning, but that wasn't something I was going to try to explain to them.

I dreaded going home because of what awaited me there. But I knew I had to.

Practice would make perfect.

Practice would make me get used to them.

Practice was going to drive me nuts....

Even though I didn't have to yet, I put my headgear on too, right after I got home and had put the twin blocks in. It made for another barrier to help keep me from ripping out the devices. And the familiar feel of the bridle and bit was a sort of comfort that made it slightly easier to handle the Twin Blocks. Though it also made me drool even more.

As usual, Jacob kept his distance that first week when we weren't allowed to have sex. I struggled a bit on my own, trying to get used to them. Like usual when I couldn't spend as much time with Jacob I had arranged to go out with friends. Now I was faced with the dilemma of having to go out and face them wearing these. All the time except for work, Dr.Wrighting had said. I knew that going out drinking with some girlfriends was not even close to something that could get me excused from wearing them. So I kept them in, and tried to explain what they were and why I had to wear them. "Because they make me bite down a certain way, they align my jaws," I said. One of my girlfriends had a niece or something who had them too, she said. The fact that the girl was ten did not make me feel any better.

I wasn't usually too self-conscious about my braces. I liked them, after all. My teeth bling. They were cool, even if not everyone agreed. But with the Twin Blocks in my mouth I did feel more self-conscious. I might as well go out in public wearing my headgear, I told myself. But I didn't do *that*.

For the first time I was *really* counting down the days on the calendar until I was going to be finished with part of my orthodontic journey, at least for the first few days. Getting used to eating with them was the hardest part, but even drinking required more effort. And speaking was tough, too, so I practiced talking to myself at home, or singing, which actually helped. At least after three or four days I didn't sound completely hopeless, and my friends didn't laugh about me quite as much.

And amazingly I did get used to them. Even eating with them. Well, eating most things. Some were just impossible. But I grew to like the feel of the plastic. Not really *like*, but I appreciated it. Waking up with the feel of those plastic surfaces in my mouth, or closing my mouth and feeling how my jaws were forced to stay in the one position because of the way the Twin Blocks came together. It took two weeks, but suddenly I found myself thinking that these appliances were…o.k.

It helped when Jacob finally came over after the first week was over and I could release him from his cage and he could plow right into me, then they were *really* o.k. He thought so too.

23.

I only *had* to wear my headgear when I slept on weekdays now, but a lot of the time I did put it in just to wear around the apartment too. Jacob liked it when I had it on, but even when I was alone, I liked the feel of it.

Dr.Wrighting has an elaborate site for her patients, too, and each one gets her own page which documents her orthodontic progress and shows what she's wearing and how long she has been at it. It's a useful way to keep track of how many hours one gets in on the devices – with the number in warning red if one is below the target time. As my next appointment approached I kept checking my page. With only 60 hours of mandated headgear weartime a week now I wasn't racking up the hours nearly as fast as before. I wasn't going to be much over 900 hours of total weartime by the next appointment and so I actually desperately hoped that Dr.Wrighting would let me continue to wear the headgear, so I could reach 1000 hours.

1000 seemed like the minimum for any sort of badge of honor. That was like a real accomplishment. There was a separate page ranking all the headgear-wearing patients' current weartime, and while new patients were always being added starting at zero, I remained pretty far down the list. Now that I was only wearing it eight or ten hours a day more patients were passing me every week, too. I knew I would never be very far up on the list – lots of patients were well into the thousands, and there were even quite a few with over 5000 hours of accumulated weartime, which meant a full year of 14-hour days, or seven months of full-time wear – but 1000 hours seemed both respectable and achievable to me.

I really wanted to reach it! Dr.Wrighting had a good idea with these ranking tables. Girls who really had to wear the headgear needed all the help they could get to convince them to endure wearing this thing, and I think this slightly competitive way of doing it was great.

I didn't know what to expect at my next appointment. Dr.Wrighting had said the Twin Blocks were standard equipment for two whole months, so I could count on them for another month. Surely there wasn't anything she could add to my mouth, was there? Which only left subtraction. And I really found myself thinking that I really didn't want to be out of the headgear just yet. Sure it was inconvenient, but honestly, I liked the feel of it. And now that I just had to wear it more or less when I was in bed Jacob and I could be more flexible in our use of it. I could take it out for our rougher tumbles in bed, and then put it back in for the night without feeling guilty.

"So I've been reading your notes," Dr.Wrighting said.

I blushed. I always blushed when I thought about her and Dr.Allegretta reading all those intimate details about my sex life and about what I was feeling. I tried not think about who was going to read it when I wrote everything down, but afterwards.... I always imagined everyone gathered around the TV, watching tapes of me and Jacob having sex.

"So you *want* to keep wearing the headgear?"

I admitted I did. "Is that weird?"

"I always take it as a positive sign when my patients enjoy wearing appliances. Of course, the ones I want them to be most enthusiastic about are their retainers, when the braces come off. But getting them excited about headgear wear is good too."

"Watching those hours accumulate is a good incentive, I think."

"Yes, I can see you've been wearing it more than you have to."

"Just around the house." Duh. "I usually figure I might as well put it on after dinner instead of waiting until I go to bed."

"And the Twin Blocks?"

"It took a while. A long while. But I've adjusted to them, I think," I lisped. "More or less, as you can tell," I added. "I still don't like going out wearing them, because they are sort of super-retainers that get in the way of too many things, between eating, drinking, talking. And just closing my mouth."

Dr. Wrighting nodded. "Yes, the adjustment curve is a long one. I'm still working on how to get my patients to manage it. I do find forcing them to wear it basically non-stop from the very beginning, instead of letting them slowly try to work their way up to fulltime wear generally meets with greater success. But they are worth it, when I can get my patients to go along with it."

"So, I get to wear them for another month?" I said.

"You know it."

Dr. Wrighting did her usual check of everything in my mouth, removing all my accessories and then putting them back in place. I wondered whether there was going to be any change, but surprisingly she told me that for the next month everything was going to stay like it had been so far.

That was o.k. with me. I felt I had gotten the hang of the Twin Blocks, and I sort of liked their smooth plastic feel now, and wearing the headgear pretty much as I pleased – as long as I wore it every night – was just fine too.

Jacob sound a bit disappointed, but I think he was relieved too. Each new appliance came with so much anticipation and heightened his lust that I didn't think his nerves could take the monthly escalation so many months in a row.

I became a bit less self-conscious about appearing in public with the Twin Blocks, though sometimes when I got home and looked at myself in the mirror I realized what an odd impression I must make. First and overwhelmingly there were the two glittering rows of silver bands and braces, which were already strange enough. Then the elastic connecting the upper and lower braces, stretching and revealing themselves whenever I opened my mouth. And then the bits of plastic, between my teeth and covering part of my palate, causing a lisp and preventing me from closing my jaws completely, an obstruction between my upper and lower teeth.

I pitied the girls I saw in Dr. Wrighting's office who were sporting a similar getup, sometimes completely forgetting that I was one of them. True, I didn't have to go to school – or my version of school, work – like that, but with my friends and boyfriend and every other stranger I was just like them, and I must have made the same impression on everyone that saw me. Jacob could appreciate it, in his own perverted way, bless him, but for everyone else I realized that I must seem like a total freak. Looking in the mirror, it was impossible to find any normalcy in that face that grinned back at me. But the face grinned irrepressibly happily because I loved all this metal and plastic firmly fixed into my mouth. I might be a freak, but I was the happiest braced freak imaginable.

I was reminded of the dichotomy between how I felt and how I was perceived when I spent a weekend with my parents again, the first time they saw me in all my Twin Blocked splendor. They were relieved when I told them that I only had to wear the headgear at night now, but then they saw those other plastic additions and couldn't hide their shock.

I realized how differently we look at kids with braces too. Kids are a different species. Smaller, with a different routine of school instead of work and long summer's off. Still discovering and working out so much about the world. Fix up a kid with braces and even accessories like mine and you felt sorry for her but it wasn't that strange. Just something they had to put up with and go through, imposed on them by adults who thought they knew what was good for them.

At my parents I was in that weird in-between world, of being an adult but also being their child. Which was of course how a lot of their friends and neighbors saw me too. My braces weren't seen as some adult decision, but more like a return to childhood. Part of which I liked, and part of which I didn't.

Of course none of them could conceive of what was really going on in my head, or that I had a boyfriend who lusted after this. All of that was unimaginable. When I ran my tongue across the mouth-filling plastic, or the beautiful smoothness of the uneven metal bits covering the front of my teeth, I sometimes worried that my secret was too easy and obvious for all to guess. Couldn't they see how I was bursting with happiness at having all this in my mouth? And how could they not be just as thrilled as me? How could they not lust after it?

From the way men looked at me, especially the disappointment as their eyes moved from my chest to my mouth, I could see that the braces weren't the same enticement and prize for everyone. That for most they really were a wall, a barrier, a turn-off. A black mark. Not like a real chastity belt, which was just a tempting barrier that aroused that eagerness for penetration all the more. A chastity belt was just a temporary hurdle, making the mouth water as one considered how to unlock it and get behind it. But braces were an absolute and complete barrier. There was nothing to conquer there.

Sometimes I thought I detected a lingering look from a man that implied some real, deeper interest, and that he wasn't turned off by the metal in my mouth but rather that something clicked and exerted a magnetic pull. Sometimes. But no one dared admit it to me. Or maybe to themselves. Not that I would have let them act on it. I think. I mean, I had Jacob, and what more could I want? But it was nice to feel desired by others, too. And I would have liked to flirt with this power I exerted, if the power was as strong as it was with Jacob.

B.B. – before braces – men constantly hovered and gazed and strutted around me. A lot of it was like a game, the back and forth of mild flirtation and innuendo, but I liked that I exuded that attraction. That men *wanted* me. A.B. – after braces, or with braces – that vast circle within which every man seemed drawn to me and that always seemed to surround me shrank in force and diameter. Men would still perk up, even at a distance or when they got their first glimpse. They were still drawn to me – but not as strongly. It was like I gave off a warning smell: even before they saw my braces they could sense and feel something was wrong or off. That I wasn't the prize I should have been. The lustful eagerness everyone around me exuded B.B. fed on itself, and drew in even those who were farther away. A.B. there was no such feeling in the air. Instead, those closest to me were the least eager and excited. They saw exactly how much metalwork and plastic there was. They heard my lisp. They saw that instead of some perfect specimen I was one who needed massive fixing, a whole construction site in her mouth.

The unobservant and the reckless would still swoop in at times, not sensing what everything around me should have told them and only coming to an abrupt halt when they saw close up what they were confronted with. Some gulped and went through their usual patter anyway, so used to spinning their lines and lies to every woman they came across, but you could tell their hearts and cocks weren't in it any more. And the more I smiled and laughed – and I had to, when I saw their faces drooping – the worse it got, their eyes growing bigger as they stared at those metal bands covering all my teeth and those wires and elastics and everything else so brightly on display until they stuttered to a stop.

So that was sort of amusing, but I did miss being a real object of desire. I never realized what a power that was. What an easy feel-good moment it was, available whenever I was in public. To know you're desired. And, sure, I told myself it was demeaning that it was mainly because I was seen as a *sexual* object, but I wasn't fooling anyone, least of all myself. It still felt pretty damned good. For months now I hadn't had that. Jacob made up for a lot of that, because his lust was so deep and broad and unbelievably intense. I melted under his gaze, that's how intense it was when he glimpsed my braces. But I had to admit I missed finding anything like that elsewhere, when I had had it at my beck and call since I was in my teens. Instead, the treatment I got was of the sweet loser tween girl going through her awkward braces phase who could only dream about being noticed by the cool kids.

24.

When I thought about it, or looked at myself in the mirror at home, when I had put my headgear back on, I realized it was ridiculous, but I liked where I was. Who I was, orthodontically outfitted like this. Looking in the mirror, at that ridiculously braced face, my upper and lower jaw held slightly apart by the blocks of plastic between my top and bottom molars, keeping my teeth apart, and that facebow coming out of my mouth and arched over my cheeks.

Yes, if I had to choose a perfect *me* moment, of who I wanted to be, this was it. I wanted to be that braced woman, as incongruous and crazy as it was. Nothing could be better than now. The braces didn't hurt. Everything sat comfortably and just the right amount of uncomfortably in place. I had adjusted to speaking and eating with all this hardware in my mouth, and even if I couldn't do it just right, I liked the way I was forced to do it wrong. I literally could not imagine feeling any better.

Facing Jacob like this was like the perfect validation, too. He didn't just love me, he loved me for who I was like this. He loved me and lusted for me *more* because of all this hardware. It meant as much to him as it did to me.

What more could I ask for?

But that was the thing, too. This was perfection, but it was temporary. This too would pass. I had another appointment with the Dr.Wrighting and she'd change parts of this perfect setup. I was due to be done with the Twin Blocks, for example. And then, in just a few more months, she'd change it all. She'd take the foundation that all held it place out, removing the braces themselves, and I would be left with almost nothing but my memories.

Sometimes I cried just thinking about it.

And I got nervous as my next appointment with Dr.Wrighting approached. She hadn't changed anything at all last time. What about this time?

Nervously I hooked up my headgear in front of the entrance to her practice the next time I got there, feeling just a bit more relieved once I was sitting in the waiting room with the young girls who looked at me in shock and awe. Today it made me happy to be stared at like this, and I held the gaze of the one other headgeared girl, smiling as if to tell her, *You and me, sister, and our headgear. We are the luckiest girls here.* Though I didn't get the same vibe back from her.

Strapped in the examination chair I let Dr.Wrighting slowly free me of my accessories. She unhooked and removed the headgear and then the elastics and then the Twin Blocks. Then, as usual, she peered around in my mouth to check that everything was all right. Inscrutable as usual, she gave me no clue as to what to expect.

Dr.Wrighting handed off the Twin Blocks to her assistant to wash at one of the sinks, and then she took the facebow and straps and put them in a clear plastic pouch, which she wrote something on with a pen. The assistant returned the cleaned Twin Blocks to her and she put those in a container and marked that too. Then she handed the container and the pouch to the assistant who walked away with them.

Was that the last I had seen of my headgear and my Twin Blocks? It wasn't a surprise that I was done with the Twin Blocks, but the headgear too? I was surprised by how disappointed I felt.

"So we're going to try something new this month," Dr.Wrighting finally admitted. "No more headgear. No more Twin Blocks. Instead…."

But she didn't blurt out what was coming next. She waited for her assistant, who had obviously been instructed with what to get. She returned with a container in her hand, leading me to think for a moment she had brought the Twin Blocks back. But I saw it was a different color when she handed it off to Dr.Wrighting. And deeper.

Dr.Wrighting smiled and opened it. "From Twin Block we're moving on to monobloc," she said, pulling out a large, pink, retainer-like appliance.

As she held it up I could see that it was like an upper and lower retainer that were joined. A large upper and large lower retainer, arching and curving. Honestly, it looked too large to get *into* my mouth.

"As the name suggests," Dr.Wrighting said, "the monobloc is a one-piece appliance. So let's see how that fits."

I had my doubts, but obediently I opened my mouth. It wasn't enough of course, and I could feel the plastic against my teeth as Dr.Wrighting pried my mouth open wider. Once past my teeth, however, my mouth easily closed around the huge plastic bloc, and I could feel it snap into place on my upper braces.

Like with the Twin Bloc, I couldn't really close my mouth for my teeth to meet. There was like a plastic wedge, all around, between my upper and lower jaws. And there was all the plastic covering my palate, and my lower arch as well. It was like to giant co-joined retainers.

There was a slit in the front, between the plastic. I could feel it with my tongue. And I could breathe a bit through it, too.

"So how does that feel?" Dr.Wrighting asked.

"Huge," I tried to say, but I could neither pronounce the word nor really form it with all that bulk in my mouth.

Even more than the Twin Block, the monobloc held my jaws in a specific place. I couldn't move them at all side to side. Dr.Wrighting showed me I could open my lower jaw a bit, my teeth coming out of the underside of the device, but the top teeth were securely anchored in the appliance.

Drool started to accumulate, and it was even harder to swallow. Biting down into the appliance, my teeth felt secured but also rooted in place. How could anyone wear anything like this?

Dr.Wrighting asked me again whether it hurt anywhere, but I shook my head. All the surfaces felt wonderfully and awfully smooth. It fit perfectly. And horribly.

"Good," Dr.Wrighting said. "Now let's see how this goes."

She picked up a small and pretty thin flat piece of metal, maybe an inch long, and inserted it in the front of the appliance. I could feel it enter the slit at the front of it.

Was this for some sort of headgear attachment or something like that?

But Dr.Wrighting turned it like a key, and I felt some sort of mechanism in the device activate. Dr.Wrighting asked me whether I felt any pain now, but it felt just the same as before. She pulled out the strip of metal, smiling. "Great!"

I was less convinced.

"Why don't you take a seat outside for a while, just to get used to the feel of it and see whether it does bother you anywhere," she suggested, beginning to unstrap me.

Like I had a choice or any say.

Like I could have said anything anyway, with this mouth-filling piece of plastic in my mouth.

Dr.Wrighting smiled encouragingly as she shooed me out of the examination room. I didn't know what to say, but since I couldn't say anything it didn't matter.

I sat down in the waiting room, not nearly as confident as I had been when I had come in for my appointment. I could barely keep my lips closed around my braces, because the device held my upper and lower jaws apart so much. I mean, it was only like a quarter of an inch, but that's enough.

The mother of the girl who had headgear who had been waiting recognized me and smiled at me. Her daughter must have gone in for her appointment, and she was waiting for her now. "No more headgear?" she smiled.

I nodded.

"I'm afraid my daughter isn't going to be so lucky. Dr.Wrighting says she's in it for the long haul. But I think she's gotten used to it."

I tried to shrug encouragingly.

"But it must be tougher at your age," the woman said.

I smiled a bit, and then she saw the plastic between my teeth. "New appliance," I tried to explain, pointing at it. I could move my lower jaw down, so I could get some sort of noise out, but it sounded more like *Ooo ahians*.

"Oh, that's new?" she asked.

I nodded. "Monobloc," I tried to explain.

"Like a retainer?" she asked, not understanding what I had been trying to say.

Super retainer, I wanted to say, but I just nodded. Fitting my hands together I tried to explain how it was just one piece.

133

Amazingly, she actually put two and two together. Or one and one. "Like a one-piece retainer?"

I nodded.

"That must be hard to adjust to."

I nodded again. It was amazing how frustrating it was to be unable to speak. I felt like I was gagged. Which is what I was, come to think of it.

And I suddenly realized that I didn't even know how to take this thing out of my mouth. I probably could just rip it, just pulling at it until it comes off, but I knew I couldn't try that. Dr.Wrighting might have some special mechanism of how it hooked into my braces. It certainly sat there very securely.

Dr.Wrighting made me wait for a while, too. The girl with the headgear came out, still wearing it. Her mother wished me good luck as they were leaving. I don't know who she felt more sorry for. But the girl now had to walk out into the street wearing her headgear. I at least had my new device well-hidden in my mouth, and obviously this was something Dr.Wrighting couldn't make me wear fulltime. Or even like half time, like the Twin Blocs. I couldn't eat with this, for example, that was clear.

Finally Dr.Wrighting called me back. She didn't even take me to an examination chair, but led me to the back corner of the office where there was a mirror.

I caught a glimpse of myself. I looked like I had just taken a way too big bite of something, and my mouth was filled like a chipmunk's with food. Even with my mouth closed, my profile looked totally different, because of the way my jaw was being held open.

Dr.Wrighting smiled. "All right, let's show you how to work this," she said. She held up the thin piece of metal again and inserted it in the slit and turned the other way. Then she reached for the sides of the appliance, and pulled it loose from where it was anchored in. Then she pulled it out, which meant I had to open my mouth really wide again so she could do that.

My jaws relaxed, suddenly able to meet again, my mouth suddenly feeling like a giant, emptied cave again. Which was a lot better.

"The first thing we have to practice is putting it in and taking it out," Dr.Wrighting said. She showed me how to hold the device and force it into my mouth, and then push it against my upper teeth until it clicked into place. And then how to release it from there.

I did that a couple of times until I got the hang of it.

"Now, what's special about this appliance," Dr. Wrighting explained, holding it up in front of me, "is that in order to make it easier for patients to wear it has a locking mechanism." She put the piece of metal in the slit, turned, and I saw how small metal rods on the wiring moved into place. It really was a key. Turning it in the other direction, the rods moved out of place again. "This way parents just fasten the appliance in, and we don't have to worry about compliance issues."

It sounded like cruel and unusual punishment to me.

"Now let's try it when it's in place." She had me put the monobloc in, and then lock it into place. Now I understood how this worked. And it really worked. The appliance was definitely immovably locked in place.

I practiced locking and unlocking it a few times. It was pretty straightforward.

Locked in place, Dr. Wrighting took the key from me and put it in the round container that had originally held the appliance. There was a piece of plastic on the inside of the lid which it could be snapped into. Then she handed me a strong cardboard letter-sized envelope. "A spare," she explained, holding it up. "You don't want to lose these, or lose track of them."

Definitely not. I practically grabbed for them, eager to be able to take the device out as quickly and as soon as possible. But Dr. Wrighting wasn't ready to hand them over quite yet. First she explained about how and when I had to wear this thing. "Eight hours a night, without fail. Twelve hours on weekends. And weekdays at least another hour during the day. Half an hour at a time, especially at first, so you can get used to it. And, yes, always locked in place, so it's not too easy for you to take it out. When Jacob is over, I suggest he be in charge of the key."

My eyes widened. That was a lot to take. And a lot of power to give up.

"Any questions?" Dr. Wrighting asked.

She wasn't making it easy for me, but then she didn't want to. But she knew that I had no real questions, so it didn't matter whether or not I could articulate them.

And just in case I didn't get the message, she reminded me as she handed over the container and the spare key, "And you'll wear this on your way home now. The sooner you get used to it, the better."

When I got outside the door of the practice, on the street, I was tempted to unlock the device and take it out, but then I thought of how I'd look fumbling with the key and maybe dropping it and then two of Dr.Wrighting's patients came towards the door and I knew I couldn't hesitate in front of them, so I just smiled at their moms as I walked by them and made my way home with this humongous piece of plastic in my mouth, hoping no one would stop me to ask me anything on the way.

It was a strange feel, a smooth plastic cave that my tongue could explore without being able to reach anything beyond it. It was all one smooth, curved wall, except the slit and small opening, through which I could suck in air, and breathe it out. It was such a weird contrast to the uneven metal surface of the braces, which were unreachable by my tongue now, but which I still felt against the inside of my cheeks and against my lips.

My mouth cavity was much smaller now, plastic covering so much of the surfaces. The monobloc didn't totally fill my mouth. It wasn't just a huge, solid piece of plastic. But it took up a lot of space and separated my tongue from where it usually roamed, my palate and my teeth.

I could move my lower jaw up and down, a bit, releasing it from the bottom of the device, but when I bit down at all I couldn't move even the slightest bit side to side. Much more than the Twin Blocs, this dictated and controlled all my jaw movements, and held my mouth in place.

And it was a gag, stifling me. I wanted to take it out, but I couldn't on my way home. I saw people looking at me and wondering why I held my mouth in this weird position, like I had too much gum in my mouth and wasn't able to chew it.

At home I did take it out right away. My mouth felt totally empty without it, even with the retainers still there. In my hand I marveled at how big it was, and how it could even fit in my mouth. It wasn't that bulky, but it was big, covering all my teeth and much of my palate in a layer of pink plastic.

Sitting in front of the mirror, I put it back in again. Once I had forced it past my teeth it snapped into place on my upper braces easily. Once in place my lower jaw, tense from being open so wide, sunk easily into the bottom half of it.

It felt weird not being able to close my mouth completely. I was sort of used to that from the Twin Blocks, but this was different. It looked as weird as I expected, too. Even with my

136

mouth closed, you could tell I had something huge in my mouth. There was no way of hiding that.

I took the metal key again and fit that in and turned it, feeling the mechanism in the device move. And tugging first lightly and then harder on the device I saw that it was really locked tight.

Damn.

I'm not too much of a mouth breather, but the thin slit meant it was hard not to breathe almost entirely through my nose, and it was a weird feeling of being gagged and blocked. For a few minutes it didn't seem too bad, but to wear this all night?

I quickly unlocked it again. It didn't make much of a difference, since it was quite firmly snapped onto my braces and palate, but psychologically it helped. The knowledge that I *could* remove it with a quick maneuver, and that it wasn't under lock and key, made me feel slightly better about it.

I tried to keep it in for a while. I knew it was all a matter of getting used to it, like with all the other appliances. But that still was difficult.

It really was like a sort of gag. One of my boyfriends had had a ball gag, a rubber ball with a leather strap through it that could be tied around my head. We tried it out a few times, but that filled my mouth in a totally different way. This monobloc was like a *concave* gag, more mouth-blocking than mouth-filling. Which didn't make it an easier to have it in my mouth.

I put it in a couple of times in the evening, while I was doing the dishes and then watching TV. But I took it out almost as fast. It was difficult to get used to, even though I kept reminding myself that I had to try. But I just kept fiddling with it in my hands, not my mouth.

I knew I should be locking it in each time, too. The additional step, if I couldn't just snap it out, might make me hesitate a bit more and longer and keep it in. But I couldn't bring myself to do it. And I watched the clock nervously, counting down to bedtime, to when I *had* to put it in in order to get the necessary eight overnight hours of weartime.

I went through my bedtime washing and cleaning rituals even more slowly than usual. Like a little kid who wants to stretch out the time before she's sent to bed. I didn't put it in after I finished brushing my teeth either, waiting until I was under the covers and only then taking the monobloc and reluctantly snapping it in place. I picked up and put down the key several times, but finally forced myself to insert and turn it, feeling it grab hold in my mouth. I put the key carefully back into the container. *That* was something I didn't want to get mistakenly swept on the floor in the night or anything like that. I wanted to be able to reach for it and have it *instantly*. I had the spare, in the other room, just in case, but I wanted to make sure it was just a matter of second before I could unlock the device, if I had to.

I sat up in bed a bit, writing down all my thoughts in the journal I was keeping for Dr.Wrighting and Dr.Allegretta. At least writing about it sort of got my mind off it, in a way. Except, of course, that I kept coming back to it. And just getting used to breathing – through my nose, and with that whistling sound through the small hole in the appliance itself – was a constant reminder of what I was dealing with.

25.

No, I didn't tell Jacob about what had happened at my appointment with Dr.Wrighting. Of course he knew I had the appointment. The thing is, we hadn't been getting along so well recently. Sure, the braces were great. We could agree on that. We could really get together on those. We loved everything about those. But as much and as often as we fucked each other silly it suddenly seemed there was less and less else there. Between us.

Normally you might figure braces would be what gets between people. The sort of thing that splits teenagers in puppy-love apart. Though teenagers are so fickle anything splits them apart, right? But in our case it was the braces that were drawing and keeping us together. They exerted an almost irresistible pull on Jacob. But suddenly everything else we did seemed repellent. Everything else was pushing us apart. And at some point that added up to even more than the incredible pull of the braces. And that's the point we had reached.

Which sucked.

I still lusted after Jacob. But I was really unsure about everything else. How much did we really have in common? Was there any future here? Or was it really all about the braces?

138

And we had even reached a point where, even if it *was* all about the braces that wasn't enough. That couldn't be a good sign.

So I spent my first night with my monobloc alone, and the first days after that too. Not sobbing in sadness, which would have been really hard with that mouth-blocking device in place anyway. More confused than sad, really. About my own feelings and expectations and desires.

I was used to going cold turkey as far as the sex went when I got a new device. That had been the monthly ritual so far, so I knew what to expect. Now it also gave me time to think about the future.

I liked living in the present. This present, especially, for the past few months. Having braces was incredible. Getting them again seemed like the best thing I had ever done. I *loved* having them. Even when that also meant dealing with the less appealing appliances like this stupid monobloc. There were even times when I fantasized about just keeping them. About spending the rest of my life braced. I knew it wasn't a realistic dream. I knew that I had to move on with my life, and that part of that meant leaving the braces behind. And it wasn't like I'd be totally without anything. I'd have retainers. Dr.Wrighting would see to it that they satisfied at least some small part of my remaining orthodontic needs. And removable devices would give me control over when and where to wear them again. Though of course part of the fun and thrill of the braces was that I was stuck with them and couldn't escape them. That's something I wouldn't have any longer.

I knew that when it came to Jacob what we had to consider were our feelings for one another entirely aside from the braces. We had to take everything orthodontic out of the equation. Even the retainers I could count on in the future. What we had to figure out was whether there was enough there to make us want to be together just as we were. Or as I would be. Braceless.

I felt too close to it to be able to figure it out. I think he did too. In a way, the braces *were* the problem. They were larger than life. They were so overwhelming, so much the center of our lives and relationship, that it was almost impossible to think beyond them. Even when we did regular couple thing, like take a walk or go to the movies or go to a party, the braces were always so much a part of everything. But like at a party with the music so loud that you can't talk, even if you give in to that and just

139

dance and sway and enjoy the other's physical presence, at some point you want to have a quiet, normal relationship.

I think Jacob felt the same way. I think we liked each other even aside from the braces. We had gotten together before we even knew how we felt about them, and we had had a good relationship before I got them, so there was some foundation there. But could we find that again? And did we want to? Maybe this was just meant to be a one-year orthodontic fling. A fantasy we lived out but which it was wiser to then just leave behind us.

I was surprised he didn't call or text or anything, to find out what had happened at the last appointment. I knew he could hold out for a few days, but he was silent for over a week. Finally I was the one to give in. Sort of. I emailed him. Not telling him what Dr.Wrighting had done, but trying to let him know what I was feeling and what was going through my head.

It was a day before he replied:

I know what you mean. I'm confused too. It's so difficult to work out. I really want you, and I want to be with you. I really want to be with the braced you, and I really want to see beyond the braced you, into the depths of your soul, and be to be part of that too. But the braces are like that wonderful temptation where everything stops and starts and I can't get beyond them unless I'm away from them. With them you're so perfect in that one way that nothing else matters. And honestly, I think I need other things to matter too. I want to be able to see and hold and be with you with my heart and head, not just my cock. And when I see you now, when I'm with you now, everything is driven by nothing else except that almost insatiable and overwhelming and wonderful lust.

The braces have taken an emotional and physical tool. I'm spent and exhausted. And even so I'm still so *eager*. I want you so badly, but I know I have to step back and reflect and put back the pieces so that it's not just that one beautiful, gleaming, silvery wired piece that dominates everything. It's *so* hard. I don't even dare ask what Dr.Wrighting had in store for you this month, out of fear that I'll just buckle and throw myself at you in abject desire. My cock is throbbing at the thought of what is in your mouth, or strapped to your head.

I have to take this step back, ok? And I hope I can step back to what we had. Or maybe take the next step.

I know that this is something we should work on together, but I need to do it alone for now. Away from you, because I can't think straight when I'm with you, deafened by your retainer slurred words and blinded by the shine of the silver in your mouth and paralyzed by the thought of my tongue feeling the rough metallic and smooth plastic surfaces surrounding your teeth.

I think a little distance will do us good. It's really hard for me too, but I hope you agree. And it's ok if you test other waters. Maybe it's even a good idea for us to try something different again, to be with someone else. So that we can see what about this is each other, and what is just the braces. I hope you understand.

I knew what he meant, I thought. Maybe he was right. No, he was probably right. We had gotten so caught up in this unreal moment that it's like we'd fallen down some well and couldn't imagine anything beyond it. It was probably good to reassess everything before the year was up and we had to go cold turkey, my braces suddenly gone.

But this testing the waters stuff? Being with someone else? In my mad fit when we had argued and stormed apart I had flung the key to his chastity cage after him, offering him a total release from everything that bound him to me. He should do whatever he wanted, I angrily thought.

I could imagine him just wanting to sleep with a regular woman. One with all the usual hang-ups and problems but also with one less. No braces. I could imagine Jacob would really, really like that one-night fling with someone who not only came with no strings attached, but also with no braces attached.

I couldn't even blame him. It seemed totally reasonable.

But me? I didn't really have that option. I saw how men looked at me. I could see them puff their chests and raised their chins as they looked me up and down and thought, *those legs, those tits, yeah, I'll take a shot at that*, and then if I parted my lips or replied to their come-on and they glimpsed my railroad tracks how it stopped them in their tracks. Jaws would literally drop. Sometimes you could see men were intrigued, but even then I felt more like an exotic animal than just some broad they'd like to sleep with. The one they considered going after so they could add it to their list of conquests. *I bagged a lesbian. An exchange student from Africa. This woman with – get this – heavy-metal braces.*

The thing is, that didn't even bother me that much. A part of me liked the idea of being a trophy. Even if it wouldn't be much more than a joke to the guy. There's something to be said for meaningless sex. And at least there was an element of desire involved. It wasn't like the guy slept with me because I was the next or last best thing left in the bar that night. He *wanted* me.

Even if it was just so he could add me to his list of unusual sexual partners.

But did I even want to sleep with anyone else? A part of me did. Or thought it did. I didn't even know if that feeling was real. After all, I was so certain that the braces were a practically impregnable barrier to any chance at coitus that I knew, deep down, that it couldn't possibly happen. So it was safe to imagine it, because it wouldn't ever get beyond the daydream stage. Lying in bed, my mouth filled by the mouth-filling monobloc, all smooth plastic and obstruction, I could let my imagination run wild in complete safety.

But what about Jacob? What was he doing? What could I do about him? What did I want to do about him?

26.

The monobloc was terrible and great. I only had to wear it nights, and a bit during the day, and then more on weekends, but in practice, once I had gotten sort of used to it, I would force myself to put it in first thing when I got home, turning the key that locked it in place and storing that away. It was like a form of self-punishment. There was something immensely satisfying about being so perfectly gagged like this, my mouth immovable and filled. It was what I deserved, I somehow felt.

I would take it out for meals and sometimes when I snacked in front of the TV, but I would strictly limit the amount of time I didn't wear it. It was frustrating having this huge object in my mouth, but it was also the best kind of frustrating. I masturbated all the time, working myself into a sweaty frenzy, drawing breath in and out so quickly through the small opening in the monobloc that it whistled, punishing myself by not allowing myself to remove the monobloc after I climaxed, even though I badly wanted to every time.

I went out with friends sometimes. It was funny how confused they were by my braces. They were sort of embarrassed to be seen with me, and sort of embarrassed for me. It was easier going out with couples. When I just went out with my girlfriends they were worried that it would be too much of a turn-off for and scare away all the eligible men. I tried to convince them that standing next to me would just make them look better, but it didn't really work out that way. Even if the

142

braces repelled most men, they were a conversation magnet. Anytime we spoke to any guys their eyes would involuntarily gravitate to the braces, and though some tried to talk about everything else they eventually all asked, *So what's with the braces?* And so instead of my horny friends getting the attention, it was me. Or rather my braces.

I had moments of weakness. Moments where I was talking to some guy and I knew that if he said the right thing I'd let him take me home with him. Of course, it was mostly a sort of wishful thinking. Ninety percent of these guys had no interest in getting any closer to my metal mouth. But sometimes their curiosity went further.

I had liaised with Erik for one of the PR events we were doing for the company he worked for for weeks, but our meetings had always been professional and quick. He always had a ton of work to quickly get back to, and we always had a lot of work to rush back to after those meetings at which his bosses came to us with even more demands. So we only got around to a personal conversation the day of the event, when everything was taken care of. Good planning meant there were no last minute hitches, which was a first for me and which meant we actually had some time on our hands. He invited me for a coffee.

"Can't do coffee," I stupidly instinctively said, pointing at my braces. Great. Like my braces weren't obvious enough. I have to go an point them out and focus even more attention on them. "The orthodontist won't let me."

He tilted his head like I had said something moronic. Which I had. "By 'coffee' I just meant ... something. Too early for a beer, but you get the idea."

I blushed and nodded.

When we found a table at the local coffeehouse – I had a pastry and some herbal tea – he couldn't help but start with the obvious.

"So what is up with the braces?" he asked. Like almost everyone did.

"The usual," I lied. "Crooked teeth that needed straightening."

"But can't they do that less noticeably now? Don't take this the wrong way, but that's a lot of metal. And quite a bit of plastic, too, right?"

I blushed some more. And I don't know what possessed me then. "My boyfriend insisted. If I was going to get braces, then they had to be the biggest, baddest around. He was tired of my getting hit on, and he figured this would do the trick."

"Did it?"

"Oh, definitely. Believe it or not, most men do not find the metallically super-accessorized look and artificial lisp attractive. It's *not* the teenage look they're looking for even when they like that nubile look."

"I get that," he nodded. "Not that they're...," he hastily added, stumbling over his words in trying to reassure me.

I laughed. "It's ok. I know how awful they look. They're braces, after all. And it's sort of a neat experience, too. For once, not being an object of desire."

"Ah, people seeing the real you...."

"Well, maybe not. Mostly they just catch sight of these things and run the other way as fast as they can."

"So your boyfriend is pleased with the results."

"No," I shook my head. "We both forgot the obvious. That not only would the super-braces ward off all possible suitors, but that he wouldn't like them much either."

"You're kidding? So he dumped you?'

We...parted ways, I guess you'd say." I was stretching so much of the truth I figured I could stretch this too.

I was a bit disappointed that Erik didn't let on if he saw this as some sort of opening. That's what it was intended as, after all. "That's harsh," he said.

"Serves me right, I suppose. For letting him have a say. But it's not that bad. I only need them for a year, so there are only few months left. And the heavy-duty material means it went quicker than it would otherwise," I added, trying to justify why I had these ridiculous braces.

"Well, that's good."

We talked some more, but soon we were both starting to get nervous about the event that evening, and even if there was nothing more to do we both wanted to double-check everything and so we got back down to business quickly. The event itself went off great, and he came by to congratulate all of us and thank us, and after he did he sort of pulled me aside and asked whether I wanted to go out to dinner later that week.

A date! Of course I was open to that. A bit scared, and feeling a bit like I was cheating on Jacob, even though I hadn't heard from him in weeks. But maybe it was the right step forward. I hoped so, because I said yes without any hesitation.

It went ok, but not great. He picked me up, and we went to a place where I was relieved to see I could order food that I could eat without totally grossing him out. There was enough on the menu that *wouldn't* gum up my braces. We got along well, our conversation mostly that getting to know you kind of back and forth, about family and school and jobs. He tried hard to keep his eyes on mine, and not my braces, though he couldn't help but glance at them every couple of seconds, a slightly worried look on his face that he bravely tried to cover up.

I excused myself after desert and brushed my teeth in the ladies' room. In case there was goodnight kiss coming, or in case things went any further. I wanted to be sure there was nothing except the scrubbed, bare metal there to gross him out.

So we got to my building and he leaned in to kiss me goodnight, and he did. But as soon as my lips parted slightly, as soon as the metal of my braces brushed against his lips he drew back like he'd gotten an electric shock. He looked me in the eye, and then he looked down at the sidewalk, awkwardly shifting from foot to foot. He clenched his teeth. "I'm sorry, Sally," he said. "I...I really do like you, and how we've worked together. And I had a great time tonight. But I can't...God, this is so silly, but I can't get by the braces. I know I'm a terrible person, but...it's just too much for me. I'd like to...get closer, but those things are...."

"The ultimate turn-off?"

"No, no. You're...it's just like everything is fine until I try to take that closer step to intimacy. Suddenly it's like...kissing my sister. Not that I have a sister, but that's sort of how I imagine it. Like a taboo."

"Sure. My wonder braces. An invisible shield – no, strike that, a super visible shield, keeping me safe from love, lust, and happiness. With teeth straightening bonus!"

He looked sad that he'd disappointed me. "I wish...."

I let him off easy. "Come on, it's fine. And like I said, I only have them for a couple of more months. Then I'll be fighting off all the men with a stick."

"If you want to give me a call then...," he suggested. Which was just more than I could take.

"I have your number," I said pretty coldly, turning around fast. "Thanks for dinner," I said over my shoulder as I turned the key in the door.

I felt a measure of relief, too – I wasn't sure hooking up with Erik was what I really wanted – but there was no getting around the fact that it also hurt to be rejected. Here was someone who liked me for who I was, but not enough to blind him to the braces. So it was probably for the best, since over the long term I wanted to be with someone who could put up with me regardless of what. And someone who could handle something in my mouth, since I was going to be wearing my retainers religiously at night, even after the braces came off.

But a little fling would have been nice, too. A one-time thing. I didn't really see myself as that kind of girl, but I could see how a few times in your life something like that would really hit the spot.

I just tossed my purse aside and didn't even take my coat off when I got inside. I just rushed to my nightstand and fumbled open the container and pulled the elastics off and snapped the monobloc into place and locked it. Sighing with relief to feel the comforting bulk in my mouth I sank down on my bed, waves of disappointment alternating with ones of satisfaction. At least the braces and the monobloc provided a secure hold. As long as I had them, I was ok.

27.

The four weeks with the monobloc dragged by incredibly fast. I mean, they were over in an instant, and yet there were moments daily that seemed to go on forever. The mouth-filling plastic was impossible to ignore, and time seemed to move so slowly when I had it in sometimes, and yet when I had to take it out, in the morning when I got up, or in the evening when I went out somewhere I almost always wanted to prolong the strange but comforting mouthful feeling just a bit longer and I had to practically force myself to remove it.

The day I had my next appointment with Dr.Wrighting I went home from work to get the monobloc, and I put it in right there, wearing it the whole way to her offices, hoping no one stopped me on the way to ask me anything.

In the waiting room I could see the other girls stare. They knew I had something in my mouth from the way the monobloc made me look. I smiled, revealing my braces and the plastic of the monobloc between my teeth, but I think only those who had had one themselves could recognize it.

I was looking forward to being strapped down again. I wanted to take out the monobloc so I could tell one of the assistants that she should just strap me down and Dr.Wrighting could take all afternoon before she should bother getting to me, but of course they wouldn't do that. They wanted a constant turnover of patients in the chairs.

But in the notes I made that Dr.Wrighting and Dr.Allegretta read I constantly mentioned how much I looked forward to just lying there strapped down at my appointment, so I hoped Dr.Wrighting would give me a few moments of that satisfaction.

I guess she did know. When I was called in her assistant strapped me in and got me ready, and then Dr.Wrighting came in. "How are we doing?" she asked, looking down at me, and I nodded to signal I was doing ok.

"I still have another patient to see," she said. "Do you want me to take that out, or do you mind waiting like this a bit?" she asked, pointing at my monobloc.

I clenched my teeth even tighter around it, if that was possible, and shook my head vigorously. Dr.Wrighting smiled. She got the message, and she left.

I breathed easier, sinking into a blissful state, restrained, mouth filled, the metal of my braces pushing lightly against the inside of my cheeks and lips so I wouldn't forget them either. Coming here was like heaven. I didn't need yoga or a spa or psychiatrist. I just needed to be strapped down at my orthodontist and all my troubles seemed to go away.

I don't know how long Dr.Wrighting took. Not long enough, of course, but it was ok. I opened my mouth so she could remove the monobloc.

"So how did it go with this appliance?" she asked, waving it in front of me.

"Kind of a tough one," I admitted. "No talking, no eating. Mouth-filling."

"But you wore it a lot more than you had to," she reminded me. She kept close track of all of that, and I recorded all the times in the notes she read.

I nodded. "That's not a problem, isn't it? I haven't just totally messed up my bite, have I?"

Dr.Wrighting shook her head, smiling. "No, it's fine. But did it have anything to do with Jacob?" she asked.

147

I shrugged as best I could under the harness holding me in place.

"How long haven't you seen each other?"

"At least a month," I realized.

"And how is that going?"

I tried to shrug again. "I guess you're getting a lot less data on the sexual impact of these appliances," I tried to joke.

"That's not a problem," she reassured me. "Are your trying to work out whether the braces have anything to do with it?"

"On and off," I said. "More off, recently, I guess. he said the braces have something to do with it. You know, are we just together because of them. Were we."

"And how does that make you feel?"

"I think it'll just take time to sort out. Or not."

"Does it make you reconsider having them? Do you wish they could come off now?"

I shuddered, panicked for a moment. God, that was the last thing I wanted to happen now. I didn't know what I would do without them. Which I only realized right there. I shook my head. "No way, I want to go through with this just like we planned."

"Good," Dr.Wrighting said. "Because I certainly wasn't going to remove them before the year was up."

Which made me realize that the year would be up fairly soon. Another three months or so. And I felt that twinge of regret and worry. What was I really going to do without them?

Dr.Wrighting examined my teeth and braces, scraping and prodding a bit. I wondered what she had planned for me.

"So we have a new device for you this time, too," she finally said. "This one was more difficult to adjust to your requirements. Since we want to avoid actual tooth movement."

She went to one of her cupboards and pulled out a larger wired device in a plastic bag. She opened it and pulled it out. "This is a reverse pull headgear, she said. "Except that in your case we want to avoid the pulling part. Normally this front bar would be connected to the braces using two elastics. Making for the pulling action. But as you can see we've attached a solid piece, connected to a retainer."

It took me a moment to figure it all out. There was a small top retainer, but instead of just the wire and clasps which attached it to my braces there was also an extension right in the middle extending out. About an inch long, it was a thin strip of

148

plastic that encased two wires, for stability and strength I guessed. This attached to a flat curved thin piece of metal that had a pink chin cup at the bottom, and a strap on the top. I realized how it would fit on the front of my face and strap onto the top of my head, and I opened my mouth so that Dr.Wrighting could fit me with it.

The chin cup and the front part of the head strap were padded, and after inserting the retainer Dr.Wrighting had me close my mouth and adjusted the positioning of the cup and strap. The piece protruding from my mouth and connecting the retainer and the facemask felt a lot like when I had my regular headgear, except that with the plastic there was more to it.

It felt a bit weird, but there was no new pressure on my teeth, which is what Dr.Wrighting asked about. She wanted to be sure it more or less just sat securely in place, but without doing anything.

The adjustments took a while, and she took it off and put it on a couple of times to make sure everything was in its proper place. Finally she was satisfied, and I was unstrapped and sent to wait in the waiting room. I knew this was the usual walk of shame, to force patients to get used to a new device, and to be seen wearing it before they even knew what they looked like. And even though I thought I had gotten used to showing my braced self I felt more embarrassed than usual. I had only seen a couple of girls wearing a reverse pull headgear in the office before, and I knew it was the most noticeable of all the orthodontic appliances, even more than the full headgear I had had. I knew I looked pretty silly. And the looks I got from everyone in the waiting room certainly reinforced that impression.

Finally after half an hour the assistant came out and took me back to the mirror so I could learn to put on and take off the device. That first look in the mirror was sort of a shock. With this metal bar running down the front of my face, curved over my nose and down to my chin, and the bright pink chin cup and then the strap around the top of my head. It was a lot to deal with. Taking it off and putting it back on was easy enough, but I admit I was a bit numb about looking like this.

The assistant took me to Dr.Wrighting's office. Wearing the device, of course.

"Twelve hours a day," Dr.Wrighting said. "Eighteen on weekends, plus any time you have to make up from during the week. Ninety-six total, every week, without fail."

I nodded. This was another of the devices I couldn't wear in public. But I could probably just manage the prescribed hours every week.

"You didn't have too much trouble sleeping with the headgear, did you?" Dr.Wrighting asked. "You sleep on your back, right?"

I nodded.

"Since it's on the front of your face, this headgear can seem more in the way, but I think you'll adjust to it quickly."

I shrugged. Sure. Maybe. Whatever.

I got a case to put it in when I wasn't wearing it, and of course I pulled the appliance off as soon as I was out the door of the practice and quickly stored it away. I wasn't sure how I felt about this one. But I realized I couldn't dawdle on the streets. I had to get home and put it one to get in my required hours.

It turned out to be a lot like the regular headgear, except it was a bit more in the way. I couldn't eat while wearing it, or drink except for using a straw. For a while I worried about it falling off when I moved my head or anything, but I realized that between the strap going around the top of my head and the retainer it was held securely in place. It just didn't feel as secure as the regular headgear, with its snug straps holding that in place.

But otherwise it wasn't really much of a bother. I was used to wearing a retainer. I always had to wear some sort of retainer. And though there was that metal bar running down my face it was right in the middle and I barely even noticed it.

The fact that it was so forgettable, except for when I was in bed – I did have to be sure to stay sleeping on my back, or not to try to pull my blanket up over my face – did make me even forget sometimes at first. Both that I wasn't wearing it, and that I was – like when I was watching TV and went to get a snack, only to smack my hand into the facemask as I brought the food to my mouth.

I went to visit my parents for the weekend again, and had to wear it most of the time there. That was embarrassing, but I also enjoyed there unease about their adult girl wearing this weird device.

I got an email from Jacob, asking how I was doing, and we emailed back and forth some and he asked to see me for coffee after work. I wasn't sure what he wanted. Or what I wanted. Would I take him back, if that's what he wanted? The itch between my legs wasn't the best reason to do so, but it was something to consider too.

He was already there when I got there, sitting at a quiet table in a corner. We greeted one another warily, after almost six weeks not seeing one another. I did go a little soft in my legs when I saw him. No question, I still had a lot of feelings for him.

"So how are you doing?" he asked.

"Pretty much as usual," I said.

"How are the braces doing?"

I flashed them, all metal and elastics. "Perfectly, as always."

I could see him twitch. "Dr.Wrighting have any surprises for you?"

I hadn't told him about my newest accessory, or the monobloc. If he wasn't part of my life he didn't deserve to know.

"She continues to put me through the wringer," I said. "Sometimes it's a lot to take, but I'm still enjoying it."

"So some new devices...?" he said, wanting me to tell him all about them.

"Yes. Every four weeks a new challenge. Some of which have proven really challenging."

He could tell I wasn't going tell. "I miss you," he said, sounding sincere and hurt.

"I miss you too," I admitted.

"But seeing you...God, I'm sorry, but it's so hard seeing anything but the braces. I am throbbing so badly with desire for you. For them."

I was throbbing pretty badly too, but I tried not to let on.

"I feel...I think I feel so much for you, but at the same time I'm blinded by the braces, you know? I mean, I know I want the braces, but I think I'm in love with the person behind them but I can't be sure because I'm so staggered by the braces. And I don't know what to do about it."

I laughed, and I could see him quiver with delight at the full sight of my braces. "So you broke up with me because you fell in love with me?"

151

"I didn't break up with you. I don't want to be broken up with you. I want to be with you. But I also want to be sure. That's why I wanted you to come here."

"You think we should just hop back into bed together again?" I sounded offended, but part of me liked that idea a lot.

"No, no. Exactly not. That's why this is so hard. I want to be sure. So I don't want to hop right back into bed. I mean I do, I really do, but we can't." He fished in his pocket and brought out the small key for his cock cage. "Here, take this," he said.

"Are you all locked up?"

He nodded. "But I just couldn't keep from temptation." he leaned forward. "Every morning. A couple of times every night. Sometimes at work in the bathroom. Always imagining you. I mean, one look at that braced smile on my phone or iPad and I just had to masturbate. I had no self control whatsoever. So you take it."

"And?"

"And...but...I don't think we're ready to see each other. I'm not. I'd just be overcome by lust. Like I am here and now, I just want to take you right here, on the table, in the corner...."

His glazed eyes indicated that he really meant it. He shook his head and tried to focus again. "Can we just...communicate without seeing one another for a while? Just get to know each other aside from the braces and the sex?"

"You mean like just talk on the phone?"

He made a face. "Not even that...the sound of your voice, the thick lisp from the retainers....Maybe just start with email and instant messaging, and work our way closer from there?"

Thinking about it for a second it seemed to me he might be on to something. "That actually sounds like a good idea."

It was, too. I sent him an email when I got home, wearing my reverse pull headgear but still not telling him about it, and in the days that followed we wrote and IMed back and forth constantly. The first few days we avoided mentioning anything sexual or orthodontic, but after a week I began to tease him with what Dr.Wrighting had been doing to me for the past two months. After another week we went to dinner, and somehow everything was more under control. We'd begun to be able to compartmentalize the different parts of our relationship, and Jacob was coming to grips with my braces. He still loved and lusted for them, but he could set that apart from everything else too. He admitted he had been seeing Dr.Allegretta, who had helped talk him through this and figure out how to deal with it.

We went to dinner again, and discussed whether he should come over to my place afterwards. I said firmly that sex was off the table and that he'd stay locked up, and he agreed with that. And I reminded him that I'd have to put on my appliance. He still don't know what it was I had to wear, and I wouldn't tell him. We agreed he'd come over for a drink. There was a TV show on that we both liked, and he'd watch that with me, and then he'd go home.

Jacob grew progressively more nervous as we got closer to home, but he was trying very hard. I told him to make himself comfortable while I went to brush my teeth, and I heard him turn the TV on as I hooked up my headgear in the bathroom.

"Ta-da," I said when I showed myself.

You could see his eyes get all big and he seemed to sway, unable top say anything.

I let myself fall down beside him, staring him in the eyes. "As you can see, it's the perfect chastity device for us at this stage. Even kissing is off the table, barred by the bar…."

He nodded, very slowly. I could see the bulge in his pants, and felt bad for what he was going through. I sort of wished he would take me right there and then, but I knew we had to keep ourselves from straying from the path we had decided on.

He turned to look at the TV. "So what's it like having that?"

"I think it's the most boring one so far. Even the real headgear was better. But I guess it's also the most…prominent? one so far."

"It is very prominent," he agreed. "How much do you have to wear it?"

"Pretty much every minute I'm at home. Twelve hours weekdays, eighteen on weekends."

We watched the TV show pretty much in silence, but of course neither of us could have told you what happened on the show afterwards. Jacob got up to leave right when the show ended, the bulge in his pants still enormous. He looked dazed as we said good-bye at the door. For a moment he leaned forward to kiss me, but then remembered all that stood in the way. "This was nice," he said, his voice cracking.

"It was." I didn't add anything. We needed this to settle in before we thought about the next step.

We IMed back forth the next day some but also decided a day apart was a good idea. No need to rush things. I cried myself to sleep in lusting frustration, Jacob admitted, so he clearly needed at least a day to gather himself again. I didn't want to torture him too much. I felt guilty about masturbating after he had left, and again the next day. I have to admit, I don't know what I would have done if I couldn't get that release. And it sounded like it was much worse for a guy not to be able to do that.

We had dinner again, and went to my place again the next night, and this time we talked more, and by the weekend we felt we were ready to be more intimate again.

I think the headgear helped. "I can't take it off," I told him. "I need to get my hours in, and with going out with you I'm behind...."

Unbuttoning my shirt he looked a bit disappointed at first, but then smiled. In a way this was better. It took the whole oral connection of the table. We could focus on the rest, which was probably better anyway.

He took off my shirt and then my bra, and kissed and sucked and bit on my breasts while he slowly disrobed. We took our time. I only had my hands at my disposal, since my headgear prevented from using my mouth or tongue. It was frustrating, but it was also nice being served, and I had my own oral sensations to satisfy me, running my tongue across my retainers and the metal of my braces.

Finally we were both completely naked, except for the cage that held his fully erect cock. I fondled it and smiled. "So we're really letting it come out to play?"

He nodded.

I had him close his eyes while I went to get the key, and made them keep them closed as I unlocked him. Kneeling there, I desperately wanted to take that throbbing, wonderfully funky smelling shaft that I released from its prison into my mouth but of course I couldn't. Jacob trembled with his eyes still closed as I opened a condom package and then unrolled the lubricated latex over his beautiful pulsing column.

When I was done I lay down on the bed on my back. "Alright, come take me," I commanded.

Gently Jacob guided his rock hard cock into me. I knew he was set to explode at any moment, the buildup just too much and long for him to contain. He knew it too, and so he carefully and slowly thrust deep into me, trying to hold back as long as

154

possible. It wasn't possible for very long, but even just those three or four thrusts were immensely satisfying.

After his long groaning ejaculation he pulled himself out. Taking two long breaths he plunged back in face first, now his tongue darting in and out and in and out and circling at my edges. I lay there, eyes closed, back in a heaven I had missed for so many months now.

After a few minutes or an eternity I heard the rip of another condom package and I spread my legs wider and he plunged back into me, this time pounding away much longer until I came and came and came again before he did.

Exhausted we lay there, our fingers intertwined, happy again.

28.

It was several more dates and half a dozen fucks before we kissed again for the first time. The headgear had priority. I had it on when he came over, I had it one when he left. It was by silent mutual agreement, I think. There's an intimacy to kissing, too, that we knew we had to be careful with. Kissing brought the braces right back into the middle of everything, and we both knew we weren't ready for that.

So it was only the next weekend that I said I thought I had gotten enough hours in, and we could even spend some time together, alone, without my wearing it.

"Are you sure?"

"We have to try making out at some point," I said.

He smiled, eager, watching with fascination as I undid the strap around my head, and then popped out the retainer, and the whole facemask with it. I smiled at him, with my familiar braced smile.

Jacob leaned in slowly to kiss me, and we sank into one another, happy and united. We explored each other with our mouths, which I was finally able to do too, and it culminated in yet another wonderful fuck. We were still panting, side by side, when Jacob handed me back my headgear – giving me one more kiss before he did. I put it back on. Yes, everything felt right again.

The reverse headgear was just the right appliance to be stuck with these weeks. It erected another barrier, preventing the

155

casual kiss that so often led to intense making out and then straight to sex. We talked more, sitting side by side, holding hands or my legs draped across his. It's not that we weren't in heat like all the time. I could see his cock bulge under his pants often when we got close, but we managed to show restraint too.

And we did seem to get along as a couple again. We were really making that connection beyond the braces. It made me really hopeful, even as I was getting more and more nervous about the approaching removal of my braces.

I guessed that at my next appointment I would get my next to last new appliance. Maybe something added to the headgear? But I was kind of hoping that I would be done with this headgear. The tongue-blocking, palate-covering intraoral appliances were much more fun that this extraoral one. Though the regular headgear was fine too. Maybe I'd get some all-in-one reverse *and* regular headgear – complete with mouth-filling mouthpiece…. Well, a girl can dream.

When I went to my next appointment I only put the reverse headgear on right in front of Dr.Wrighting's office, fumbling with it just as a headgeared girl came out with her mother. Both shook their heads at my lack of dedication, since it was clear I hadn't worn the device all the way from home. I felt a bit guilty, but there was no way I was walking around wearing that. It felt like punishment enough to have to sit wearing it in the waiting room, alongside some mothers who weren't that much older than me.

Of course, it was worth that quarter of an hour or twenty minutes of embarrassment for the blissful relief that came as I was strapped in to the examination chair and left alone except for the assistant discreetly in the corner to watch over me. Then the hold of the facemask of the reverse gear sat comfortably there, and I almost regretted that it might be taken away from me.

Almost.

Dr.Wrighting came in after ten minutes and asked how I was doing. I was bubbling over with nervous excitement, babbling about how well everything was going.

"So you and Jacob are doing fine now?"

"Better than fine," I insisted. "Really well."

"I'm so glad to hear that!" she said, and she sounded like she really meant it.

She unhooked the headgear and had me open my mouth so that she could pop the retainer out. After putting the appliance on the tray hovering in front of me, she turned back to my mouth and began her usual poking and looking around it.

Dr.Wrighting handed off my reverse pull headgear to the assistant, saying, "We won't need this anymore." So I guessed I was done with that. Then Dr.Wrighting removed my elastic, and my lower retainer. Then she got a cheek retractor and put that in place. It felt good to have my lips held wide apart like that again.

I could tell she was opening my brackets and bands, so that she could remove the archwires, which she hadn't done in a while. She took both the top and bottom off, and I felt a little exposed. Suddenly I worried my mouth was too bare. Were we already beginning the transition to when the braces came off?

But Dr.Wrighting did have the assistant get something for her. I gave a sigh of relief. There was more coming.

It was disappointingly small, however. Dr.Wrighting took out what looked like two small, metal tubes, all silvery, each about an inch and a half long, with a bit of metal like a small button or something on each end. She held one up for me, as I stared gaping open-mouthed, unable to say anything.

"This is a kind of Herbst appliance I have modified for you," she explained.

I had no idea what a Herbst appliance was.

"We're attaching the top and bottom parts to the bands on your top and bottom braces, one on each side. Now as you can see, it's like a tube within a tube." Pulling one of the devices apart, I saw that a slightly thinner tube fit in the big one. So it could be stretched out to almost three inches in length. "It's going to restrict your jaw movement a bit, but otherwise shouldn't be too much in the way."

I couldn't say anything or ask any questions anyway, and Dr.Wrighting got right to work. I wasn't sure about getting these small poles installed in my mouth. Even if they were extendable and collapsible. But, like always, my fate and future, at least for the next month or so, was entirely in her hands.

Fitting and attaching these was more work than most of the recent appliances had been, since these had to be securely attached to my braces. Lying there with my mouth held open I could feel her progress from one piece to the next, but it took a while until all four ends were attached. Then she put the archwires back in place. But no retainers. No elastics.

I was relieved when the assistant did bring one more small plastic bag with what looked like a retainer, but it was a small upper one that barely covered more than the area behind front four teeth. "With the Herbst we're just going to have you wear this small bite plate," Dr.Wrighting explained, pressing it into place.

Then she took out the cheek retractor. The two tubes ran at an angle between my upper and lower jaws, roughly where the elastics had been. But they extended far more away from my teeth, and I could feel them rub against the inside of my cheek as I opened and closed my mouth. I could also feel them with my tongue, and compared to the elastics they really were like massive poles. Carefully moving my lower jaw around, I could feel how the appliance only permitted so much movement. The biteplate was just a little bit of plastic behind my teeth, the smallest of the retainers I had had so far.

Dr.Wrighting explained how if I opened my mouth really wide, or it got jerked to one side or another, the inner tube would come out of the outer one. She demonstrated, and suddenly I had the two top tubes just dangling from my teeth, and the bottom ones separated from them. "If that happens," Dr.Wrighting said, "and it probably will, then you just have to open your mouth very wide and guide the one tube back into the other."

I had to open my mouth *really* wide for her to get the tubes back in place, but at least it was clear that it could be done.

Dr.Wrighting left me alone for a few minutes, to see how I got used to them. If it was headgear or something like that she would have made me wait in the waiting room, but here I had almost nothing to really be embarrassed about, so she decided I might as well just stay strapped down in the examination chair.

"So, any problems?"

I shook my head. "They feel a bit strange, but they're almost no bother at all."

"Disappointed?"

"A bit," I said, laughing.

"I wish all my patients were as eager to be outfitted with *less* comfortable and attractive appliances," Dr.Wrighting laughed.

Twirling a bit on her seat, she reminded me, "You only have a bit more than two months left, you know."

I nodded. I didn't even want to think about it.

"So you're going to have these for four weeks, and then we have time for one last set of appliances. And for that I think it's only fair to make it patient's choice. Anything we've used to date, or even variations on those. Then you can spend your last month – well, it's more like six weeks, actually – wearing just the bare-bones braces themselves, if you like. Or any combination of appliances and accessories, one last time. The only demand I have is that whatever you select, you wear it that full length of time, exactly like you ask for. So if you say you want headgear that you wear twelve hours a day you can't change your mind after a couple of weeks and only wear it nights."

I *loved* this idea, and could barely keep myself from shouting all the things I wanted back in my mouth.

Dr. Wrighting saw how I was ready to burst but put her hand up to slow me down. "Think about it, Sally. You have about two weeks to think about it, and then you should let me know *exactly* what you want and we'll try to fix that up at your next appointment. But for now, it's just these Herbst appliances for the next four weeks. And since they're mounted on, there's not much for you to do with them."

I thanked her as she unstrapped me, barely able to keep my mind from mapping out exactly what and how much I could wear for that precious last go around in braces.

For once I could just stride out of the office without worrying at the door about taking out or concealing the appliance I had been outfitted with. Besides, there was nothing I could do about the Herbst. It felt weird, these two metal bars, but almost boringly weird. There wasn't really that much to them, and I had gotten used to there being a lot to my appliances. I had liked it, too.

I examined what I looked like at home. It was sort of how I did just with my elastics, except the silvery tubes were a lot more noticeable than the thin elastics. It was a bit irritating how they stood out from my teeth and pressed against the inside of my cheeks, but all the metal bits were completely rounded off, so they didn't hurt or anything. Eating was going to be a bit difficult, I realized. Again it was going to be like with the elastics except about ten times more pronounced. The metal tubes were going to have a lot less give and so they were going to be a lot more in the way.

I called Jacob, who tried to act like totally indifferent, even though he knew that I had had my appointment with Dr.Wrighting today and everything that meant. I knew that he was dying to know what I got this time. And we both knew a new device meant the start of a weeklong lockdown for him. But he was totally casual and just asked how everything had gone, and he even interrupted me when I wanted to describe what Dr.Wrighting had installed. "I'll see when I see you, right?" he said, willing to put off knowing, even though we both knew it was killing him. I had wanted to immediately tell him about what Dr.Wrighting said about the final phase of my treatment, but then I was glad he cut me off. That was going to be a nice surprise for him, and I wanted to give it to him in person.

"I like," Jacob said when I let him in. He stood there, his hands on my hips admiring the smile I couldn't hide. "A classic, braces dominated look, with some nice additional metal on the sides for emphasis." He kissed me, his tongue darting into my tongue and around the posts of the Herbst. "Sure, there isn't much smooth retainer surface area to enjoy, but it's a nice stark contrast to the previous months."

I smiled, happy that he wasn't disappointed that I wasn't even more wired up. We kissed. Carefully, both a bit on guard that Jacob wouldn't get too worked up. Though that was a hopeless cause. It was clear that his cock was as hard as it could get in its metal cage. But he didn't complain.

We ordered in, and I tried to get used to chewing with the two metal pistons on each side of my mouth. It was strange. I often ate something with elastics stretched just about in the same places, but they weren't nearly as much in the way. The Herbsts were like real metal posts, unlike the elastics, and without any give. Unlike the elastics. So my chewing ability was constrained. It took me a while to begin to get the hang of it.

While we were eating, and once I wasn't totally focused on figuring out how to chew my food, I told Jacob the good news about being able to choose what I would wear the final weeks.

He dropped his knife and fork, which clattered on his plate, and he clapped his hands. "Oh, man!" he said, shaking his head. "The possibilities...."

"I know."

"I can't believe it's almost over, but oh, this helps ease the pain. What a way to end things. I mean, you do want to return to some of your favorites, right?"

160

I never want to let them go, I wanted to say. But I knew we couldn't cling to that idea, so I was resolved just to get the most out of that last month that we could. "Oh, yeah! I just don't know which combinations."

"The headgear, right? Definitely, right? Please tell me you miss the headgear."

"I miss the headgear," I admitted.

"And some of those lisp-inducing, mouth-filling smooth plastic devices...."

I don't know if his mouth watered more or mine at the thought of them. We both sat there, dreamily staring off into space and letting the food get cold while we imagined the possibilities. Knowing that it was all going to be gone so soon too intensified the feeling of nostalgia and desire.

Of course it wasn't that soon. About ten weeks, in all. So I still had a lot of time to enjoy my braced mouth to the fullest.

I could sense Jacob's restlessness as we cleaned up. I didn't have to watch him shuffling uncomfortably in his pants to recognized that groinal itch he was feeling. Not that my own situation was much different. The difference was that I could slip my hands into my sopping moist patch and eventually find relied, while he just had to grit it out, regardless of the intensity of his desire.

He looked almost feverish by the time he left. I would have liked him at my side all night, but I could see it would be too much for him. At the door he could barely get his eyes off my braces as I smiled. I have to admit I liked the intensity of the passion I saw in his eyes and felt in his trembling hands. If he had any way of escaping from his cage he would have ripped the clothes off me and ravaged me right there. And I would have loved it. But he was resigned to his locked-up fate, and went home disappointed. I let myself fall on my bed, closed my eyes, and slowly, slowly satisfied myself. As much as I could.

It wasn't like having Jacob thrusting deep into me, but it offered some relief and pleasure. Enough to tide me over, but not so much as to not leave me on edgy excitement for the time a few days later when Jacob could have his way with me.

29.

We emailed back and forth all the time for the week we had to wait until we could have sex again, discussing what combination of appliances I should finish my treatment off with. That probably wasn't a good idea. It riled us both up, into a sex-starved frenzy. We probably should have waited until we were fucking on a steady basis again before we moved on to considering what our options were. But we couldn't help it. It was like a second genie coming after the first had already granted us our fondest wish, allowing us to fine-tune it one more wonderful time – even as full enjoyment of our first wish was being withheld in a cruel weeklong countdown.

The Herbst was sort of difficult to get accustomed to. I mean, everything orthodontic was strange, and usually in a good way. The Herbst, too, in its own way. It was weird when it came apart, the metal tube and post dangling there. And it was weird how it opened and closed but also constrained my jaw movements. And it was definitely annoying while eating. But everything orthodontic was annoying while eating. Still, a lot more could wrap itself around these than the elastics.

Jacob liked them. The bulky metal appealed to him. "It just makes it look like there are *more* braces," he explained. "And more braces are just better braces."

I could see that. Especially when I looked in the mirror. When others looked at me, on the other hand, I could see that this wasn't the majority opinion. Everyone seemed to think less braces were better. Even after all these months with my full-metal mouthful some of my friends still cringed a little each time they saw me. And I heard the pitying *You still have those?* more often than I could count.

I went to a club with some friends, and they brought along a girl I didn't know. She had braces too, but her top ones were the sort of translucent kind. Her bottom row was all metal brackets, but she tried to hide that. They all pitied me for not being able to have *presentable* braces likes her. They really said that! *Presentable*! And she felt bad for me too, and said how brave I was. "I don't think I could have gone through with it if I would have had to get braces like that," she said.

162

I could just laugh, and I liked that that exposed all my metal in all its gleaming wonder, the two pistons stretching near as far apart as they could. Didn't she realize how glorious it was to have a whole mouthful of such shiny silvery wonder? I felt sorry for her. I was the lucky one, and the only reason I envied her at all was because she was going to be able to keep her third-rate train tracks longer than I was going to be able to keep my grand equipment.

I was really, really tempted to tell her that I didn't even need mine. That I wasn't just wearing these voluntarily, but because I *wanted* to wear them. Desperately wanted to…. That would have blown her mind.

Sure, it bothered me some that people looked at me askance because of the way I looked. I guess what really bothered me was that they felt bad for me because of my braces, while I felt so good because of them. The only time it really made me feel sad was when I saw a teen or tween girl with a similarly glorious set of metal bands and wires and I smiled proudly at my orthodontic sister and she would grimace and turn away, put off, I guess, by any reminder of what she looked like. I always wanted to grab those girls and shake them to get them to understand that this was the best thing that could have happened to them and they should enjoy it while they could because it was going to be over before they knew it. I knew that was silly, of course. There weren't many girls who could be convinced of anything other than that I was nuts. But I knew I was right. And sometimes those girls, even as they grimaced, couldn't help but stare back, and I imagined that in their minds there was a faint glimmer of recognition, of what a wonderful experience having braces could be if they just allowed themselves to give in to it.

I tried not to let what people said and how they looked at me get to me, but no matter what, occasionally there were times when creeping doubts slowly expanded in my mind. I hated that. The way it took away from my happiness. But fortunately my doubts were short-lived. After a week, when Jacob finally could spend the night and we could finally do everything we wanted to again, my certainty blossomed right back along with my pleasure. Here, in Jacob's arms, and under his caresses and kisses and with him between my legs, pounding into me, I had confirmation. This was the best of possible worlds. Being braced, two wire tracks firmly banded to my teeth, this was physical and sensual perfection. Here, wired up, was perfect happiness.

Our post-coital talks, and most of our others talks continued around what we should settle on for those precious last few weeks. It wasn't like there were really that many options, but I also wanted to experience what I still could to the fullest.

How much was I willing to challenge myself?

How much could I put up with?

But the limits on how far I could go where what was imposed on me by day to day life. If it weren't for my professional interactions I could have let my mouth be filled unspeakably and spent all those last weeks blissfully, completely braced. But work threw a wrench in those works, so the menu of what was available was much more limited.

Not that there wasn't enough to get me through it all with an ear to ear wired grin....

But the choices were pretty obvious, and after playing around with the unrealistic choices we made what was a pretty easy decision. I submitted the list to Dr.Wrighting. She did email back, asking *Are you absolutely sure?* but there was no question in my mind. I did tremble a bit sending back the email that said *Yes*, but I wasn't sure whether that was nerves or simply the excitement of all my anticipation.

Once that was out of my hands Jacob and I just enjoyed the present state. There wasn't that much to these braces, but they were still a full set of braces, with the two metal pistons to go along with that. Basic, but fulfilling all our requirements. And on my calendar I could mark down the remaining days until my next appointment, and my final orthodontic adventure.

30.

I knew it wasn't my last time going to Dr.Wrighting's office. I had to go back to get the braces removed. To get my retainers. Probably for a checkup now and again. But there was that terrible sense of something winding down and coming to an end as I came to the office for that final truly orthodontic session. After this, it was all just tidying up and aftercare.

My last hurrah. Which had me feeling sad, especially when I saw the girls in the waiting room with their overbites and crooked smiles, just beginning their tortured journeys, whose wonders and rewards they couldn't even imagine yet. But at least I was going out in style. Nothing too fancy or complicated, but enough that was unforgettable – for every remaining waking moment, and then, as memories etched in my mind, for the rest of my life.

I followed the assistant really slowly when she led me to the examination room. She probably thought I was reluctant about what was in store for me, like most of the other girls she had led to their places all day, but actually I wanted to savor every moment to the fullest. I couldn't help but sigh with pleasure as she strapped me down, too. God, was I going to miss that feeling of complete helplessness and absolute security that I had when I was securely strapped in place, able only to move my wrists slightly side to side, the padded belt firmly in place between my legs.

Dr.Wrighting smiled when she saw me. "So, are you ready for the last stage of your treatment."

"Ready for what's coming," I said. "But brokenhearted that it's the last."

"Every fantasy has to come to an end," Dr.Wrighting reminded me. She looked a bit wistful, too. Like she was enjoying this and would miss it as well.

"It's rare that a patient has such a good idea of what's in store for her when she comes into the office for her appointment," Dr.Wrighting said. "Of course, I've never before let one order what they want installed, either. Like from a menu."

"I think a lot of your patients would surprise you, if you gave them the option, once they were nearing the end of their treatment. If you gave them one last opportunity to really enjoy what they've been through, safe in the knowledge that in a month or six weeks they would be finished with it."

"You might be right. I should try that. Offer them a parting gift like that."

"I know I'm not your usual kind of patient, but I certainly couldn't dream of anything better. Or anything much better. I mean, if I could *really* have what I wanted, and not have to worry about the impression I make at work...." I sighed.

"It's probably good to set some limits," Dr.Wrighting said.

She got the cheek retractor and spread my lips around it and that feeling of happiness surged even more strongly through my body, like when you've smoked a joint and that feeling of feeling fine just spreads to every bit of your body.

Dr.Wrighting was right that I knew what was coming, but that didn't really diminish the excitement I felt. Even if you know you're getting a certain device, you can't really prepare for the complete feel and experience of actually having it. I just knew it was going to be a good feeling.

Dr.Wrighting removed the Herbsts, and then the small biteplate I had. I was glad to be rid of all of it, and looking forward to the more solid feel of the more substantial appliances that were in store for me. I could run my tongue around my emptier mouth, but I didn't even feel a bit of a twinge of relief. I wanted there to be more back in there, despite the hardships and inconvenience that also came with it.

I cheered up when Dr.Wrighting got the small metal bits that she then proceeded to attach to some of by bands. The bits that would help anchor and secure retainers. With the sharp edges that could only be retracted by the retainers holding them down, when they were in my mouth. Otherwise, if I wasn't wearing the retainers, they would jut painfully out into my cheeks. The bits that ensured I would wear the retainers, come what may, the painful alternative unbearable except for the brief moments when I took them out to brush my teeth.

I was sweating a bit when Dr.Wrighting got up again. To get the retainers, I knew. I shifted uneasily in the seat, the pressure of the padded strap between my legs more noticeable than ever, my own moistness down there lubricating me in excited anticipation. I closed my eyes for a moment, drifting into fantasies. I imagined my legs spread wide apart, like in gynecologists' stirrups, and Jacob thrusting into me while Dr.Wrighting snapped the retainers into place....

I sighed, then opened my eyes with a start to find Dr.Wrighting looking down at me, smiling. "Everything ok?" she asked.

With the cheek retractor in place I couldn't tell her just how perfectly ok everything was, but I nodded.

Then my eyes saw the two pink retainers Dr.Wrighting had placed on the tray hovering in front of me. A shudder went through me. They were beautiful. Their curves, their crannies. The silver wire and clasps. And I could see that the upper retainer was bulkier than the first retainer I had had. I knew that was risky. The smaller ones had already affected my speech a

166

bit, and made it more difficult to eat. Dr.Wrighting had warned me that adding any bulk to it would cause me to slur my words considerably more. She reminded me that she had made the initial set smaller so that it wouldn't be an issue at work, and she said we should probably stick to the same size, but I insisted she make the top one just a bit larger. A slightly more pronounced lisp, a bit more slurred speech...I wanted to finish up my orthodontic treatment with exactly this kind of in your face reminder to everyone who I spoke to what I was going through.

Dr.Wrighting reminded me that after the braces came off I would be getting retainers, and that I was going to have to wear those retainers regularly forever. "We could make those bulkier," she suggested. But it wasn't going to be the same thing. I knew those were going to be removable. Really removable, without any consequences, whenever I wanted. I wanted to be *forced* to wear something that was harder to put up with and more embarrassing to try to talk with. I wanted to be well and truly braced, one last time. To really indulge in that most pleasurable of suffering.

Dr.Wrighting picked up the lower retainer and snapped it into place. Then the upper. They fit perfectly, without pinching or poking anywhere. Dr.Wrighting removed the cheek retractor and I closed my mouth around them, thrilled by the sudden larger obstructions for my tongue and that wonderful feel of the smooth acrylic. "Perfect," I said, thrilled by the sound of my slurred voice. Yes, these were just the right size, I thought, swallowing again and again as the saliva quickly built up with the devices in place. Oh, how I had missed them!

Dr.Wrighting had me open and close my mouth a few times, to make sure they fit like they were supposed to. Then she put the cheek retractor in place again and popped both the retainers out, putting them back on the tray.

My heart pounded more strongly as I watched Dr.Wrighting go to another cabinet to retrieve the next appliances. She came back with a small, clear plastic bag, and I could see the wire and clear acrylic through it. I closed my eyes. Even though I knew what to expect, it all seemed too good to be true.

Dr.Wrighting took two pieces of wired acrylic out and placed one on top of the other in the palm of her left hand. Two oversized retainers, the one fit neatly over the other, much like my Twin Blocks had. That's what these were, too, except that Dr.Wrighting had done as I had asked and made a much more substantial version. The bulk of the top device alone was nearly mouth-filling, I could see, and it had a huge bulge where it fit into the horseshoe-arch of the lower half.

Dr.Wrighting first inserted the lower appliance. It wasn't that much bigger than the retainer I had just had there, but the blocks of acrylic that covered part of my molars made it a bigger appliance.

Then came the upper appliance, and it was huge. I closed my eyes and took a deep breath after Dr.Wrighting had clicked it into place. It seemed to fit as perfectly as the retainers had.

Then came the moment of truth, as Dr.Wrighting removed the cheek retractor and I brought my jaws together and the two devices came together.

I couldn't close my mouth completely, because of the blocks of acrylic between the two appliances. But the upper fit perfectly into the lower, and when I clenched my mouth it was like I had one solid block of acrylic there, like the monobloc. Except that here it did come apart, into two, the upper and the lower. "That's great," I said. Except of course I could barely form anything like words. A garbled *Ads glay* was what it sounded like. But even if she didn't understand the words Dr.Wrighting could see from my broad smile that this was exactly what I had wanted.

"Great!" she said.

Opening and closing my mouth, my tongue held back even when my mouth was more open by the curved acrylic that came down in the middle of the top half of the device, I wondered for a moment if it wasn't all too much. It was and it wasn't, and that's what made this perfect. That's one of the things I I always loved about my braces. That they could be both so awful and noticeable and irritating, but almost at the same time be the best feeling the world.

I wasn't done yet, either. Now Dr.Wrighting came back with the headgear and that wonderful harness. I opened my mouth to let her put the facebow in. That small sliding of the wire end into the tubes attached to the bands of my braces. It's such a little thing, but once both ends are in you can feel this larger thing suddenly anchored there, and it's just another of these wonderful feelings of being even more intensely *braced*. I lifted my head from the headrest so she could strap the harness back on. I loved the feel of those straps around my head and neck again. And then, when she hooked the final end in to the

168

facebow and the whole contraption was secured in place my happiness was complete. I almost started to cry.

"So there we go," Dr.Wrighting said. "Oh, right, the elastics, too. But you know how to put those on, so we'll set that aside for the moment." She looked at her clipboard. "So we have the headgear down for 106 hours a week. Fourteen hours every weekday, and eighteen hours Saturdays and Sundays. We have the functional appliance weartime scheduled at ten hours a day during the week, and fourteen on weekends. Basically during the week you should put them in after dinner, and wear them through until breakfast. Then we have elastics: fulltime. And the retainers: fulltime any time you're not wearing the functional appliance. Understood?"

I nodded eagerly. Jacob and I had made up the schedule, so I knew exactly what was expected of me. Swallowing, or trying to with the functional appliance in place, I knew it was going to be a challenge, but I knew that I wanted that challenge.

"Alright then," Dr.Wrighting said. "Alright." It was like she realized the finality of this too. That we were almost at the end of the road. She unhooked the headgear and removed the facebow, and then removed the functional appliances, replacing them with the retainers. Then she hooked in the elastics, one on each side diagonally connecting top and bottom braces. Then the facebow went back in. Then she hooked up the straps again. The retainers felt almost small compared to the cumbersome functional appliances, but they too took up a lot of room in my mouth.

I swallowed hard. Repeatedly. Dr.Wrighting took her time cleaning off the functional appliances and then put them in a protective container. I got a pouch for my headgear as well.

"I guess we're done," she said, looking around like she hoped she had forgotten something. But she hadn't. She unstrapped me and I got up, a bit dizzy.

She handed me the container with the functional appliances and the headgear pouch. "I put the bags of elastics in the pouch," she said.

"Thank you so much," I said, truly grateful. I couldn't keep myself from hugging her. "Thank you!" I said.

She smiled, a bit embarrassed. I don't think too many of her patients with a headgear strapped on hugged her at the end of their appointments. Unless she had to comfort them as they sobbed about what they had to wear. But then I wasn't her average patient.

"I'll see you in two weeks," she said. "Just to check how everything is going," she said when she saw the flash of panic in my eyes, as I worried she meant that that was when everything was coming off. But, no, I still had six full weeks of this. *Full* weeks!

"And remember to meet your weartime quotas. If you don't, there will be consequences. And since I'm limited in how I can punish you if you don't meet your quota, rest assured I would do something that you would not like and that you want to avoid."

It was true she couldn't punish me by prolonging the time I had my braces. I could live with that. I probably wanted to live with that.... So it would be something different. Like stripping me of all these wonderful accessories for the remaining time. Something like that.

When I walked out I was still hit by that wall of self-consciousness when I saw everyone in the waiting room look up and see me with my whole bridle and bit. But it was o.k. That was part of the experience too. I got my appointment slip from the reception desk and then left the office. I leaned against the wall outside, looking up and down the street whether any of Dr.Wrighting's patients were coming before slowly unhooking the headgear. I couldn't bring myself to wear it all the way home, but it felt right to not furtively rip it off as quickly as possible but only slowly take it off.

I called Jacob on my way home, too happy to contain my elation. "It's done. Exactly like we planned. Exactly like I hoped for. Everything's great," I told him. I was pleased by the slight lisp the retainers gave me, and the smooth feel of the acrylic covering my palate again.

"I'll bring some champagne," Jacob said. I could hear him panting slightly. Excited. Frustrated, because he had to wait to see me, and then because he was going to have to wait to be able to fuck me. And I think both our voices had that edge of regret. Our celebrations, even if they were at their height, were winding down. The number of days left for us to indulge in my braces were falling away faster than we could bear it.

At home I hooked in the headgear as soon as I closed the door behind me. Even before I took my coat off. It felt like a relief to have it in again. To feel the wire from the inside bow across my braces. To feel the gentle pull of the straps connecting it to my head.

I opened the container with the other, larger retainers. Pulling them out I admired the bulk and smooth curves on them. I shuddered with delight at the thought of them in my mouth again. And with fear, knowing what it meant to have such enormity in there. Knowing how hard it would be to talk and swallow. How humiliating it would be to try to speak.

With all the other accessories, the headgear and the elastics, I couldn't quickly switch out one set of retainer for the other. It was better that way too. I wanted to get a feel for these intimidating devices, but I knew that it was better to wait until I had to put them in, and then not be allowed to take them out until morning. I knew how hard it was going to be. But I also knew how good it was going to be.

Usually when getting dinner ready or doing housework I lose track of my orthodontic outfit. You just forget you're wearing headgear, or whatever. Not this time. Not yet. I constantly sank in that feeling of pleasurable wonder of those retainers back in my mouth, of the headgear strapped to my head. I was so thankful to have all this, on top of the wonderful braces themselves.

It was a relief to realize that even when the braces came off, at least I'd have that small consolation of retainers I could wear whenever I wanted. They couldn't make up for the metal bands and the protrusions and the wire stretched across them covering my teeth. They couldn't ever be nearly as much as my braces. But it would be something.

Jacob beamed when I opened the door. He kissed me gingerly, the wire of my facebow between us, yet our lips stretched over it, touching. I could feel him trembling as he held back his passion. I knew the intensity with which he wanted to kiss me. But with the headgear only so much was possible.

He popped open the chilled champagne. I even had two glasses that were the right shape. We clinked glasses, and then I carefully leaned my head far back and dribbled some into my mouth. The only other alternative was a straw, but I couldn't see myself drinking champagne with a straw. It was hard to drink this way too, and I spilled some of course. But we laughed, and I got enough of the bitter-sweet taste and the prickling bubbles on my tongue.

I had to bare my mouth repeatedly so that Jacob could take in the elastics and the headgear and the retainer surfaces. I had to show him what I had to put in after dinner. He sighed, and I could see the bulge in his pants, struggling even more. The sight of my orthodontic work was like instant Viagra to him, putting him in a perpetually erect, ready to fuck me silly state. Except that for now he wasn't allowed.

I finished cooking and served the meal, only taking off the headgear when everything was on the table. I wanted to put it away, but Jacob held me back and said I should leave it here on the table. "Not as good as in your mouth, but at least it's still there." It's like he didn't want to miss a second of any of these last braced impressions. And before I served the food he pulled me to him and gave me a real kiss, his lips and tongue against the rough surface of my braces. Neither of us wanted to stop, but we knew we had to. Especially since we also couldn't go any further.

When we were finished I looked at my watch nervously. "I'm going to have to put in the other set of retainers now," I reminded him. "I'm not going to be able to talk very clearly when I have those in."

Jacob smiled, excited. "I know," he nodded. "Go ahead," he said, "I'll wash up."

That was a first, that he was eager to clean up.

I picked up the container with the clear retainers and went to the bathroom. Unhooked my elastics. Popped out the pink retainers and brushed them clean under the warm running water. Then I brushed my teeth. Probably longer and more intensively even than usual.

I opened the container and looked at the two devices. But I knew I had no choice. I had to plunge in. Or plunge them in. I snapped the bottom one in place. Then the top one. Then put the smaller pink retainers in the case and shut it tight. I had to swallow before I even got around to putting the elastics back on. And I could feel my tongue against the enormity of my retainers. I shivered a bit. *What have I done?* I asked myself. But there was no turning back, just like there had been no turning back once the braces were cemented in place. And looking at my reflection in the mirror, at those two wonderful rows of bands and wires, I knew these too belonged. Then I had to swallow again, and again.

I hooked the elastics in place and then went to face Jacob.

"Well, here they are," I said. I grinned, my jaws clenched together, but my teeth not touching because of the mass of plastic in my mouth. And of course what I said sounded more like *Weh, he ay ahh.*

Jacob took me by the hips and drew me closer. I could feel the cage his cock was trapped in pressing against my abdomen. He looked so pleased. "Open up," he requested.

I did, the elastics stretching. He sighed with pleasure when he saw how much plastic there was there. He ran the tip of his finger around the inside of my mouth, and I couldn't feel it because he ran it only over all that plastic. Then he leaned in and kissed me, and thrust his tongue deep in, and between that soft warm flesh in my mouth and all the hard, smooth plastic I lost myself in ecstasy and pleasure. I didn't want to let him go. I didn't want to let him stop.

But it was Jacob who gently pulled back. "You have to put your headgear on," he reminded me.

I sighed. Yes, we were limited in how much pleasure we could take in each other. With his penis under wraps he couldn't get the release of fucking me. And with my headgear on I couldn't get such a passionate and fulfilling kiss from him. But I did as I was told and as I knew I had to.

31.

During the day, in public, the retainers and elastics were not much different than anything I had appeared with before. I quickly and happily adjusted to having this particular setup in my mouth. There was pressure to go and stay home, since I had to get my headgear weartime in. Sometimes it annoyed me again that it limited what I could do. "But you can always wear it in public," Jacob repeatedly reminded me. But that wasn't something I could bring myself to do. Wearing it wasn't a problem. I liked strapping it on. I liked the cozy feeling of the device hugging my head. It was annoying not to be able to snack, or to easily take even a sip of water, but otherwise it was worth it.

After dinner was tougher. The oversize retainers were a lot to put up with. In some ways I loved the feel of them, even as I kept swallowing, and even as I could barely say anything. But they were so huge and *there* and dominant. But I always put them in like I was supposed to, and kept them in through until the morning.

A few days after I got them my sister called at about 9:00. I saw it was her on the Caller ID, and I considered undoing the headgear and popping out the retainers before picking up, but I didn't think I could do it fast enough. I considered just letting it go to voicemail. But then I picked up, headgear and mouth-filling retainers and all.

Of course, my sister barely understood me. It took me a few mumbled, jumbled *My redainahs* to get her to understand why I was not enunciating clearly.

"You're wearing your retainers?" She finally got it.

"Uh huh."

"Can't you just take them out?"

"Naw allowed," I told her.

"But you've had retainers with your braces, and they don't affect your speech this much," she said. "Don't you wear them during the day, too?"

"Dees ah spesha oneth," I tried to explain. "I ha to weh them ah nigh." *These are pecial ones. I have to wear them at night.*

"Honestly, Sally, I can't believe what you're willing to put up with. There's got to be an easier way. I couldn't imagine ever forcing my kids to put up with all that you've gone through."

"Id's ok," I assured her. If she only knew, I smiled to myself.

It was one of those calls where she just needed someone to talk to, so she let my braces be and just went on blabbing about her problems. My mumbled pieces of advice took a bit of back and forth to decode before she figured out what I was trying to say, but mostly she just wanted to hear her own voice anyway.

After that, if someone from work or one of my friends called after I had put the big retainers in I'd let it go to voicemail and, if it was important, unhook and remove all my apparatuses when I called them back. If it was my sister, or my parents, or Jacob I'd just answer, speech inhibiting devices firmly in place. My sister warned my parents, and the first two or three times they encountered my super slurred speech they kept saying how weird I sounded, but after that everyone treated it like it was almost normal. It helped that I began to be able to speak a bit more clearly. But I didn't speak a lot more clearly. It still sounded like I had a mouth full of plastic. Which I did.

174

Jacob enjoyed teasing me when I had them in, after dinner. We could lightly try to kiss, with the headgear facebow between us, and he would dart his tongue adventurously past it, into the recesses of my plastic-filled mouth. But it wasn't entirely fulfilling kissing. I always wanted more. And he laughed about that, and my struggles to articulate my desperate desire. It wasn't like the shoe was totally on the other foot. He was still as frustrated with his caged-up cock, which I still wouldn't release, but I certainly had a better idea of how he felt now.

The frustrations of being unable to speak and swallow normally, of unfulfilled kisses with a headgear bar blocking lips from softly melting onto other lips, the pull of the elastics always a cruel reminder of my jaws not entirely being free in their range of motion, and the braces, those incredible braces themselves the uneven metallic surfaces instead of my smooth teeth a reminder of how different and childish and imperfect I looked, like a teen still in the making: all this and more was what I loved about the experience of having them, even as it all frustrated and humbled me.

How was I ever going to live without the intensity of these feelings? With enormous satisfaction I clenched my jaws together, top retainer guided into the grooves of the lower one, plastic obstructing everything. I didn't know how I was going to live without these feelings, but I certainly could enjoy them for now.

Once the first week was up Jacob showed up eagerly, knowing we could finally again consummate our orthodontically enhance relationship. I didn't make it easy for him, insisting that he wait and watch as I did a strip tease in front of him, and only then unbuttoning his shirt, then his pants, and pulling them down, until we both stood there naked except for me with my headgear and he with his cock in its metal cage.

"Well, where's the key?" he asked, his voice breaking.

"Patience," I smiled, still swaying back and forth. He may have been most turned on by my braces, but he liked the look of my breasts as they perkily swayed to the music too.

I unhooked the headgear. I would have to make up the weartime another time. I wanted nothing to get in the way of our sex. I took out the retainers too, but I switched in the larger ones.

"Ok," I slurred, "come an geh me." *Come and get me*.

"But this…" he said, pointing helplessly at his erect cock in the unforgiving cage.

"Oh, you'ah goin to haf to wahm me uh maw if you wahn me to take thad off," I teased, putting my arms around him, and losing myself in a deep, long kiss. *Warm me up*, I insisted.

My breasts against his chest, my legs around his hips, he could barely contain himself. He kissed me, and he fondled my breasts, and kissed them too, and again and again he just wanted to ram himself into me, before remembering, again and again that the cage wouldn't allow him to feel any of the release he longed for.

I wouldn't release him either, holding myself tight to him even as he begged to be allowed to fuck me and even as he continued to kiss and fondle me, unable to take his hands off me.

Finally, when he was shivering with excitement I got the key and released him. He took a deep breath and sigh, which gave me just enough time to lean back and spread my legs wide before he plunged into me like he wanted to split me in two.

With a few loud grunts he came almost immediately, of course. I had expected that. But I only gave him a few moments to recover before I began to do those things that I knew would quickly arouse him again. And when he was hard enough again I guided him back into me, and more tired and relaxed he made love to me more gently, until we were both satisfied.

Were the weeks after that the happiest in my life? I think so. I couldn't imagine being more completely happy. Sure, the sex had a lot to do with that. We now knew each other so well that we were totally in tune, and the physical part of our relationship was perfect. But it went way beyond that. Maybe because we looked forward to the physical part so much, we also got along incredibly well otherwise. And even though I had always felt comfortable with my braces, regardless of how people looked at me or what they said, now I felt completely comfortable in my braced skin. I was at one with my braces. I finally knew what that idea of *being at one* with something meant, because I truly was completely at one with my braces. They were not just part of me, they were the pinnacle of me.

It was all like some incredible drug-induced high, except for instead of any drug it was the metal and plastic in my mouth. The only bad part was that time zipped by without my even realizing. Everything was going perfectly, but it was going, going, going…and, I realized with a start every now and then, would soon be gone.

176

After two weeks I had my next appointment with Dr. Wrighting. I had gotten in all the weartime with the different accessories that I was supposed to. There was certainly no reason to try to pull any sort of fast one. Part of the pleasure was that I *had* to wear this stuff, and that I knew I had Dr. Wrighting's wrath to fear if I didn't. But I wanted to be the model fake patient. I was happy to be that.

Dr. Wrighting was pleased, and she soon let me go. There was nothing for her to do, after all. Getting unstrapped, I began to feel that sadness again, of how this was one of the last times I would be going through this. Walking out I stopped in the waiting room and looked at all those lucky girls who still had so much longer to go with their treatment. I didn't mind standing there, and them and their mothers staring at me in my headgear. I realized how lucky I still was. But in a month I knew I would give anything to change places with any of them.

32.

That last month passed even quicker than I could imagine. On the one hand, it was nearly perfect. Jacob and I had our routine down, and rode a roller coaster of emotion and sex and lisped pillow talk as I still struggled to speak with the huge retainers in place. The brief times I had my headgear off he'd run his index finger over the surface of my braces and gently kiss me, almost tearing up with emotion about the wonder of them on my teeth. We'd make love repeatedly, and at incredibly drawn-out lengths.

For a while Jacob constantly was taking photographs. Close-ups and headshots. Trying to capture the perfect keepsakes. But the two-dimensional richly color pictures, even at their sharpest, paled beside my real-life orthodontic rigging. We both knew that. Still, they would be nice memory aids. Something to show the kids....

And then time was almost up, and I was nearly in a panic. This, I realized, must be exactly how some kids felt when they had their appointment to *get* braces. Facing that life-changing event. *If they only knew!* I told myself. They were the lucky ones. Those thousands of girls around the world who at the same time that I was losing mine were taking that wonderful first step and getting braced.

177

Dr.Wrighting had made the appointment for a Sunday, when the office was usually closed. She wanted to be able to dedicate herself entirely to me and to getting this awful deed done. Jacob offered to come along, but I couldn't bear the thought of him watching as Dr.Wrighting ripped out everything that had meant so much to us for so long.

We had almost perfunctory sex in the morning, both lost in the same thought elsewhere. After he showered Jacob obediently came back to bed to have me lock his cock in its cage again, but I put it aside and told him there was no need for that. We were going to be done with all these attachments and accessories, after all. Despite how much he hated the metal cage and always railed and complained when I locked him in it, he still looked disappointed.

I slowly made my way to Dr.Wighting's, and at the entrance to the office put in my headgear and hooked it up. One last time, I realized. Then I went in, to face this particular dark doom.

The practice was dead quiet. That funereal atmosphere was appropriate. I went to the empty waiting room, calling out, *Hello?* to see where Dr.Wrighting was.

It was her daughter who came out. I had met Natalie a couple of times. She was in her late teens, probably a high school senior now, with two beautiful rows of banded teeth much like mine.

"Hi, Sally," she said. "So today is the big day."

I gave a resigned nod.

She noticed my reluctance. "You scared? Or disappointed?"

"Oh, I'm not scared. But, yeah, it feels way too soon."

She grinned at me with her full glistening silvery mouth. "I know the feeling. I'm dreading the day when mine have to come off. I've convinced Mom to prolong my treatment a couple of times already, but I know she's going to tell me it's all over one of these days."

It was good to talk to someone who understood and shared my longing.

Natalie led me to an empty waiting room and had me sit in the examination chair. She strapped me down quickly and efficiently, and I immediately felt more at ease. Lying there, the headgear still strapped around my head, the retainers in my mouth…it all felt like it was meant to be.

Dr.Wrighting came in soon and said hello and asked how I was doing. "Alright," she said then, "let's take this off," she said, reaching for my headgear. I flinched a bit. This was it. The last time it would be in my mouth. The last time it would be pulled free. I pressed my eyes closed, to prepare for the terrible moment.

I was used to the feeling of the headgear being unhooked, the straps pulled off, the facebow pulled out. I had done that several times a day for a long time now. But the finality now began to hit me. Looking at the apparatus on the tray that hovered in front of me, next to the container with the two large retainers. The detritus of my orthodontic adventure was accumulating.

Dr.Wrighting unhooked the elastics. And then she took out the smaller retainer, adding them to what was already on the tray.

And then, before I could even say anything or realized it, she went to work on the braces. Efficiently and steadily, removing the archwires, pulling off the bands. It was a strange blur to me, as she went through the same process, with pliers and other metal contraptions, freeing tooth after tooth, vacuuming out, cleaning, swabbing.

It might have taken her an hour in all. It was a relief to be able to turn away from Dr.Wrighting intently staring into my mouth and watch Natalie watch with bated breath, frozen there like a statue but at least revealing her own braced look, which I was growing more envious of by the second.

I barely knew or felt what Dr.Wrighting was doing. I had gone all numb. Paralyzed and lost in my thoughts. It didn't hurt – though I don't know if I even would have felt any pain. But sitting there, letting this be done to me, I realized that this was the worst thing that had ever happened to me. The worst loss. And I was part of it, allowing these braces to be pried from my mouth. I knew it was necessary. I couldn't go around for the rest of my life with them on my teeth. But this was the worst sort of rite of passage I could imagine, taking away from me what was most precious to me.

Even after the brackets and bands had been removed, Dr.Wrighting scraped and buffed and had me rinse repeatedly. I could already feel the smoothness of the surface of my teeth. But I didn't feel unburdened or free or prettified. I just felt like I had lost everything.

Finally, Dr.Wrighting leaned back and allowed me to close my mouth. "All done," she announced my fate.

I felt my lips suddenly closer to the smooth, flat surface of my teeth when I closed them, not caught up in all the previously protruding metalwork. I ran my tongue over the slimy smooth surfaces, amazed at how roomier my mouth suddenly felt.

Dr.Wrighting went to a cupboard and got something out, sitting down again. "I never indulge my patients' vanity and let them see what they look like once the braces have come off, but I'll make an exception here," she said, holding up a mirror for me to see the transformation that had taken place.

I opened my mouth, stunned at how different I looked. Pretty much like how I used to look, almost exactly a year ago, but it was still unexpected. Pure, clean white, all straight and flat. No metal whatsoever. My smile looked beautiful and radiant. Everyone's ideal. And I could imagine nothing worse.

I broke out sobbing, everything I'd lost suddenly clear to me. Dr.Wrighting got out some tissues and helped me blow my nose and wipe away my tears, since I couldn't while I was strapped down like this. I felt a bit silly, because I couldn't stop. I was so overcome by emotion.

"It'll take some time to get used to," Dr.Wrighting said. "At least a third of my patients go through a deep depression after they get their braces off. And almost all of them say they miss them, even those that initially looked forward to this day. It's a tough adjustment."

When I had finally calmed down a bit, only sniffling some, Dr.Wrighting got the impression materials so she could make impressions of my newly freed teeth. Natalie mixed the alginate for her in the small bowl, and then she filled the impression tray with it. First upper and then lower teeth.

"So, I'm going to make you a set of retainers now," Dr.Wrighting explained. "Usually, I'd have you come back in a day or two, but if you want to wait here...."

I nodded, desperate to at least remain tied down like I was and not escape even for a moment without some mouthpiece to fall back on.

"Here? Or in the waiting room?"

"No, here, like this, is just great," I said eagerly. "And...,"

"Yes?"

"Could you like put in the cheek retractor or something?" I asked, blushing a bit. I still wanted to feel like a patient.

Exposed. And without being able to feel my newly denuded teeth.

Dr.Wrighting smiled understandingly. "Of course." She got out a cheek retractor and stretched my lips around it, and I immediately felt better. She hooked up the vacuum tube to suck the spit that accumulated, too, and then she left with the two impression trays, with Natalie left there to watch over me.

Natalie sat down next to me and stared and smiled. "They do look great, if it's any comfort," she told me.

I grunted that it wasn't. Sure, it was nice too. A perfect smile is something people like to see. It was going to help at work. But the sacrifice I had to make in order to get it....

Natalie continued to smile down at me, revealing her two rows of glistening silver. She could see my eyes were focused on them. She knew that's what I needed to see. That even as I was jealous of what she still got to wear, at least I got to stare and admire them. So instead of pacing around and cleaning up she patiently sat there the whole time and let me stare, and imagine, at least in my mind, that my wonderful adventure wasn't completely over and that braces weren't entirely out of reach.

I don't know how long it took Dr.Wrighting to make the retainers, but she was away for a long time. Finally she came back, and put the two pink appliances on the tray. They were about the size of the retainers I had been wearing during the daytime up to now. Maybe a hair bigger, especially the top one. But I was still disappointed.

Dr.Wrighting probably realized that. "These are for everyday wear," she explained. "Since we haven't moved much around, we could probably get away with your only wearing retainers at night, maybe after a one or two week adjustment period. But I like to make sure everything really stays in place, so I want you to wear these 24/7 for the next three months. And I can make you another, more substantial set for nighttime wear, if you want that."

My mouth still held widely open, I nodded vigorously.

Dr.Wrighting smiled and fitted the retainers, asking me whether there were any sharp edges or anything anywhere. But like with all her devices, they fit perfectly.

So she removed the vacuum tube and the cheek retractors and I closed my mouth and gave a small sigh of relief when my tongue came up against the plastic of the retainers and I could feel the wires running across my teeth against the inside of my lips. It was nothing like the braces, in all their wonderful metal bulk, but it was something.

As Natalie unstrapped me, the tears began to flow again. This was it. The end of my braced fantasy, with just some retainer off-shoots to tide me over.

Dr.Wrighting made me an appointment for Wednesday, to pick up my other retainer, and she gave me a case to put these ones in if I took them out. "You can, briefly, for special occasions if you have to, but otherwise I really do need you to wear them 24/7 for the next three months."

I was happy to. They weren't braces, but at least they were something.

Utterly dejected I walked out into the street. I smiled at the entrance. At least I was able to walk out with my head held up high and I didn't have to worry about quickly taking off my headgear before anyone saw. And yet, what I wouldn't have given to still have needed to wear that headgear....

I couldn't bring myself to go straight home and face Jacob. I wandered aimlessly around, window shopping and watching the kids play in a park. The retainers were a blessing. I don't know what I would have done without that reassuring plastic in my mouth. The full orthodontic monty would have been too much to bear all at once.

Finally I went home to Jacob. I greeted him with a sad smile. "At least we still have these," I said, revealing the two wires of my retainers." He nodded and hugged me, holding me tight.

I went to the bathroom to see what I looked like with the retainers. At least there was some silvery wire there, stretched across my teeth. But it was so much less than my glorious braces had been.

I took the retainers out, to see my completely freed and unencumbered teeth again. This was the sight that every patient who had braces supposedly longed for. The triumphant straightened smile that signaled the final conquest over malocclusion. Unfettered freedom finally achieved again. And yet it was the last thing I wanted to see. I sobbed again, and quickly put the retainers back in again. What a relief at least those wires running over my teeth were! Even if they fell far short of the archwires and the supporting metal bands and brackets that I now missed so.

Talking to Jacob and telling him about the procedure I was happy to see that the top retainer was a bit bigger than the one I had before, and that it did inhibit my speech slightly, giving me a small but pronounced lisp. A welcome constant reminder that I wasn't entirely orthodontically free. I think Dr.Wrighting knew how necessary that was for me.

Jacob comforted me, and then kissed me, and his tongue running over the surface of my retainers, and over the wires running across my teeth felt so good. But as he pulled me to the bedroom I had him stop and I popped out the retainers. "We have to try," I explained. "See what it's like without them...."

He nodded gravely, and we undressed and kissed and fondled. It felt so strange, like I was missing an arm or leg or other vital appendage. Which I was. My most vital appendages of all. But Jacob was up to it. Eyes closed, and keeping his mouth away from mine, so as not to remind himself of what was now absent, he focused on the actual fucking , and that was fine and that was good and even if it wasn't as completely satisfying as exactly the same thing was when I had my mouthful of metal and my bridle and bit strapped on it was good enough.

But it came as a relief to be able to reach for the retainers and pop them back in and just be wearing them.

There was a lot I was going to have to adjust to.

33.

One of the weird things was how excitedly everyone reacted. Everyone that saw me congratulated me on finally being *done with those horrible braces*, and even as they sympathized that I still had the two wires running across my teeth, those were *so much better*, and at least the *hard part was out of the way*, and all sorts of things like that. People finally felt free to tell me how horrible they thought the braces were too, and they all did. My friends and parents and colleagues all said it was *such a relief*.

All I could do was wince inside. No one understood. Instead of being something to celebrate, I was mourning. I felt no relief. I had not been unburdened. Instead, there was this yawning void within me now. I had been in heaven, and now all I had was a set of retainers to show for it.

Going to Dr.Wrighting's a few days after the dreadful day put me in a slightly better mood. I was getting a bigger retainer, which was something I looked forward to. And even if I was no longer part of that orthodontic world, I could at least surround myself for a short time with other patients in the middle of their treatment. So I sat happily in the waiting room, looking at these girls in the prime of their orthodontic treatment, few of them realizing how lucky they were. I wanted to go up to each of them and tell them to enjoy the experience to the fullest. Even I was surprised how rich an experience it could be.

I felt like so much was missing when I was led to the examination chair and strapped in. Just wearing my retainers felt completely inadequate in this holy place. I felt like I was letting Dr.Wrighting down by being such a trivial patient, without two full sets of train tracks or some serious accessories.

Dr.Wrighting asked me how things were going, and I admitted my disappointment. She told me that she was surprised by how many of her patients felt that way. Even when they came back years later, for routine check-ups, they would get all sentimental and regret that they hadn't had their braces for just a year or two more.

Dr.Wrighting took out my upper retainer, and then brought a small plastic bag in which there was another, bulkier one. I sighed with happy relief and expectation as she took it out and pressed it into my mouth. "Yeth!" I lisped. This was much mouthfillingly better.

"Good," Dr.Wighting said. "And I have a surprise for you, too." She popped out the retainer and held it up for me to see. "Notice anything special about it?" she asked.

When she said that I immediately did. There was a small metal tube on the clasp that went over my back molars, one on each side. And some sort of reinforcement near clasps closer to the front of my mouth. I knew what that had to mean, but it seemed almost too good to be true. "Headgear...?" I barely dared whisper.

She nodded, glad to see how pleasantly surprised I was.

She brought out a facebow, and showed me how it locked into the retainer. I almost melted in my chair. This was awesome. She brought out the full bridle, too, and hooked me up, and with my lips around the two bits of wire connecting the facebow to the bow that fit on the retainer, I couldn't have been happier. "Thank you!" I sighed, sitting happily there in headgear once again.

"That's not all," she said. She went to her cupboards and got out another small plastic bag. Out of this she pulled what looked like a functional appliance, a bulky one-piece retainer which my lower jaw would bite into. And I saw it had the same tubes as the retainer I was now wearing.

Dr.Wrighting took out the retainer with the headgear and the lower retainer, and put in the functional appliance. It was a huge, tongue blocking device, but it fit perfectly and beautifully. Once she saw that it fit ok she took it out and removed the headgear from the retainer and snapped it onto this device, and then put it back in my mouth and attached all the straps.

"This is great for nighttime wear," she told me. "As a retainer, and to keep you jaw in perfect alignment. You don't have to wear it with the headgear on, but it helps hold it in place...."

"Ith no poblahm," I burbled. *It's no problem*. No problem at all, I thought, closing my eyes, happy to find myself with at least some solid orthodontic accessories to fall back on, come what may. Reclined and strapped down in the seat, the feel of all this orthodontic hardware once again having its hold on me, I could pretend my fantasy lived on. And it could live on, a bit. Nothing could replace the braces, of course, but this was more than I had dared dreamed of.

At home I had Jacob sit down on the couch as I brought out my surprises one by one. He had been expecting the larger retainer, and of course immediately wanted me to put it, but I told him he had to be patient.

I tapped the small tubes on the side of the retainer as I held it up for him. "Recognize what these are for?"

His eyes lit up. "Really?'

I pulled out the facebow, and then the straps of the headgear.

"That's fantastic!"

"And there's one more thing...," I said, finally bringing out functional appliance and showing him that it too came headgear-ready.

He hugged me, and it felt like he was just as relieved as I was. We didn't have to go cold turkey. We had something to hold onto. Even a bit of the spice of variety!

"So how do you decide what to wear, and when?" he asked.

"I guess just when and what I feel like," I said, attaching the headgear to the retainer and then swapping it with the smaller everyday retainer I had been wearing. "Chust whe an whad I feew wike," I said, hooking up the straps of the bridle and beaming at him.

He kissed me gently, happily, and we ordered take-out, fooling around while we waited. Removing the headgear and switching retainers again when the food arrived we talked more seriously about it.

"How about when we're together, just the two of us, you decide?" I said. "Whatever you say goes."

"Really?"

I wanted him to have that control. I liked the idea that it was out of my hands, to some extent. That I *had to* wear this, or that, regardless of whether or not I really wanted to.

He thought it over for a moment. "Ok," he said. Then he went to my bedroom and came back with the empty cylindrical mesh that had been the cage for his cock all these many months. "But then you get to decide when I have to wear this."

"Quid pro quo?"

"We're in each other's hands."

"That sounds fair."

We both were slightly nervous about giving up some control, but also mildly excited by it. And by the thought of continuing our games.

And nervously I asked him after we had finished eating, "So which device do I have to put in now?"

"Or devices," he laughed, before tapping the container with the larger retainer.

"With or without the headgear?" My voice trembled a bit as I asked. I wasn't sure which I preferred.

"Without, for now," he said.

I brushed my teeth and put in the bigger retainer. When we had finished washing up, we made out and then we made love. A calm, easy-going fuck, like that of a couple familiar with all each other's moves and happy in one another's arms. I didn't ask whether I should put on the headgear during the night, and Jacob didn't command me to. We slept happily in each other's arms.

After he showered in the morning I motioned with my index finger that he should come back to the bed. His towel wrapped around waist he looked unsure of what I wanted, but the slight bulge beneath it suggested he was ready for a quick fuck before going off to work. Instead I reached over to the nightstand and held up the metal cage.

He groaned, even though he still had a smile on his face. "Really?' he asked, half annoyed but clearly also secretly pleased that I was exerting my dominion over him. Groaning louder, he obediently dropped his towel and let me sheathe his now erect cock in its cage, and then lock it shut. He laughed and kissed me, and then went to get dressed.

34.

I don't know what I would have done without the headgear to strap on at home, or the functional appliance to fill my mouth with. The retainers were fine. Something that could tide me over. Especially as long as I was required to wear them constantly. But often I longed to get home and put the more massive retainer in and strap the headgear, or once I was at home looked forward to going to bed with the mouth-filling appliance snugly in place. They eased what otherwise was just too sudden and enormous a change, from a mouth full of braces to a mouth entirely without them.

At least I had the pictures of me in all my different braced beauty on my computer. Nostalgically I would click through them, remembering what it had been like. This vicarious thrill wasn't nearly as good as the real thing had been, but at least it helped me cling to my memories, which I was so afraid of losing.

Both Jacob and I had exit interviews with Dr.Allegretta and Dr.Wrighting about the past year. They had us fill out long questionnaires, and then they met with us individually and asked us all sorts of other things. It was always more embarrassing trying to answer the probing and revealing questions in person, instead of just writing down what I felt, but I wanted to be as helpful as possible. Dr.Wrighting had done so much for me.

We weren't entirely done after the big debriefing, either. There were still follow-up questions, especially about how we were progressing through the post-braced transition and all the withdrawal symptoms we were going through. And both I and Jacob separately continued to see Dr.Allegretta regularly for therapy sessions for months. Not to cure us of our strange obsession, but to help us make the most of it without making too much of it. And to allow us to fit it properly into a healthy relationship that didn't revolve entirely around what was or wasn't in my mouth, but instead one that appreciated that but also went beyond it. I think she helped us both a lot.

Dr.Allegretta and Dr.Wrighting sent us offprints of their article when it finally appeared in some fancy specialist journal. Jacob and I both looked at the scholarly paper, and then at each other, and decided we didn't really want to read it. There had been so much that was magical about that year that we didn't want to demystify it. We didn't want explanations. I think we were both even afraid of explanations. We didn't want to be told why a few bits of metal and wire on my teeth, and varieties of oral and extraoral accessories were so meaningful to us. We didn't want to know what childhood experience or chance encounter or repressed memory had triggered our desires. Maybe knowing would suddenly deprive everything orthodontic of its hold over us. And, at home in the evening, popping in the retainers I no longer wore in public, or strapping on the headgear, we both knew we wanted their allure to remain undiminished. So we thanked the good doctors for sending the article, but then we put it away. But, yes, we both discussed our reasons for not reading it in our therapy sessions with Dr.Allegretta....

35.

Three months after the braces had come off Dr.Wrighting said I didn't have to wear my retainers 24/7 any longer. She actually said I *shouldn't*. I knew the time was coming, but it still came as a shock. I still didn't feel like I had even begun to get over not having the braces. But Dr.Wrighting said it was time to wean me off them. And I knew she was right. For work, for all my public life, it was time to put even these behind me. For the world at large I should just be another girl with a beaming straight smile.

Dr.Wrighting usually makes even her patients who are long out of braces and have just been wearing their retainers at night for years wear their retainers in the waiting room and then on the way home after their appointment. To set an example for the other patients, and to remind the patients themselves that the retainers remained an essential part of their lives and daily routines. But I didn't need that reminder, and Dr.Wrighting made an exception. She knew it was important for me to take those first completely orthodontically unsecured steps, and so she put my retainers in their case and handed it to me and instructed me *not* to put them in until I got home. "At your next appointment you should come wearing them," she said. "But today – you're done!"

It was harder than I expected. I felt naked walking home without them. I wanted to stop as soon as I got out of the office and furtively pop them back in, just as I had so often furtively stripped off my headgear in that same spot. But I forced myself to keep them in their container, even as they rattled in it with each step like a call to be put where they belonged. In my mouth.

At least I had what I had at home to fall back on. They weren't braces, but they were still a satisfying sniff of that orthodontic nirvana I had once enjoyed, and pleasing in and of themselves too.

I don't know where Jacob and I are headed, but it looks like we are headed there together. We get along well even now when we go out and I can't flash my braces to excite him – or run my tongue over them to excite myself. We have the most wonderful of shared memories, but I think there are more memories for us in the future too. Just of a different kind. With a bit less stainless steel – or titanium… – to them.

A few weeks after I had reluctantly gone cold turkey and stopped wearing my retainers in public we had lunch in a sidewalk bistro. It was a glorious, sunny day, and when we got to desert a gaggle of teenage girls sat down at the table next to us. Jacob and I turned our heads like synchronized swimmers at the sound of a tell-tale lisp, our eyes immediately catching the sparkle of the rows of silvery braces on the girl who had spoken and was now laughing, before she was quick enough to put her hand over her mouth.

Jacob and I exchanged knowing, happy glances. We paid our bill and slowly walked home bathed in the warm sun. We were in no rush, enjoying basking in our shared anticipation.

I don't know how much or little we'll have in the future, but we'll always have this mutual bond over braces. Like braces themselves, its hold is firm and strangely beautiful, a wonderful thing I wouldn't give up for anything in the world. And even if so few others understand it, that doesn't matter. It can't diminish how much it means to us, and how much it moves us.

My braces don't define me any longer. Not to others, anyway. Most people have already started to forget I had them again. But in my heart and mind I'll always have them, in a way. In my memory. And, if I need a stronger reminder, in the appliance I put in my mouth, or the bridle and bit strapped to my head.

I'll always treasure the memories of this year, and I'll never forget what it was like to live my braced fantasy. Often, a dream coming true can't live up to the hopes one has pinned on it, but my braced year was everything I ever hoped for and more.

— T H E   E N D —

About the author

Catherine Aimes was born and grew up in
Michigan. She now lives in England with
her husband and their two daughters, who
both had braces.

Catherine Aimes can be reached at:

info@intraoralpress.com

For additional information

Visit our website at:
www.intraoralpress.com

Living the Braced Fantasy is the fourth book of orthodontic erotica from Intraoral Press, and the tenth Dr. Samantha Wrighting book.

Visit our website for all the latest information about author Catherine Aimes, and the complete line of Dr.Samantha Wrighting novels as well as our new line of orthodontic erotica.

Look for new novels
from the Offices of Dr. Samantha Wrighting

74734628R00118

Made in the USA
Middletown, DE
30 May 2018